Praise for B... W9-BGQ-448

Twenty-Six Lies/One Truth

"Ben Peek is a writer I fully expect to blunder out into the scene like a runaway brontosaurus one of these days. He has titanic talent generally leashed to micro-detail projects when his true canvas is probably something much wider and deeper. *Twenty-Six Lies/One Truth* is a gently experimental text that uses a glossary of terms from A to Z to create vignettes, one-liners, and other supports for loosely connected narratives. Some are funny, some are most definitely not funny. All are lively and deserve your attention."

—Jeff VanderMeer, *Locus Online*

"I emerged from the book feeling somewhat dazed and exhausted (having read it from beginning to end within a twenty-four-hour period), and I'm not entirely sure what I feel about it. Impressed, certainly. Curious, definitely. A little pissed off . . . well, maybe."

—Tansy Rayner Roberts, *ASIF*

"What I got from it is this: that truth matters when it matters, and doesn't when it doesn't. And that each of us must find our own path as to where that distinction lies. *Twenty-Six Lies/One Truth* is an intelligent, playful, funny, challenging, thoughtful and deeply moving work. It is a book filled with outrageous lies. And it is a book filled with truth."

—Ben Payne, *ASIF*

"It ought to fail miserably. But, curse his eyes, Mr. Peek has written a fantastic book. And despite its structure, *Twenty-Six Lies/One Truth* has a powerful narrative drive. Mr. Peek has deftly woven a story into his encyclopedia, complete with character development, unfolding themes, and a hard shock of an ending."

—Chris Lawson, The Talking Squid Blog

"Quite extraordinary."

—Clare Dudman, author *of One Day the Ice Will Reveal Its Dead* and *98 Reasons for Being*

"Ben Peek's *Twenty-Six Lies/One Truth* is a memoir in the form of alphabetical entries, ten or so entries for each letter. The book is also semiotic, social commentary, a meditation on the truth-telling responsibilities of a writer, a part-time comic book, funny as hell, profane, and melancholy. Like the best memoirs it's deeply personal yet engaging and universal. Peek lays out the truths and lies and is smart enough to trust the reader to fit everything together. Powerful stuff. Highly recommended."

—Paul G. Tremblay, author of *In the Mean Time* and
—*Swallowing a Donkey's Eye*

"This is a clever, moving, funny and insightful book. I laughed, and I would have cried, but I'm too fucking hard for that sort of shit. See, I understand, relate and empathize with a lot of the truth in this book, the truths I know are true."

—Paul Haines, author of *Doorways for the Dispossessed*

"Recently I read Ben Peek's *Twenty Six Lies/One Truth*. Yes, it's full of bluff and bluster, Peek coming across as a hard-ass, and yes, it's very fucking good. There are moments, in fact, of brilliance."

—Rjurik Davidson, author of *Unwrapped Sky*

"A bit too clever."

—Dan Hartland, *Strange Horizons*

"Ben Peek's *Twenty-Six Lies/One Truth* is inebriating, an absinthe of self-deception, a smoke-filled room of conflicted emotion, a hall of mirrors, each of them distorting both perception and reality. Ben Peek dances on the stepping stones of Ben Peek's supposed life, leaping from philosophy to pop culture, from insight to angst. As one reads this remarkable work, the question arises, 'What is the line between the art and the artist'? Peek knows. I know. But you cannot know, for certain, until you pick out the lies. Do you trust your judgement that much? Do you trust Ben Peek? What makes you so certain that you can crack the code of *Twenty-Six Lies/One Truth*? I'd be careful if I were you. Deception awaits."

—Forrest Aguirre, World Fantasy Award-winning editor of
—*Leviathan* 3 and 4

Black Sheep

"With the gravitas of a Margaret Atwood or Kazuo Ishiguro, Peek, in his debut novel, *Black Sheep*, crafts a quietly horrifying world displaced from ours by a century of time and an implosion of globalist attitudes."
—Paul Di Filippo, *Barnes and Noble Review*

"There's a clear critique operating here of contemporary Australian society, with its expectation that newcomers leave their cultural background at the door on entry. . . . *Black Sheep* is one of the more interesting novels I've read in recent times."
—Ben Payne, *ASIF*

"This is an angry young book . . . it blazes across the page with absolute intensity. It's also one of the most interesting and politically challenging science fiction novels to come out of Australia in a very long time. It's a novel that has something to say."
—Tansy Rayner Robers, *ASIF*

Above/Below

"Continues to press the nerd pleasure centers of my brain."
—John Scalzi

"Cleverly and at times beautifully written.
—Not If You Were the Last Short Story on Earth

"An old-fashioned flip book. . . . An interesting concept. . . . Overt politics in SF, making a clear statement. . . . Highly recommended."
—The Writer and the Critic

AND OTHER STORIES

ChiZine Publications

FIRST EDITION

Distributed in Canada by
HarperCollins Canada Ltd.
1995 Markham Road
Scarborough, ON M1B 5M8
Toll Free: 1-800-387-0117
e-mail: hcorder@harpercollins.com

Distributed in the U.S. by
Diamond Book Distributors
1966 Greenspring Drive
Timonium, MD 21093
Phone: 1-410-560-7100 x826
e-mail: books@diamondbookdistributors.com

Library and Archives Canada Cataloguing in Publication

Peek, Ben, author
Dead Americans / Ben Peek.

Short stories.
Issued in print and electronic formats.
ISBN 978-1-77148-171-7 (pbk.)
ISBN 978-1-77148-172-4 (ebook)

I. Title.

PR9619.4.P43D42 2014   823'.92   C2013-907738-3
        C2013-907739-1

CHIZINE PUBLICATIONS
Toronto, Canada
www.chizinepub.com
info@chizinepub.com

Edited by Stephen Michell
Copyedited and proofread by Kelsi Morris

Canada Council   Conseil des arts
for the Arts   du Canada

We acknowledge the support of the Canada Council for the Arts which last year invested $20.1 million in writing and publishing throughout Canada.

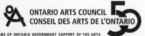

ONTARIO ARTS COUNCIL
CONSEIL DES ARTS DE L'ONTARIO

50 YEARS OF ONTARIO GOVERNMENT SUPPORT OF THE ARTS
50 ANS DE SOUTIEN DU GOUVERNEMENT DE L'ONTARIO AUX ARTS

Published with the generous assistance of the Ontario Arts Council.

Printed in Canada

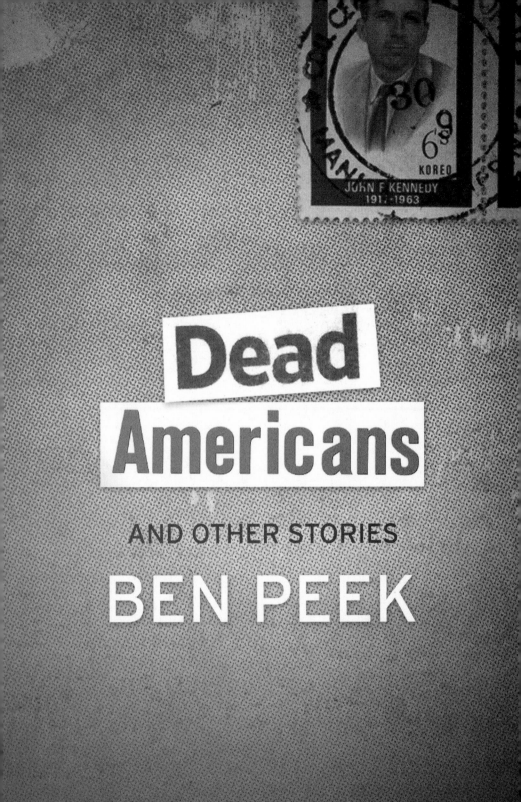

Dead

Americans

AND OTHER STORIES

BEN PEEK

For Nikilyn Nevins

Contents

Ben Peek: Liminal Artist

An introduction by Rjurik Davidson

Parramatta road runs west from central Sydney, out into a vast urban and suburban sprawl. It's a liminal space, between the city and the bush. Roads climb and fall over the small hills, they wind through the districts with their little shopping centres and vast malls. Freeways bypass the area altogether, as if some of us weren't meant to venture there. In one of these little dense knots of population lives Ben Peek, a man accustomed to the liminal zones.

Peek is a large man with a quiet voice. He rarely drinks, has excellent taste in both music and literature. Over the years, he's made both friends and enemies. This is in part because of his forthright opinions, many of which can be seen on his well-read blog. Peek is not one to compromise and that's to some people's taste but not to others. Intransigency is not an admired trait in so-called civilized society, though it is one we are sorely lacking. To begin with, Peek has been openly critical of awards, for he sees them as contingent affairs that don't represent much at all.

For over ten years, Ben Peek has been quietly writing his dark and intense fiction. For over ten years, he has been making himself into one of Australia's pre-eminent writers. For over ten years, he has been under-read and underappreciated. His early dystopian novel, *Black Sheep*, examined an Australia where 'multiculturalism' was a crime. Despite laudatory reviews, the book was lost in small-press isolation and quickly disappeared. His brilliant postmodern novella, *Twenty-six Lies/One Truth*, told a story in fragments, each piece headed by a letter of the alphabet. It was a literary triumph that made small waves among a select readership. Peek's equally ambitious book *A Year in the City*—a section of which is printed here as "The Dreaming City"—rewrote the geography of Sydney through the eyes of Mark Twain and aboriginal myth. Like his lucent Red Sun book—showcased here in the exciting "Under the Red Sun"—it is yet to find a home. All this is about to change, as Peek has sold a major fantasy series and soon his work will be sought out. Some of this early work will yet see print.

From this short précis you might gather Peek is a genre writer but, like the suburb he inhabits, he stands on the borderlands of the literary. In a sense he is the archetypal speculative fiction writer. He likes to experiment with form and he has read widely outside genre. In this collection of stories you will find—in "Johnny Cash" and others—the influence of "literary" writers such as Murikami, Peter Carey, or science fiction's great experimentalist, J. G. Ballard. Peek's love with headings and sub-titles implies a meta-narrative distancing, a self-conscious eye overlooking the very stories they are a part of.

Take the opening story of this collection, "There is Something So Quiet and Empty Inside of You That It Must Be Precious." Each subtitle resonates with the story adding the self-referential depth. The story takes the form of a police procedural, resonating with Chandler and Ellroy, and yet subtly shifts into the kind of magic-realism you might find in Peter Carey. The true centre of the story, however, lies in the character of Williams, a drawn-out forty-year-old. His world-weariness is so finely crafted that we can practically feel the weight in his bones as he moves around.

Which brings us to the question of voice—an area of writing difficult to analyse, hard to teach, yet crucial to the success of any writer. Peek found his voice early: distanced and ironic, and yet in some contradictory way still powerful and intense. If the distance and irony come from the self-reflexiveness, the muscular intensity comes in the prose itself, the attention to detail, the inner life of the characters.

In his stories, Peek likes to refer, however tangentially, to cultural icons: John Wayne, Lee Harvey Oswald, Johnny Cash, Octavia Butler. It's a manoeuver that appeals to the wider world beyond the text, with all its meanings, and so adds to the self-reflexivity, the ironic distancing.

In Butler's case, the reference is to science fiction's greatest female African-American writer, and highlights Peek's ongoing concern with race and multiculturalism. Each of his novels in some way meditates on this concern, in Peek's distinctive way. Peek is an iconoclastic progressive, belonging to no discernable political tradition, but rather having fashioned a political outlook of his own making.

A collection of Ben Peek stories is long overdue. For over ten years, he has stood at the forefront of a new wave of Australian short story writers. In this book, you'll find his best short work, though certainly there will be more to come. It will take you away from your everyday life and throw you into unknown, dark worlds. Peek will impress you with his technique. He will make you think about life and death, race and gender, hope and despair. With the recent sale of his fantasy books, he is no longer the proverbial "writer to watch." He no longer needs to show what he can do. He has done it. He has been doing it for more than a decade. Here is a selection of the fruits of that labour. Prepare yourself.

—Rjurik Davidson is a freelance writer and Associate Editor of *Overland* magazine. Rjurik has written short stories, essays, reviews, and screenplays. His collection, *The Library of Forgotten Books*, was published in 2010, and his novel, *Unwrapped Sky,* will be published in 2014.

There Is Something So Quiet and Empty Inside of You That It Must Be Precious

The Mosque That He Did Not Know You Visited

After the fire in the mosque burnt itself out, Pete Williams, Red Grove's local representative from the San Bernardino County Sheriff's office, found himself staring at the cindered, broken skeletal remains of the building long after all others had left, the site lit by the bright headlights of his truck. It was a stark sight, coloured in blacks, grays, and whites, and boxed in by lines of tape that secured it from no one. He had been standing there for an hour: the splinter of moon above him had pushed its way through a portion of an ugly cluster of stars, but the shadows over the Calico Mountains to his left had yet to be disintegrated by the clean, bright light that would reveal it and the tangle of cheap housing, local owned stores, and dust that was Red Grove running beneath it. Until then, the only thing that punctured the long empty darkness were headlights coming off the I-10.

Williams' solitude was due, he knew, to the remains that had been found inside the mosque. Unsurprisingly, the body had been burnt, but that fact was looking to be as if it were an event after the actual killing, an unpleasant attempt to disguise what appeared to be a brutal attack to the head of the victim. He'd asked Jesse, who doubled as mortician and coroner, to let him know for sure after the autopsy, which had been unnecessary given that they were identifying the body through dental records and he'd be receiving the paperwork anyhow; but Williams was the kind of man who said the unnecessary things at times. He liked to talk, and he did, muttering to himself when alone—"I don't like this one. Something's not right. Her *face*."— a habit he had never tried to break. There was something about the body, about the anger that was written across its blackened head, that left within Williams a series of questions about the mortality of the individual that he couldn't quite shake, and it was digging inside him. He had passed it off as a joke at first: being forty-one now came with a predisposition to linger over life and its meaning just as it came with a renewed interest in woodwork, but the joke didn't stick. He made shit jokes, anyway. But yesterday, he would not have thought about how easy skin went black and crisp and when touched broke to reveal something so pink and red underneath; and he would not have thought how in death every expression was stripped back to a grimace, as if the recently departed knew that he or she was being taken away to some place worse, or taken away from the one good thing they had, the thing that they neither had to barter or earn, and it bothered him that the thought was there. He had been exposed to violent death before: car and farm accidents, mostly, but also to the suicides of men and women his same age and older, and kids who hadn't gotten enough in life. It was part of his job and he had thought—when he had given it thought—that he possessed a coldness, an impersonality that allowed him to keep those thoughts from him.

"What if you couldn't switch it off anymore?" his wife asked him, six months after they moved from L.A. to Red Grove, and settled into their small house. "What if you wake up and it's not there anymore?"

"Why would it change?"

The memory was of the two of them lying on the bed, naked, smoking pot and drinking beer. It was hot outside, and that third element, combined with the previous two, left them uninterested in sex, wanting nothing more than to touch, to talk. That was seven years before she left, fifteen years before he stood before the burnt out mosque, fifteen years before the memory returned. His hair had been full, then, black as grease, and the skin under his jaw did not sag and he, in general, had not sagged; nor had his teeth been a partial plate that aged him another ten years in the mirror when he took them out.

"A moment." He did not know what she looked like now, just what she was then: pleasantly plump and white, with dark hair, and a tattoo on her left shoulder in the shape of a paw print so bright and new that it was as if blood had seeped out of her skin to reveal an inner, bestial quality. Which is exactly what she wanted everyone to think. "A *moment*. Like an epiphany. A moment where something inside you just changes, where you lose something and gain something, but you'll never be sure why it all changes, and why it means so much to you."

"What am I going to do then?"

"Yeah."

"I got no fucking idea."

They had laughed, then, a good easy laugh aided by everything in the room, and despite the nature of their parting, and the cruelties that both had visited on each other since, Williams smiled faintly at the memory, though, so self conscious of his fake teeth was he that even alone, he did not smile wide enough to reveal them.

Burnt Down with the Body of a Girl You'd Never Met Inside

The burnt body had, only recently, been named Amanda Currie. She had been nineteen.

In the colourless bright light of the afternoon, Williams drove to where she lived, a spare key from the landlord, talking it out to himself—"Burnt down as a cover, killed cause she was too beautiful, maybe; beautiful to someone, anyway"—beneath the drone of the radio. Currie had a roommate, but no one had answered when the real estate called so, on instinct, he decided to go and have a look. Instinct, that was all. He did not know Amanda, did not know her family, and he took that to be a sign that she was a decent, reasonable human being, and someone who was not prone to burning down a mosque because she was too white and too Christian to leave the petrol can at home. Not that he thought she did that, anyway. The burnt out mosque was just a setting, a place where the event happened, where her burnt face had pressed itself into his mind, and he had not found a way to leave it behind, yet.

Amanda Currie's place was a tiny, two bedroom, tin roofed house on Shepherd Street, the lawn a mix of dirt and dried grass, and the garden weeds and tiny cactus, like old, sun faded ornaments painted green and left to fade away in the front. They were the final vestiges of an attempt at a waterless garden, an idea that Williams himself had had for his similarly small house, but one that had never gotten to the point of killing the weeds that clung to it stubbornly. Inside, the differences between the two homes became even more pronounced: Williams' place, while not empty, and certainly not cleaned regularly, contained very little outside the couch, TV, his bed, and an always made, never used spare bed in the second room. On the dining room table there were reports, each of them waiting for him to sit and complete, half-heartedly, while eating one of his limited recipes in the evening. Currie's place, in comparison, was a cornucopia: three guitars lay in the living room, one on the old couch, two on the floor, all of them surrounded by CDs, cans of Coke and bottles of water, and empty plates, a jacket, and so on and so forth in such a way that all the items blurred to Williams as he picked his path to the bedrooms, murmuring the names of things that caught his eye as he went, forgetting them instantly until he came to the first. Inside, he found a fourth guitar, acoustic, two amps, broken and full strings on the dresser table, books of music, CDs, a tiny stereo, a notebook, and a single, unmade bed. With plastic gloves, he pulled open the draws and wardrobe and found a range of clothes. Blacks and reds, mostly. Everyone had a set of colours that they liked to wear, Williams had found, and it was when those colours began to change that you could find a corresponding change in the individual. At least, that was the theory he had developed, just over eight years ago, and it hadn't failed him yet.

In the second bedroom, his slow, murmuring—"Door shows its been kicked at the bottom, someone smokes"—stroll found a dismantled drum kit, the snare covering stabbed in by a pair of sticks. The rest of the room was dominated by an unmade double bed with red sheets and the hint of perfume beneath the cigarettes. The closet, when he pulled back the flimsy wooden doors, was empty of everything but clothes hangers, two dozen of the metal holdings hanging from the bar like the petrified remains of ancient, ugly birds. It wasn't proving difficult for him to have a suspect for the violent trauma to the back of Amanda Currie's head and spine, it seemed. That didn't surprise Williams: there had been five murders in Red Grove in the last fifteen years, and each of them had been done by a family member, either by blood or marriage, each of them done in that intense hatred that only having someone in your life so meaningfully could inspire.

From the bedrooms, he made his way across the thin red and brown carpet—"Where is the roommate?"—and into the white lino floored kitchen. There, the sink was empty. The fridge, too, or mostly. A can of

Coke, a piece of meat going brown, a Babe Ruth. The cupboards were full of plates, cups, glasses, nothing unusual. There were some drugs—aspirin and the like—in the cupboard above the fridge. Nothing unusual there, either. In fact, the only unusual thing he found in the kitchen was a photograph, unframed, and with a curiously fragile nudity to it. A CD lay beneath it, the cover a collage of withered flowers. The photo, however, revealed two girls, twins, and identical; one held a guitar—she was in red and black—and the other held drumsticks. "Just black for you, then." Williams picked up both CD and picture in his covered grip. The girls were pretty in that way that local teenagers often were in Red Grove: white, but browned in the sun, and with dark hair, nice breasts, and a figure that time and children would take from them. They were his type, but separated by a generation or two and a full head of hair and full set of teeth. One of them was Amanda Currie; the one holding the guitar, he figured. He was a little confused, however, by the fact that none of her personal details supplied at the office had noted that she had a twin. A mother, yes. A father, deceased. Nothing else. Strange, but not the first time, he supposed, and tragic if the sister was dead herself or responsible.

"Wouldn't be the first time, either."

The CD, which Williams opened with a casual flick, was for a band called Dried Flowers, and had the same photo on the inside jacket. The girls had a band of two, it seemed. A closer look at the actual album revealed it to be self-produced, the label listed as TwinsOne, the address for ordering was the house he stood in. With a shrug, he closed it, and kept both. He'd be back to dust the place, if he felt it necessary; but first he'd let the real estate know that they couldn't come in, then call up Steve, the part timer on today—he had four part time sheriffs, each of them young and with brutally short haircuts as if they came from the same white kid machine— and have him tape down the house, and then he'd call Amanda Currie's mother. That was a conversation he didn't want to have.

Twisting the key to start the engine, he slipped the album into the truck's player and, with half an eye on the road, listened to it for the fifteen minutes it took him to reach the office.

"Shit," he said, five minutes into the drive, "you girls couldn't play a note."

You Never Knew Her Mother (Who Did Not Weep)

Helen Currie, a small woman with discoloured teeth, and who had lost her looks to sag, expansion, and sun, sat on the white cushioned fold out steel chair in Williams' stark office and held her leather handbag tightly on her lap, her knuckles a stark white against her white skin. "I don't have to see her, do I?" she asked, finally, her tone suggesting that if the answer was yes, then she would do it only with submissiveness born out of loss. "Not like that?"

It was hard. It was *always* hard, these moments, but Williams had relied upon his ability to switch it off to get him through. He could view it abstractly, and from a distance no matter how close he was physically. He'd lost that, somehow, in the look of Amanda Currie's ash stained teeth gritted so tightly, and without his distance, he was uncomfortable, *fucking uncomfortable* he murmured inside his head. What made it worse was that he could never predict how people were going to react. It was always different. Most cried, sobbed, needed to be held—and Williams did that, he held the ones, male, female, young, old, whoever, whatever, who needed to be held. Others were quiet and asked to see the body and stood there in silence and did their grieving elsewhere. In a few rare cases, people accused him of making a joke. A sick joke that he, Williams, came up with because he had nothing better to do than to sit around after work and think which family he'd be cruel to the following day. But he understood that. He understood all the reactions. He had distance. He could see the hurt. None of it touched him, except in the briefest, lightest touches of sympathy for a fellow human. Not here, though, he thought. No. Not here. He pulled open the drawer of his table, lifted out a slim bottle of Southern Comfort, and said, "No, you don't have to see her. Drink?"

The only cups he had were plastic, from the coffee and water machine, but Helen Currie took one and held it with a frail sense of gratitude.

"I got some questions." He was drinking himself. "That okay?"

She nodded, sipped from her cup, left her eyes on it.

"Mind if I record?" After a shake of her head to say she didn't mind, he flipped the small recorder on, and said, "Who did Amanda live with?"

"Sarah."

"Sarah who?"

"Her sister, Sarah."

Not, Williams thought, *my daughter, Sarah.* "You know where she is?"

"If she's not at their house, no." The plastic cup swirled, then she lifted it. Once lowered, she said, "I don't know who her friends are."

"You're not close?"

She shook her head.

"Most of her stuff is gone."

That made Helen look at him, a quick, but wary rise of her eyes from the cup. "Are you saying—"

"All I know is that she's not there, but I'd like to find her. I'd like to speak to her." He paused then, deliberately, to both catch his thoughts and let his words settle in Helen. He sipped the Southern Comfort, wished he had some Coke, wished he knew how long he'd been keeping a bottle in the drawer at work. Four years? It wasn't more than five, he knew that. "Either of them got a boyfriend, girlfriend?"

"Amanda didn't have time for relationships." Helen settled the plastic cup down on the table, a thin layer of liquid able to be seen staining the bottom through the bright light of the room. "She had music to write. Music to play. That's all she cared about. I don't even think she'd kissed a boy."

"Sarah?"

She shrugged.

"Helen," Williams said, "I need your help here."

She nudged the plastic cup towards him, a signal. "Do you have children?"

"I have a son," he replied. Southern Comfort slipped out in a wet line into the cup. "He lives with his mother in L.A.."

"Do you ever feel like he isn't yours?"

Williams shook his head. "No." Even though he hadn't seen Samuel for six years, hadn't spoken to him in five—if you could call speaking to a then three year old a conversation, he didn't know—and though he told himself that it was for the best that he kept his distance, that he didn't track down where they had moved a second time, not after the letter that told him about the new man, the new family, and that it would be a kindness if he didn't confuse the boy, a kindness she was going to force upon him . . . no, not after all that, had he ever thought that his son wasn't part of him.

"I look at that girl," Helen said, drawing the cup to her slowly as if it were full of bitter pills. "I look at her and I can say I don't know her, that she's a stranger to me. That I feel nothing towards her. Isn't that awful? It should be. It should be awful. It's an awful thing to know. But I don't feel bad about it—I just don't feel anything about the girl. With Amanda it's different, but with Sarah?"

"I'm not—"

"And it's returned," she continued, her voice a monotonous recital of thoughts she had had for years. "I'm nothing to Sarah. She said that to me, once. She told me that I wasn't her mother, that I was nothing to her. I couldn't even argue." She looked up at him then, the confusion in her eyes seeking justification, salvation, or absolution. "I don't even have a birth certificate for her. I lost it. What mother loses her daughter's birth certificate? A mother who knows that she has had something that's not right, that the daughter she gave birth to is not part of her, that—that it's like she's been forced on me, somehow. I don't know. I just—I don't know what I'm trying to say. I don't even know if this is making sense to you."

A little, he thought, *a little to piece together motivation*, but you can't tell a mother that. You lie to her about that. "How was her relationship with Amanda?"

"She loved her."

"And the music?"

"Amanda was the music. Sarah loved it all." She drank the Southern Comfort with one swift movement, the medicinal way. "Their world was music and each other, like they were born in it."

"You ever hear them play?"

He couldn't help it: the words slipped out, a mistake born out of curiosity, but when Helen Currie met his gaze, there was, in her pain and confusion, an acknowledgment of what he had heard on the way to his office.

"Yes," she said, softly.

You Never Knew Her Sister (Who is Lost)

Dried Flowers played in Jacob's Barn two weeks before the fire in the mosque.

Jacob's—the Barn was habitually left out—was Red Grove's nothing bar, a place that was a long, dirty passage between two restaurants, one serving cheap Italian food, and the other greasy pizza, also cheap. Williams had been to all three more than once, the pizza place more than twice and, if he were being honest, Jacob's more than both put together. The inside of the latter was a long bar with old wooden stools lined up against it, cigarette troughs on the floor, and dead animals on the walls. Trophies hunted in catalogues. There was an old TV beneath a dusty bull's head, and at the very end, a tiny stage next to an old jukebox. It was the kind of place that thrived because it had cheap drinks and, in Red Grove, cheap drinks brought in the men and women who couldn't find steady work and the kids who weren't legal and didn't have the money, ID, or appreciation for the other two bars in town. Music also brought in the last group: Jacob's was the only local place where a local band could get a spot on Friday night and show their stuff, guaranteed.

"Yeah, I remember Mandy. Fuck, but she was shit on stage." Mike Carey, owner of Jacob's, was a big white guy covered in coloured tattoos of snakes and skulls down his arms and across his chest, so thick and heavy a collage of blue, green, and red that not a hint of his white skin was exposed except on his hands and neck and face, where a greying, but still mostly brown beard, and long, balding hair hid most of the skin. "Kinda surprised me that they were so fucking awful, I have to say. She was so fucking intense on it. You should've seen this girl, Pete, she had nothing but music in her. I thought I was going to find the next big fucking thing."

"You didn't get her to play first?"

"That's not how Friday night works." Carey placed a beer in front of Williams, asked for nothing in return. "You put your name down, you get up, you start. We get shit, we get fun, we get okay—we never get good, but that's not the point. It's a place to start, if you're serious; a place to have some fun if you aren't. It's just something to do on a Friday night. Thought I was going to get more this time, though."

Williams drank his beer and Carey kept talking, profanities lacing the details of a bad set. *A real bad set, yeah, no surprise.* Both men had known each other for a long time and were friends, which was why Williams drank for free, and why he overlooked the underage kids drinking when bands played (and when they didn't). The last had never got him too troubled, anyhow: in Red Grove kids either stole their parents liquor, had older kids buy it to drink in empty paddocks, or drank in Jacob's. Stop the last and there was still the other two. Stop the first and there was still the second, and there would always be the second. "What was the sister like?" he asked, eventually.

"The sister?"

"Yeah." He paused, sucked on his false teeth, a habit just developing, then pulled out his notebook. "Sarah. That's her name."

"Right. Fuck. I blanked on that for a second."

Me too. Odd, but nothing worth worrying about. "Remember her though?"

"Yeah, she was the drummer." Carey nodded at an elderly, heavily lined man who entered the otherwise empty bar. "She was an angry girl, that's what she was. Her sister got on stage, had disks they wanted to sell; started off all right, since she was comfortable on stage. But five minutes into it and they were being booed and told to fuck off. They must've known it would happen. It happens once a month here, and I'd seen Mandy before, Sarah too, I reckon, but maybe I just only ever saw one and not the other. But Friday is Cheer or Boo night and once the booing started, it was Sarah who cracked it at the back and started abusing the audience."

Half a glass left. Williams said, "That always works well."

Carey laughed. "Just makes them boo more. Got so bad that Mandy ran the fuck off stage, leaving her sister up there. Sarah hung 'round for a bit then gave everyone the finger and went after her."

"You see them after?"

"Yeah, and that fucking surprised me." He finished pouring a beer, placed it down in front of the old man, collected the money. "She—Mandy, she'd been crying, like you would, but when I found them out back, she still had that intensity. Still that *want* in her eyes. Kept telling me it was nothing but a minor setback. That she'd get it right soon. That I could expect to see her back, which is kinda admirable, in its own way, but seemed to me like she was ignoring the truth of the situation. Seemed she was kinda blind to it, y'know?"

Williams left shortly after that and on the street said, "Not making sense." It wasn't: according to Carey, Sarah had been standing at the back, nodding in agreement with Amanda, completely supportive. The anger that she had shown on the stage was simply not there, he said. Evaporated. Summer dams in a drought. Who knew? Certainly not him, and he half wished that Sarah would show up now, so he could talk to her and figure out how she went from that to killing her. Instead, as he stood under the clean, colourless light of Red Grove sun, Williams stared at the cafe across from him. In there, he knew, worked Emily, a girl who had just turned nineteen and who had gotten married on the same day to Robert Parson, a year older than her. He knew about it because it had made the paper, the lean white girl in her wedding gown making the front page because it was one of the few Red Grove weddings of nineteen year olds not to be done under the influence of pregnancy or religion. She would have been in the same year as Amanda and Sarah, would know the pair of them, might even know some of the latter girl's friends. Worth the walk, anyway.

Inside the cafe, Williams introduced himself to Emily who, having caught her between the breakfast and lunch crowds, was sitting at one of the tables with a glass of juice and reading an old paperback thriller, her tiny strip of a name badge before her.

With smiles, offers of food, drink, all of which he turned down, Emily Parson told him what he had heard already about Amanda: about the obsession, about the want, and about her complete inability in relation to music and the way that surprised her the first time. She had even seen the set in Jacob's, which, at this stage in her relationship with Amanda, was no surprise. Still, when she spoke of the dead girl, she did so fondly—"like she was a kid who didn't know any better"—even if she knew nothing to tell him that would relate to her murder and the fire in the mosque.

Strangely, however, she did not speak of Sarah until he bought it up. "Sarah?"

"Yeah," Williams said. "Her sister."

"Her twin, right." Emily Parson shrugged, looked a little embarrassed. "I forgot. But I'm going to have to apologize, Sheriff, because I just don't remember her at school. It was a shock to see her there; the whole time I just drew a blank, and I still do. So did all my friends. None of us could remember her from the school: it was as if she just appeared after we'd finished."

And They Were in a Band He Didn't Like

It got strange, afterward.

With Emily Parson's words lingering in his mind, Williams returned to his sparse, brightly lit office and began making phone calls. At Red Grove High, it was only Amanda who was remembered by the sad-voiced principal, Audrey Davids, and only Amanda who appeared in the files. It was an unremarkable file, lacking definition in studies and delinquency. In a year of sixty-seven, it was fair to say that Amanda Currie had been a ghost, forced to wait until after High School for colour and weight to be added to her so that she could be real. But at least she was a ghost: that trail of paper work was more that her sister had.

"If you could just walk through the door, Sarah," Williams muttered, dropping the phone into its cradle after the call, "just right through my door, that'd be real helpful."

Before Red Grove, Williams discovered as he picked his way like a vulture through the files he'd printed out, the Currie family had lived in Yermo. The father—Martin—hard worked on the military site there. Calls to the local High and Junior High Schools in Yermo did not find anyone who could remember Sarah, or find a listing for her on the roll, just as it had been for Red Grove, and when he called the military base, a sweet-sounding white girl told him that Sergeant Martin Currie, deceased for reasons she could not disclose, had one daughter, one wife.

"Through the door. Just right through the door. Come in and sit down. I'll give you a drink."

After that last frustrating call, Williams saluted the door with his plastic cup, refilled twice, and then picked up the photograph of Amanda and Sarah. It was evidence of a very tangible kind of her existence but, it appeared, he was one of the few people with it. Maybe she was a secret, then? An angry little secret kept hidden. That would go some way to explaining it: Sarah could have lived with an aunt—Helen had a sister, Martin a brother and sister—and, once the thought appeared, it bloomed inside his mind, growing so big and bright that all other avenues of thought were obscured by it. "Some mystery solver you are, just making this shit up," he murmured as he dialed Helen Currie's number, and waited while it rang.

"Hello?"

It was a man's voice, deep, but familiar.

"Yeah, hi. This is Sheriff Pete Williams. I'm wondering if I could speak to Helen?"

"I'm sorry, Sheriff, but she's asleep. I'd rather not wake her—it's been hard, y'know?"

He sympathized, but still couldn't pick the voice. "That's fine. Who am I speaking with?"

"Robert Hicks."

A big, fatty man, caught twice for speeding, once for drunk driving. "Hi, Rob. Think you might help me? I'm trying to track down who Sarah lived with before coming to Red Grove?"

"She lived in Yermo with Helen."

"Didn't live with aunt or nothing?"

"Kinda grief she gives, I wish she had, but no."

After the phone clicked, a solitary piece of punctuation to end his theory, Williams picked up the photo again.

"Fuck me," he said, finally, and tossed it across the room with a defeated flick.

He left it in the corner, a coloured, useless memory, and left the office to head home. The day was just about done, anyhow, but mostly he just couldn't handle another moment sitting in that chair, calling people, hearing them tell him they didn't know Sarah, and feeling his frustration grow. It was enough to make a man with a borderline drinking problem think he'd pushed himself across that line. Still, when he climbed into his sun-warmed truck and found the Dried Flowers album still on the passenger seat, he couldn't resist opening it, just to double check that Sarah was still on the inside. She was, of course, and that frustrated him more. Maybe this frustration was what detectives in fiction felt? He'd never been a big reader, but the thought, now there, left him feeling as if he'd missed a way to solve his problem. He even had books that he could consult, bought by his wife before they left for L.A., and still unread. Their library, despite best intentions, had been a pristine one, and she had left it with him when she took his son and her new clothes, and he thought—"It isn't going to help, idiot"—that they might provide a way for him to find his answer.

It was desperation, nothing more, he knew. Chances were that in the morning he would be back to wishing that Sarah would simply walk into his office off the street, which was worse than looking through detective novels for answers. In truth, he knew what he should do, which was to call the county's office, tell them what happened, and have them send someone who had dealt with this kind of thing before. He wouldn't, though. He couldn't. Not yet. The two girls had dug under his impersonality, his purposeful deadening of emotions in relation to his job and, as he drove through the darkened Bale Street on which he lived, he knew that he would not be able to let it go. In fact—

He stopped.

Literally.

He jammed his foot on the brake and jerked his truck to stop half way up his driveway.

There, in front of his squat, tin roofed, dark house, sat Sarah Currie. She was on the cement stairs, a thick backpack next to her, and a series of cigarette butts at her feet. She was wearing brown and orange, earthy colours, and no black; but there was no time to linger over that realization than the quick, subconscious note he made, because as his truck stopped, as the lights illuminated her, she rose to her feet, taller than what he imagined, and with a small, black pistol in her hand. Upon seeing that, there was a moment, just one, where before he turned the engine off, before the lights flicked off, he thought that he should put the truck in reverse. He should stomp on the gas, call Steve, get the gun he left locked in his office and . . . but he didn't, even though he knew she had killed her sister, even though he knew it possible that she could kill him, he didn't.

His hard soled shoes hit the gravel. "Sarah Currie," he said, trying to place as much authority in his voice as he could. "I've been looking for you."

"I know."

"You want to put down the gun?"

"No." She sounded controlled, confident, unphased by his tone. "Stay by your truck, too."

"Okay." He put his palms out, fingers wide, projecting as little threat as he could. "How did you hear I was looking for you?"

"I heard you."

"Heard?"

"Yes." She had yet to raise the gun, but he noted that her feet kept moving, agitated. "It was all I heard today."

Taking a step forward, Williams said, "Your Mum—"

"She's not my mother!" Sarah cut him off loudly, her right arm, the arm that held that gun, twitching suddenly, and causing him to tense, to halt his second step. "I could hear you, Sheriff. Hear you in your office, in the street, in your truck, wanting me to come and see you. Pleading with me. Telling me to walk through the door, to hand you an answer."

Unable to say anything else, he said, "This is not my office."

"No." She smiled, a queer, disconcerting smile. "I have some choice over what I do now. I have some free will. You're not—"

"Sarah."

"Amanda," she said. "I was going to say Amanda."

"She's dead."

"I know."

28

"You." He paused, then mentally shrugged, took another step forward, and said, "You killed her?"

Sarah's strange smile evaporated and a frown, a tiny turn of her lips, a sign of genuine regret, emerged in its place. "Not on purpose. She—she wanted to hurt herself so badly. She wanted to punish herself. It was after the gig at Jacob's, because of that. It was meant to go differently!" She shook her head. "She was so sure of that. She knew it. She *believed* it. We weren't meant to be booed off stage. We were supposed to be loved—but when that didn't happen, she blamed herself. She hadn't believed enough, she said. It made her so angry."

"I heard that was you."

The regret flashed away: the eye in her emotional cyclone. "Yes. I suppose you did."

He continued forward, slowly. "Why don't you tell me what's going on here? Why no one remembers you?"

"No."

She shot him.

Once, then twice, but not, he thought as he fell, not a third time.

"I don't need people to tell me what to do," he heard her say. "I don't need their thoughts in mine, not now. Without her around, there's no one to force people to remember me. No one to force me to remember things I never did. To feel things I never felt. Do you know what that's like? When she was angry, I was angry. When she hated someone, I hated someone. She got to be free of it, but not me, no. No. It was like she really did just make me up one day to be everything she didn't like about herself." She was standing above him now, and he looked up, looked at her from where he sat crumpled in the gravel, but could not really see her. His focus was on the blood flowing from his stomach, on the difficulty he had swallowing. But her smile, that queer smile from before, returned to her face as he looked up and it was, even distracted as he was, he was sure that it was the sign of her derangement, of her broken psyche, of the reason why she killed her sister. "No," her voice was muffled, and it seemed that she was answering him, but he hadn't spoken, for once, he hadn't. "That's not true. She really did make me up, to be what she couldn't be. So she could make that music that no one liked. That was the crazy part."

But it Made Him Think of You

When she was gone, he lay there on the gravel, dying.

No one had come to him, but even though he found it difficult to focus, he wasn't surprised. They should stay inside. They should stay where it was safe. Still, he thought. Still, if one of those people in any of the blurry-lit houses could call an ambulance, that wouldn't hurt . . . but he did not say it. What did it matter? He wouldn't die with gritted teeth like Amanda Currie. There was no reason for him to do so—and that, he realized, there, the end of his epiphany, the final part, was why she had dug under his skin. The intensity that everyone had spoke of, her desire to be a musician, it was there, even in death, marking her as something she had lost; but he had no such thing to lose. He had so little, in fact, that he could not even be bothered to crawl painfully to his truck, to radio for the ambulance. By turning his head he could see the outline of the bumper, the dent in the metal from where he'd hit a pole, parking, a little drunk. No, it really didn't matter. Inside the house was empty. One bed still made. One not. Photos still in their dusty place. He could not grit his teeth if he tried.

But.

But.

But what, he thought dimly, the sound of an ambulance not yet reaching his ears, what if that deranged girl was right, what if, through simple force of belief, you could change the world around you?

What then?

Or So His Letter Said.

The Dreaming City

In his dreams, he had always been Mark Twain; awake, he had always been Samuel Clemens.

It had been so since the day he had first used the pseudonym. At first, he thought of it as a warning, but the first dreams had been sweet like the Missouri summers of his childhood, before his father's death. There was a rare quality to them, and he awoke refreshed and invigorated and filled with the kind of joy that not even the most vivid memory of his childhood years could supply; of course, as time continued, not all the dreams of Mark Twain had been so pleasant, but even the nightmares provided him with a substance that nothing in the waking world could provide him.

And now, at sixty, asleep in the White Horse Motel in Sydney, the small, grey haired man no longer felt the slightest sense of warning as he dreamed.

It was natural, normal, as familiar as the shape of his hands. It simply *was*.

Mark Twain dreamed:

He stood on the wooden, creaking docks of Sydney Harbour. It was early evening, and the sky had been splattered with leaking orange paint, while in front of him was an ocean of closely packed, swaying hulks: rotting old troop transports and men-o-wars, their masts and rigging stripped away, the remaining wooden shells turned into floating prisons that had, one hundred years ago, marred the Thames in a cultural plague.

1788.

The Eora watched the arrival of the First Fleet from the shores of the Harbour, and were told by the Elders that they had nothing to fear from the great ships: they held the spirits of their ancestors, reborn in fragile white skin. In response, the Eora questioned and argued, but the truth, the Elders said, was inescapable.

Look closely, they whispered, *and you will recognize the members of your family.*

But how? the Eora demanded with one voice. *How can this be true?*

The Elders never hesitated with their response: *They have sailed out of the Spirit World itself.*

Introduction to *A Walking Tour Through the Dreaming City.*

The Harbour has never been a welcoming birth for immigrants. Since the day the English landed and changed its name from Cadi to Sydney Harbour, this has been the case. The cultural wars that have been fought along its banks and throughout Sydney's streets for over two hundred years have left their mark on the heart of our great beast, and the signpost for this is the Harbour. Yet strangely, the literary acknowledgement of the Harbour's significance does not begin in the journals of the naval captains who arrived with convicts, or in the diaries of the Irish or Chinese, but in this book you are holding now, Mark Twain's *A Walking Tour Through The Dreaming City:*

'Sydney Harbour is shut behind a precipice that extends some miles like a wall, and exhibits no break to the ignorant stranger. It has a break in the middle, but it makes so little show that even Captain Cook sailed by without seeing it. Near by that break is a false break which resembles it, and which used to make trouble for the mariner at night, in the early days before the place was lighted. Any stranger approaching Sydney is advised to take heed as the entrance is the only warning the city will offer on its nature; that it is filled with false hope and false promise, and that it and its citizens will break anyone dreaming who is not natural to it.'

Twain understood Sydney, in some ways clearer than those who have lived in it, while at the same time being incredibly naïve about certain aspects of it. However, he understood the importance of the Harbour, and it is from here that he launched his dissection of the city, altering it forever. It might appear strange to an Australian that such an important change in Sydney's history would begin in an American's book (and published one hundred years after the first Englishman stepped foot on the soil), but after shaping the city and its political climate, historians and academics alike have been forced into recognizing Mark Twain's legacy for years. The reader only has to walk down George Street, and into the floating mass of American culture that is presented in signs tattooing *McDonalds, Nike, Subway, Taco Bell, HMV Music*, and *Borders* onto his or her subconscious to understand the very basics of the argument.

The seeds of this gift (or curse, depending on your stance) have now been passed onto you, dear reader, with this new edition. In these pages, you will find the finest chronicle of English occupied Sydney, which began when the first of our chained ancestors stepped onto our shores, and the birth of the new Sydney when the most American of Americans began his tour.

And yet, still, the meaning of the Harbour and Sydney has not changed in all that time. It is as if it is immune, or purposefully resistant to anything that arrives. The result of this, is that time has only crystallized the fact that Sydney has never welcomed immigrants, never welcomed the poor, the hungry, or anyone who is in need, and that this mentality spreads throughout the country from here. It is a sad fact in this new millennium that examples are easy to find: Detention Camps that spring up as barbwire islands in the dusty sea of outback New South Wales, fattened with immigrants who have fled less fortunate countries than ours, are just one example. But then perhaps Twain, for all the change he brought, knew that this part of Sydney's nature would not change. After all, it was he who wrote that 'Satan made the deceptive beauty of Sydney's Harbour, which is available for all to witness on shore.' It is a sentiment that anyone who has lived in Sydney will find familiar.

1788.

Pemulwy, the scarred, black skinned Eora warrior, climbed into the thick arms of a eucalyptus tree. There, he watched his dead brothers row into the ocean on ugly, unsuitable boats, and fish.

The warrior had never doubted the Elders before, but he did now. He could do nothing but. On the ground, beside the grey eucalyptus, lay his spear, tipped with the spines of the stingray; while out in the ocean, the dead dragged one of the great fishes from the water.

The creature was huge and grey and sacred. It had been—and would ever be—since the Eora and other tribes had begun telling the story of the ancient fisherman Jigalulu. In the story, one of the stingrays gave its life to the fisherman so that he could fashion a spear to kill the great shark Burbangi, who had murdered his father and brothers[1].

Yet, from his perch, Pemulwy watched the dead kill the stingray with a knife, and later, in the evening, watched them cook and eat it.

The Elders told Pemulwy that the dead, being dead, could do as they wished with the fish, but he disagreed. It was not just an insult to the Spirits, but an act of supreme arrogance that told the warrior that the dead did not care at all for their kin.

But it was not a solitary act.

Perhaps worse happened during the day, when the dead would take the young Eora, take their food, and take their land, giving them nothing but coloured ribbons and blankets that left them ill in ways that none had ever seen before.

Finally, on the branch of the eucalyptus tree, watching the dead eat the sacred flesh of the stingray, he was forced to answer why they acted this way.

The answer was simple:

They are not my kin.

They are invaders.

1895.

....

He followed the long, twisting gangplank that looped around the hulk,

---

1. In the story, Jigalulu's spear does not kill the shark. Instead, the shark flees, breaking the spear but leaving the stingray spines imbedded, thus forming the fin that warns men of a shark's approach. While this is most certainly an Aboriginal story, the notion that the Eora of Sydney believed the stingray to be a sacred creature is not. The idea can be found in Tim Flannery's the Birth of Sydney, where he also informs the reader that the largest of the stingrays taken from the Harbour weighed, when gutted, 200 kilograms.

showing him the rotting and discoloured frame of the ship. Below him, the water was still, and pitch black, and emanated a menace that caused Twain's old legs to tremble whenever the planks he stepped on groaned beneath his weight. Half way around the hulk, Twain knew that he did not want to continue, but his feet would not stop, and he found himself muttering in disgust to them and making his way onto the deck.

The deck was ragged, empty, and filled with invisible spirits: the till turned left and right, spun by the hands of an unseen and pointless sailor; above, the remains of the rigging flapped, trailing through the air as decayed streamers and confetti; while the cabin door to the captain's quarters was twisted off its frame, and hanging on one hinge, the glass window shattered, leaving jagged points into the middle. Twain walked on rotting planks and passed broken railings that were circled with rusted chains.

It was a parade of death, cheering him towards the hulk's rotting belly with relentless determination.

The smell of unwashed bodies, urine and feces overwhelmed him when he stepped onto the creaking stairs that led into the ship's belly. Had he been anywhere else, he was sure he would have fallen, or even vomited, so tangible was the odour; but instead he continued down the stairs, one step at a time.

At the bottom of the stairs, the smell grew stronger, and the air had a heavy quality to it, but the belly of the hulk itself was empty. He had expected to see hundreds of men and women, sick, dying, and generally pitiful, huddled together, but instead he found only a thin pool of black sea water and the disintegrating ribs of the ship.

And, in the far corner of the hulk, the shadow of a man.

Twain's feet splashed noiselessly through the black water, and the silence around him grew while the oppressive odour slipped away. He was not sure what was worse, as the silence filled his head like wet cotton, and weighed down his senses until the shadow revealed itself to be a black skinned man.

He was darker that any black man Twain had seen before; black like the water he stood in, he was naked and across his skin had been painted white bones. Yet, as Twain gazed at the bones, the paint became tangible, turning the bones solid. In response to his awareness, they began to move, shifting and twitching and cracking slightly while the man's black flesh remained still.

Twain's gaze was pulled away from the bones when a buttery yellow light filled the hull, illuminating a painting on the back wall. It had four rectangle panels, each panel located beneath the proceeding one.

In the first panel were two men and two women, one black and one white of each gender. The two women held babies, and wore white gowns with hoods, while the men wore trousers and shirts and had a dog beside them. The second showed an English Naval Officer (Twain did not know who) shaking hands with an Aboriginal Elder. The third panel showed an Aboriginal man being hung for killing a white man, while the fourth panel, identical to the third, showed a white man being hung for killing an Aborigine. It was, Twain knew, a message of equality, but it felt cold, and hollow for reasons he was unable to voice.

Finally, turning to the black man—an Aborigine—he said, "Is this your painting?"

"No," he replied, the skull painted across his face moving in response, while his thick lips remained still and pressed tightly together. "It was painted by an Englishman for Englishmen, as you can clearly see."

More confidently then he felt, Twain said, "It doesn't have 'English' in big lights now, does it?"

"Look at their clothes, Mark Twain."

Unnerved by the use of his name, Twain returned his gaze to the painting: in the first panel, as he had noted, all the men and women were dressed identically, while in the third and fourth panel, the dead Aborigines wore nothing but a loincloth and the painted symbols of their tribes.

"Equality and law rise from the English viewpoint," the bones of the Aborigine said quietly, the tone laced with anger and resentment.

"That's hardly a unique experience," Twain replied, the confidence he feigned earlier finding a foothold in his consciousness.

"I am aware of this," he said. "The Oceans of the Earth speak to me, and tell me of the English, and their Empire. And they tell me how it crumbles with revolutions, but that does not happen here, in Sydney. Other things happen here."

Behind the Aborigine, the painting twisted and became alive: the white man stepped from his noose and shook hands with the officers, and they passed him a flask of rum. (Twain did not know how he knew that it was rum, but it was a dream and he knew not to question the logic of a dream.) In the top panel, the black man was beaten by the white man, and attacked by the dogs, while the black baby in the Aboriginal woman's arms disappeared, and was replaced by a baby of mixed colour and heritage which began to fade until the baby was as white as the baby next to it.

"That's a nice trick." Twain's foothold slipped into a vocal tremor as the scenes played themselves out in an endless loop. He cleared his throat loudly and asked, "What's your name, then?"

"Once," the Aborigine's bones replied quietly, "I was called Cadi."

1788.

Perched once again on a eucalyptus branch, Pemulwy, three weeks later, watched the skyline turn red and grey with flames and smoke. The cries of the dead pierced the night as they rushed from their tents to the wooden dwelling that held their food.

Pemulwy's decision to fight the dead was not popular among the Eora. Elders from other tribes sent messages and warned him that the Spirits would be furious, and many warned that his own spirit, strong now, would not survive.

Last night, an Elder had sat in front of him and told him that he would die nine years from now if he followed this path, and that he would be struck down by divisions that he, Pemulwy, created in his kin. The words had rung disconcertingly true, as splits throughout the Eora were already beginning to show.

But he had no other choice. He was a warrior, and as such, he would fight the dead like any other invader into his land: he would strike their weakest targets: the houses where they kept food, and crops they were trying to grow. He would burn them, and then he would burn the men and women, and, finally, the land itself if required. Whatever the white beeàna[2] decided in response, he would also deal with.

He drew strength from the fact that a dozen other warriors, stretched throughout the bony trees and in the bush around him, also watched the fires. He knew, gazing out at their shadowed figures, that more would come after the night. Perhaps from the dead themselves.

He did not believe that any of the dead were kin, but around the Harbour there were black skinned men that he felt a faint kinship for. It was not unreasonable, he believed, to think that they might join him—and it

---

2. The word means father, and in this case, applies to Governor Arthur Phillip. Phillip's title was given because he was missing a front incisor, which, in one of the tribes native to that part of Sydney, would be knocked out of the mouth of a boy during the ritual of manhood. Therefore, it was assumed that Phillip, who led the returning spirits, was part of the Eora.

would certainly assure some of the worries from the Elders if he could bring one back as a friend.

He would have such a chance now:

In front of him a black figure emerged from the fire lit horizon, the harsh crack of leaves, twigs, and scrubs alerting the warrior to his presence long before he came into sight. With a cautioning wave to his warriors, Pemulwy dropped from his perch, leaving his spear balanced along the branches.

The dead was a huge figure, twice the size of Pemulwy. His face, craggy and scarred, was a pitted black stone, with wet pebbles lodged deep within, suggesting in the dark that the dead had no eyes; but he did, and they blinked rapidly, scanning the trees and path around him, before settling upon the Eora. His clothing, covered in soot, smelled of smoke, and around his wrists was a long chain, attached to the manacle on his right arm.

His teeth, when the dead smiled, were yellow and misshaped. "Deve ser o bastard que põe o fogo," he said slowly. "Agradece."

Pemulwy had learned a small amount of the dead's language, but it was difficult to learn without a guide for context and meaning. Yet, knowing as little as he did, he knew that this was not their language.

Come with me, he said, pointing into the dark scrub. *I will offer you shelter.*

Around him, his warriors tightened in a ring above the dead, watching, waiting, protective. Unaware of them, the dead shook his head, and said, "Eu nao entendo o que você dizem, mas eu nao vou em qualquer lugar com você." Slowly, as if trying to conceal the action, he began wrapping the length of chain around his right fist.

Pemulwy, giving him one more chance before he killed him, tapped his chest, silently, and then pointed into the bush again.

"Tive suficiente com ser cativo. Você e o Inglês," the dead's gaze swept the surrounding area. "São somente os mesmo a mim nesta prisão."

"Inglês?" Pemulwy repeated, tasting the familiar word. "English?"

The dead nodded, his yellow teeth splashed against his skin. "English," he agreed, glancing behind him. The message was clear to the Eora: the English were the white men at the fires.

Still glancing behind him, the dead suddenly swung his chain-covered fist at Pemulwy.

The warrior ducked and, darting forward, jammed his foot in the back of the dead's knee, causing him to cry out in pain and slump to the ground. The cry sent a hot flush through him, and he bared his teeth in joy. Around the fallen man, the dozen Eora warriors emerged, one of them tossing Pemulwy his spear.

The black man—and he was a man, Pemulwy knew, *just a man*—began to speak, but the spear of the Eora warrior never hesitated.

Leaving his spear in the body, Pemulwy turned to the warriors. None of them had struck the dead, but they knew, by watching him, by hearing the exchange, that it was only a matter of time until they too killed the dead.

Running his fiery gaze along the semi circle of men before him, Pemulwy said, *The name of our enemy is the English.*

1895.

The bones across Cadi's skin snapped together in faint clicks as the Aborigine walked through the black water of the hulk's belly to stand before Twain.

Twain, despite his wariness, was fascinated by the features behind the white skull. It was the impression of a man sleeping, with the full, closed lips, smooth skin, and large, closed eyes. But there was nothing childlike or innocent about the Aborigine. Scars covered him in slender lines, as if a series of blades had been run again and again against his skin, and then stitched back together with a care that ultimately could not hide the damage.

"Revolutions." When Cadi's faint, skeleton whisper of a voice reached Twain's ears it was harsher: raw, sad, and violent, whereas before it had sounded like a man's. "I have tried to organize revolutions."

"That's a mighty large thing to do," Twain replied. "And not always altogether successful, from my understanding of history."

As he spoke, the ribs of the hulk melted away, and the black water had drained from his shoes; but rather than experience a dryness, the fluid was immediately replaced with new water that signalled, before he saw it, a continual silver slant of steady rain that ran over him.

Before him was an inn made from wood, with a wide, tin roofed veranda around it, and hitching posts for horses out the front. It had glass windows, while behind the glass was light provided by lanterns.

"I have tried to make symbols," Cadi's grating voice whispered to his left. "A revolution must have a symbol."

Twain began to reply, but stopped.

On the veranda, dark shapes slithered into view between the rain. Allowing the Aborigine to lead him through the mud and grass, Twain approached the figures and found them to be man-like, and moments later, to be men. They wore armour that covered their torso and head, and which was made from ugly black metal: it was dented, and poorly shaped, and the helmet looked like an upended tin, with a slit cut across for the eyes.

The armour was crude and laughable, but Twain could not bring himself to acknowledge the fact. Instead, he watched the figures load their pistols and rifles and step from the porch in heavy, awkward footfalls, the silver rain washing over their dark bodies.

"Symbols," Cadi repeated, and stepped before the figures. They paused, and he ran his bony fingers across the black armour. "A symbol to defy the English, that is what this is."

"There's certainly something in it," Twain replied quietly, shivering, but not from the cold.

"It would have been pure in Sydney." Cadi turned and raised his right arm, pointing behind Twain.

He gazed through the rain, at the graveyard of fallen branches and trees that littered the ground around the inn. At first, Twain could not see anything. But then, like ghosts emerging in the darkness, outlined by the rain, he saw them: Police Officers. The representation of English authority, scattered throughout the branches and trees, easily fifty in number, each with a rifle or pistol aimed at the four men.

"Here, it is an act of stupidity," Cadi said.

"Stop them!" Twain cried, spinning on him. "This doesn't need to happen!"

"It already has. All my Irishman had to do was ride into Sydney and walk down the streets, his guns drawn, dressed in this armour, demanding the release of his mother, and the heart of the nation would have gone to him. But he did not understand that, and instead, he took my revolution and wasted it here, where no one would understand."

Twain curled his hands into fists and fought back the urge to scream out a warning to the black armoured men. Instead, trying to hide his distaste in the situation, he said, "And what exactly happened to these youngsters who didn't go to Sydney?"

The Aborigine's voice was faint, and touched with sadness, "Like all Australian folk legends, they died at the hands of authority."

There was a loud crack from behind him, and, with a violent shiver, Twain felt a bullet pass through him. He clutched his chest, horrified, terrified, ready to scream out; but there was no injury, only the disconcerting echo of pain. *It's a fantasy! Nothing more than a cheap trick!* The thought, rather than calming Twain, made him angry. Around him, more guns fired, the bullets fat silver streaks in the air, and the four black armoured men raised their arms and returned fire before falling back into the hotel. As they did, the windows shattered and screaming from men and women inside the inn tore out and ignited the night.

"What is the meaning of this?" Twain demanded angrily. "Why show me this tragedy? Let me go—I've no interest in this!"

"You must understand the need for revolution," Cadi replied, the sockets of his skull gazing intently at him. "You must understand why the heart of Sydney needs to be replaced."

"I don't care!" Twain hollered. "This isn't my country, this isn't government! This isn't my goddamned concern!"

"No, not now. But it will be."

Cadi thrust his bony hand into the mud. There was a faint crack, and he straightened, lifting a smooth hatch from the ground. Inside was a tightly wound spiral staircase made from wood and iron railings.

"Come, Mark Twain, and I will show you more."

"Where're you taking me?" Twain asked, his feet moving without his consent. He struggled against them, but realized the futility quickly.

"Into the Spirit World," Cadi replied without emotion. "Where one step can be a day or a year or a lifetime. At the end of the stairs, you will understand the importance of this event, and why the death of an Irishman will always be remembered, if not understood."

Twain gazed at the inn, and watched as one of the black armoured men stepped out of the front door, pistols held in his hands. Alone, a dark, iron-covered beast torn by emotions and a lifetime of injustice, he strode down the stairs, firing into the Police.

Unable to watch him fall, Mark Twain accepted his descent.

1797.

Toongagal[3] had been turned into simple sprawl of ugly, poorly built English buildings parted by a muddy stretch of road and surrounded by dirty bush land.

Pemulwy emerged from the muddy scrub, followed by the lean shadows of twenty warriors. Each man was armed with only a knife, but also carried sticks and cloth across their backs; they held nothing that would hinder their speed or their use of the land and the cloudy night sky as cover, for their goal tonight was one that relied upon stealth.

Silently, Pemulwy lead the warriors along the edge of the muddy road, leading them around the town, aiming for the isolated outpost at the opposite end.

In the years of his war, the Eora warrior had become a fearsome figure in the minds of the English and his fellow tribesman, but he was not pleased with the progress he had made. Burning crops, stealing food, killing farmers on the edge of the townships: these were not stopping the arrival of Englishmen and women and their convicts. If anything, it only dug the farmers on the outskirts deeper into the land. And, as each year progressed, Pemulwy became increasingly aware that he was not winning the war.

To complicate matters, he was also coming to the realization that it was not the English and their weapons that he was losing too, but rather their clothing, food, and luxuries, such as tobacco pipes.

And rum.

Rum was the enemy that Pemulwy could not fight.

It was the currency of the land, spreading not only through the Eora and tribes inland, but the free farmers and convicts who worked for the English. It was indiscriminate, and endless, a dark, intoxicating river that weaved around everyone, and which flowed out of the hands of the English authorities.

He had learned of that only recently, when fellow tribesmen moved into the towns, lured by rum and tobacco that they received for erecting buildings, ploughing the land, and hunting. Tasks that tribesmen had done for their tribes, but now did for the English Redcoats.

---

3. Governor Philip officially named it Toongabbie in 1792, who took the name—and the land—from the Tugal clan living there.

Having followed the wayward Eora to threaten and force them back to the tribes, Pemulwy had instead decided upon a frontal attack on the English. The idea had come to him suddenly, a gift from the Spirits that was accompanied by the Elder's warning nine years ago, about his foretold death. Being a warrior, he pushed aside the doubt, and focused on acquiring English weapons. He would need them.

The outpost was a long, squat building that resembled a giant wooden goanna baking in the sun, or, in this case, the night. There were no lanterns inside it, but on the veranda, on a wooden chair, slept the white body of an Englishman.

Pemulwy motioned for the warriors behind him to wait, and he then slipped up to the veranda. The mud around the barracks pushed coolly through his toes, and clung to his feet, leaving muddy prints along the railing that he climbed, and the porch he stalked along before his strong fingers clamped over the Englishman's nose and mouth and his dagger sliced into the man's neck.

The muddy prints multiplied as the Eora warriors joined him, and they pushed through the door, into the dark, half empty barracks and circled the beds that held men. There, nothing more than a concentration of mud marked the struggle and the death that took place in the beds.

At the back of the outpost, behind a poorly made wooden door, the fading prints ended at the weapons of the English: thirty gunmetal black rifles and fifteen pistols, each with wooden stocks; a dozen sabres; one cat-o-nine-tails; chains and manacles; a dozen daggers; a small cannon on wooden wheels; and bags of powder and bullets and balls for the cannon.

The cloth and sticks were laid out, and rifles and pistols and sabres and knives taken. The cannon and its ammunition proved difficult, but Pemulwy ordered two Eora to carry it, and their feet, free of mud, made an invisible, slow exit from the building.

They were ghosts, unable to be tracked in the bush, the only sign of their passing for the returning English soldiers were the dark stains that they experienced with mounting terror two hours later. They knew who it was, in their bones, more spiritual in knowledge than they had ever experienced, as if something in the land was taunting them itself, and they knew what it meant:

Pemulwy was armed for war.

Introduction to *A Walking Tour Through the Dreaming City.*

There is no doubt that the protests, art, and stories of the Aboriginal culture influenced Mark Twain during his stay. The reader will note that the retelling of their stories and anecdotes throughout the book are always sympathetic, and that the tales he was told could have filled a dozen books equal to this one's size. Yet, as the book continues, the reader will find that he is particularly interested in the story of Pemulwy. Indeed, his fascination with the warrior was so intense that he took a band of Aboriginal storytellers under his wing, and made sure that the story of the Eora warrior was heard every evening before he performed.

The great Australian poet and author, Henry Lawson, in his private memoirs (collected, finally, in Lauren Barrow's biography, *Lawson, One Life*) wrote:

'Twain's adoption of an Aboriginal storytelling band was nothing short of shocking. Newspapers were flooded with angry letters from readers and blossomed with poisoned columns from writers. All of these complaints could be summarized into the catch phrase of 'How dare people pay their hard earned money to see the history of a savage!' It was quite the scandal at the time. Even I, who had never had a problem with an Aborigine that was based on the colour of his skin, wondered about the quality of the show now that Twain's ambitions had turned to a local cause.

Unsurprisingly, Twain's first shows with the band were failures, weighed down, no doubt, by an unappreciative audience; but by the third show, the great man himself joined the band on stage, and lent his own considerable skills in telling the tale of Pemulwy. During this first performance, he promised that if the audience was not properly respectful, then they would not be treated to Twain's solo performance later that evening.'

The shows were, after that, given a grudging praise, but they earned criticism due to the fact that they were not totally accurate on a historical level. In response, Twain replied that 'history [has] never been respectful to the needs of narrative.' At the end of his tour, the debate about Pemulwy and his importance to Sydney was such a topical item that many forgot that he did not, as Twain said, 'attack a King.'

The question that has interested historians and academics, however, is why Twain went to such lengths for the Aboriginal people and their culture. The press releases, and Twain's own statements before his arrival in Sydney, gave no hint to this desire. That is not to say that Twain was not sympathetic to native cultures: one can witness in *Following the Equator* his many generous and wonderful insights to the natives of Fiji and New Zealand, among others; but he never gave them as much attention as he did the Aborigines of Sydney. In response to the question, most researchers have focused upon a particular dream that Twain describes, where 'the visible universe [was] the physical person of God'. Many writers have drawn connecting lines between this and the peculiar belief of a Spirit World that was favoured by Aborigines.

For my own part, I cannot say. Certainly Twain experienced something, but what it was, and if it was linked to a spirituality, we will never know. It is possible that this 'spirituality' was linked to the grief that he still felt for his recently departed daughter, Susy. Some historians believe that it was this that motivated Twain, but it is too nebulous for me, a reason that is too easily accepted and dismissed under the same reasoning.

For my own part, however, I will agree with noted historian Jason Vella that whatever Twain experienced, it was linked to the Cross.

1797.

Before dawn, on the same night of the attack on the Toongagal outpost, Pemulwy and his warriors—joined by an addition twenty—swept into Burramatta[4].

The wooden outpost of the English town appeared in the misty morning, looking like an atrophied beast, and Pemulwy slipped up to it silently. With a vaulted leap over the veranda railing, the Eora warrior plunged his spear (brought to him by the additional warriors) into the belly of the lone Englishman on guard. Standing there, he turned to the dark figures of his warriors, white war paint curving like bladed bones across their skin, and motioned for them to sweep into the outpost, where they butchered the ten Englishmen inside.

After the outpost, they continued into the town, breaking open the pens, scattering livestock, and killing the men and women who

---

4. In 1791, Burramatta was renamed Parramatta by Governor Phillip, the name rising from Phillip's spelling and pronunciation of the Aboriginal word.

investigated the chorus of agitated animal noises that swept through the morning sky. It was there, watching the animals, and his men, and the dirty orange sun rising, illuminating the muddy streets and crude houses of the town, that Pemulwy realized how poorly he had planned the attack.

He would die here, on these streets, as the Elder had said.

Shaking his head, pushing the thoughts aside, Pemulwy gripped his spear and walked down the cold, muddy street. Around him, his warriors were firing into the houses, the battle having already broken down into individuals, rather than a combined force. Pemulwy had feared that this would happen—he had stressed that they had to fight as one, that they needed to remain together to take and hold the town, but his words had fled them, lost in the rush of emotions they were experiencing.

To his left, the cannon fired; the sound of splintering wood and a peak in screaming followed.

You will die here.

Shaking away the unsummoned thoughts, Pemulwy advanced on a white man that emerged from his house. Thick set, bearded, barely dressed, the man raised his rifle, but before he could fire, Pemulwy hurled his spear, skewering the man. The Eora stalked up to his body, retrieving his spear and the man's rifle, before turning back to the chaos of the town.

The cannon fired again, and the smell of smoke worked its way to the warrior; before him, bodies littered the ground. They were white men and women and children and between them, dark slices of the country given form, were his own warriors.

You will die here.

The thought was a cold chill, working up his spine, through his body. But he was a warrior, and he would not leave. Instead, he rushed through the churned mud and into the chaos of the battle, where he ploughed his spear into the back of an English woman.

When the shape of the battle changed, Pemulwy asked himself if he had seen the English soldiers arrive before the first bullet tore through his shoulder to announce their presence, or if he had not. In the split second the question passed through his mind, he realized that he had been so caught up in the bloodlust, in the killing, that he hadn't.

When the bullet tore through his left shoulder, he fell to his knees, his spear falling into the mud; in his right hand, he still gripped the English rifle. Around him, fire leapt from crude building to building, acting as his warriors had done when they swept into the town, but with a more final devastation.

They had failed.

Pemulwy rose to his feet, clutching the rifle.

Before losing control of his warriors, he had planned to organize a defensive structure, to take prisoners, to prepare for the wave of red coated soldiers that swept into the town.

The men that will kill you.

The bullets that sounded around him were organized, and worked in series, punching through the air and into the bodies of his warriors. Across the street, he watched a tall Eora warrior hit by a volley of bullets, his body lifted from the ground. It was the sign, the moment that Pemulwy's attack was truly broken, the moment he should have fled; but instead, he began running across the street to help the fallen, a bullet sinking into the calf of his right leg before he was half way across, and spinning him to the ground, into the mud.

Don't die face down.

Pemulwy pushed himself up, using the rifle for the leverage. The wave of Redcoats had become a flow of individuals, and he was aware, dimly, that some of his warriors had fled. Around him, six others were caught on the same street, firing into the red tide that worked itself to them like the lines of a whirlpool working into the centre. His warriors dropped slowly, as if an invisible finger, a spirit's finger, was reaching out and knocking them down, taking their life away as children did with toys in a game.

A third bullet punched into Pemulwy's chest.

Die fighting!

Roaring, Pemulwy raised the English rifle, levelling it at a red-coated figure in front of him. He took no recognition of the figure's details, of who he was, or what made him; he was English and it did not matter; he squeezed the trigger, and the soldier pitched backwards—

Four bullets smashed into Pemulwy in response.

The Spirit World.

To Mark Twain, the spiralling staircase was endless. The rickety, wooden panels sliced through the inky black world around him, dropping until his perspective refused to believe that he was still seeing a staircase, and his body trembled from fright.

There was no way to measure time. His body did not grow weak, or strong, and, more than once, Twain believed that he was stepping on the same two steps. When he mentioned this to Cadi, the Aborigine laughed, a warm, smooth, calming sound.

"Would you believe," he said, "that I am walking along the beach of my past? The sand is pure white, the water blue, and the horizon beautiful."

Unhappily, Twain muttered, "So this is for us tourists, huh?"

"In the Spirit World, you see what you expect to see."

Twain stopped and turned to face the Aborigine. The bones that had been so prominent on his skin were now sunken, having turned into a smooth white paste that covered his muscular body. His skin was no longer scarred, and his eyes, once closed, were open.

"What happened to you?" Twain asked, not surprised by the change.

"This is my world," Cadi replied. "Why would I look dead here?"

Twain began to respond, then shrugged, and said, "I don't suppose you've got a smoke?"

Cadi shook his head. "No. It's not a habit I've ever seen anything good rise from."

"Right then," Twain said, and continued his repetitious walk down the spiralling stairs.

Eventually, a light blinked into life in the inky black. Twain wondered, upon seeing it, what Cadi saw, but refrained from asking. He had not liked the Aborigine's previous response—it had made him feel young and foolish, that latter an emotion he worked hard to avoid. He continued down the steps, drawing closer to the dot, which in response, grew brighter, turning from yellow to gold.

Finally, Twain reached a position on the staircase where he could make out the features of the dot. It was a small, brown bird, the kind that Twain had seen many times. As he drew closer, he discovered that it was caught in mid-flight, unable to move, to rise or fall.

"I'm not the only one seeing this, right?" he asked, unable to conceal his irritation. "Or is this a private showing?"

"I see it," Cadi responded quietly.

"What is it?"

"A bird."

"Thanks," Twain muttered dryly. "What does it mean?"

Cadi smiled, but it was a small, sad smile. "This is the last Aboriginal myth, which took place before the turn of your century. In it, an Eora warrior, my first revolutionary against the English, is lying in an English hospital, shackled to the bed, dying."

"So the bird is his fantasy?" Twain raised his arm, reaching for the bird. "It's not terribly original."

"You misunderstand. This *is* the Eora warrior. On his seventh day in the hospital, he turns into a bird, and flies out of the window to return to his people."

Twain's fingers touched the bird, and its beak opened, and a small, angry chirp pierced the inky blackness, startling him. With a second chirp, the bird bit Twain's finger, and, flapping its wings, flew around the spiral staircase, and off into the darkness.

"The Aboriginal tribes began to die after this," Cadi continued sadly. "They were always my favourite, but it was a mistake to take one of their men as a champion. I poured into his spirit everything that the Aboriginal culture had, everything that gave them form and purpose. It was a mistake. There was nothing for the others, and he, alone, could not change the inevitable. He could not defeat the English."

Twain sucked on his finger, and muttered around it, "It doesn't sound like any of your so called revolutions worked."

"No," Cadi agreed. "Gone are the days when the disenfranchised could change a path. I must rely on a celebrated kind, now."

"And that's me, is it?" Twain asked, shaking his hand.

"You are a celebrity, are you not?" the Aborigine asked.

Twain shrugged, and then nodded. "Yeah, I am. But why bother with me? Just make your own kind and leave me in peace. People react better to their own kind."

"The Eora are Sydney's own," Cadi said softly. "But no Englishman would embrace them, just as no Aboriginal or Irishman would embrace the English. So tell me, whose kind should I make a celebrity out of?"

Twain began to reply, then stopped. He could think of nothing to say in response, and instead said, "Well, if that's the case, why even bother?"

Cadi was silent. Twain watched him look around, wondering what, on his beach, he was gazing at, for nothing was offered to him but the endless black and a spiralling staircase that stretched endlessly.

"If you could save your daughter, Mark Twain, would you?" Cadi finally asked.

Stiffening, Twain replied hotly, "Of course—"

"What if she was no longer the daughter you remembered? If she did things you didn't agree with, or understand. What if, except in name, and dim memory, the presence of your daughter was a totally alien thing? Would you still offer to save her?"

Swallowing his anger, Twain nodded in wordless response.

"Then we must continue onwards," Cadi said, pointing to the stairs that he did not see.

1802.

Pemulwy could not stop the English. They continued to spread, a white herd of disease and invading culture that knew no boundaries.

Once, the Eora warrior had believed that the strength of the English would unite the tribes, would force them all to fight, but it was not the case. Each week, young men and women left the tribes, lured by the items in the towns, and stayed there. Their family and friends would then journey back and forth, visiting, partaking in what was offered. Weekly, the base of the tribes was eroded, worn away not by individuals, but by the inevitable march of time, which Pemulwy, for all his strength, could not stop attacking even himself.

Ten years ago, he could run all day, and rise in the morning, ready to run again. Tracks were sharp, and bright to his eyes. The night wind was soothing, and he would lie naked beneath it, gazing up into the sky until he fell asleep. But not now. Now he took breaks during his running, and after a whole day, he would awake with aches, and the awareness that he slept longer. He needed a blanket at night, and the tracks he had followed so easily were no longer clear, and the horizon, when he gazed out, was now a shifting, blurring thing.

Worse, age arrived with another barb that Pemulwy had not expected: the animosity of the young.

They argued against everything he did. They brought back the trinkets of the English, and when he ordered them put aside, they told him that he did not understand. That he was *old*, that he no longer *understood*, that he was *trapped* in a time no longer important. To make matters worse, he could not pick up his spear and issue a challenge to respond to them directly. To attack the youth was to attack the future of the Eora.

Other problems had also arisen (and which, with the weave of his thoughts flowing from the fire he stared into, joined the procession like smoke) and that was the bushrangers. The escaped convicts, or white men who had taken to the bush, that, despite Pemulwy's instructions, had been shown the land by the young. These men—and they were always men—did not fall into conflict with the Eora warrior, but they showed to him the flaw in his early logic. The mistakes his hate had created, for the free men and women in the towns favoured the white bushrangers. They looked to them for protection and, in some cases, a future. From the towns, he had seen mugs, plates, and pipes work their way through the tribes, designed in the faces of the favoured bushrangers[5]. No such thing existed for him, nor for any other Eora or tribesman warriors that fought the English. But was it possible, that if he had aligned himself with the free men and women, instead of attacking them, he might have fought a more successful war against the English?

So closely did his thoughts mirror the argument taking place around him that Pemulwy did not notice it until his name was shouted through the night. That, and only that, drew his attention to the group before him.

They were Eora men and women, but they were not dressed like him. Instead, they wore the clothes of the English: buttoned shirts, pants, boots, dresses, with their beards and hair turned smooth and decorated with reds and blues. At their feet were bundles of their belongings, bulging in various shape and form, leading the aging Eora warrior to surmise that what was contained within would not be welcomed by him.

"He gives us his attention!" cried one of the Eora in English. He did not have a beard, but a moustache, and through his ears were silver rings. "The Great Pemulwy finally looks upon us, his subjects."

The words were not the same, but he knew them. *You're old, you're a relic, you don't understand*, spoken in the English language he despised. Unfolding his body from its position, the Eora, weaponless, lean, a map

---

5. Historian Robert Hughes, in *The Fatal Shore*, notes a line of clay pipes that were made the week after Bold Jack Donohoe's death at the hands of the authorities. They were modelled after his head, and came complete with a bullet hole in the temple, where he had been shot. They were bought, Hughes noted, by emancipated convicts and free settlers, but not in recognition of the lawfulness of Jack's death. Rather, they were bought as part of the celebrity cult that surrounded the favoured outlaw, and highlighted the local resentment towards the English officers.

of scars from English bullets that refused to kill him, stalked over to the younger man, who, to his credit, did not sink into the company of his friends.

Quietly, he said, *Miago, yes?*

"I am called James now," he spat in reply, angrily returning Pemulwy's gaze.

Shaking his head, he said, *It is a great shame—*

"Spare me," James retorted hotly. "Spare all of us your words. We have been perfectly content away from here."

Then leave, Pemulwy replied, his voice cool, controlled, his gaze running over the eight Eora behind James—it was such a fitting, ugly name for him—where he found them unable to meet his gaze.

"We cannot!" James said harshly. "Thanks to you and your ways!"

Pemulwy's eyes flashed with a touch of anger, and the younger Eora faltered for a moment, almost stepping back as he spoke: *I have not done anything to you. I have not seen you since after I escaped the hospital, and your father helped me with my injuries.*

"You should have died!" James cried, and the Eora who understood his words gasped. "That's what the Elders said!"

Rather than being angered, Pemulwy felt a thread of defeat work through him. Ten years ago, he would have struck James, killed him for the words, no matter his age. But now? Had he seen too much death? Was it possible that he was not only losing the war, but the will to wage it? *You would do well to watch your words*, Pemulwy said quietly. *Show respect, for you are the one who came here, not I.*

"King[6] has driven us out," James spat venomously in reply. "Because of you! You and only you are to blame for this!"

King? Pemulwy repeated, annoyed, a spark of anger finally igniting in him. *King doesn't run those towns, boy! The soldiers with rum do! He cannot do anything without their approval.*

"Not true!" James turned to the Eora behind him. "Tell him."

"It," said one, a young woman, "it is true. King has driven us out."

"He has done it because of you!" James shouted angrily. "Because of your attacks, your raids, because of everything you have done. King has driven us out!"

---

6. About the Aborigines, King wrote, 'I have ever considered them the real Proprietors of the Soil.' Australian history, however, would not remember him, or these words. King would be remembered, instead, as a politically weak man who married his cousin.

And what would you have me do about it? Pemulwy returned hotly. *I'll not bow to the English wilfully!*

"We cannot go back until one of you are dead!"

Then so be it.

Angrily, Pemulwy spun away from the young Eora and stalked over to the fire, grabbing his spear. The sudden movement caused a snap of pain to run along his chest, but it only angered him further. This was his land! Eora land! It was their past and their future and no one, much less King, would dictate how an Eora would walk across it.

Gripping the spear tightly, Pemulwy stalked up to James, who, shrinking back, knew that he had pushed the warrior too far. The warrior who, for all his age, for all his failures, had still been struck down in Burramatta by seven bullets, and when he refused to die, chained to a bed in a hospital, had escaped with the Spirits aid. The warrior who had fought the English from the day they landed, the warrior whose very name caused fear in the settlements.

That warrior, Pemulwy, said to James harshly, *Do you wish to fight me?*

The young Eora shook his head.

We cannot fight among ourselves, Pemulwy spat angrily. *That is how the English will defeat us. If we separate, if we betray our heritage, then they have already won.*

Thrusting the young Eora to the side, his companions parting before him, Pemulwy stalked into the darkness of the bush. It welcomed him and his intent with the comfort and support of a mother.

The Spirit World.

In the middle of the spiral staircase a door appeared. It was a faded red, and had a long, brass handle.

Wooden stairs were behind it, but Twain could not make out a way to reach it, without climbing onto the edge of the stairwell, and risking the grasp of the inky darkness. He considered it, arguing with his fear as he gazed downwards, but the disorientation and nausea was a powerful response, and Twain was left gripping the railing tightly, unable to climb it and step out.

"Mark Twain," Cadi said after a moment, "we wish to go through the door."

Biting his lip, he said, "Why wait to tell me that?"

"Sometimes, when a man is different, he will go around it."

"But not me?" Twain muttered with annoyance, releasing the railing. "I'm just an ordinary man, huh?"

Cadi shrugged. "Does that bother you?"

"I guess not, since I've got no desire to go 'round." Twain grabbed the door handle, and paused. "Still, there must be something about me. Being a celebrity and all, right?"

"No," Cadi replied, shaking his head. "A celebrity is just an ordinary man, or woman, given an extraordinary place. I do not understand why, or how, or what even makes other ordinary men and women so fascinated by them. It is beyond me."

"I think you just lost me," Twain replied, leaning his back against the door. "I was almost starting to come around, too."

"The knowledge is here," the Aborigine said, touching his chest, at the place where his heart beat. "It's locked away from me."

Twain shivered, and pushed aside the finger. He was aware, more than ever before, of the stretching emptiness on either side of him, of the frail stairwell he stood upon, and of the fact that there was only one other man in the world with him at that moment. "I think I ought to open this door, don't you?" he said.

Cadi smiled, but not with amusement.

The door handle turned smoothly under Twain's grasp, and when he pushed it open, he found that it lead to a set of stairs. But unlike the stairs he left, these were made from dirty grey cement, and lead downwards for five steps, before running into a narrow alley where buildings made from brick and smooth cement loomed over him, and the noises of the world reached into the alley with thin, sticky fingers.

They were familiar noises: the sounds of cars, of people, of music, and the things that mixed between, like dogs, birds, and cooking. But there were other sounds, familiar in the cacophony, but yet, at the same time, alien: beeps, strange, tinny musical tunes, sirens that were not quite right, and more that he could not distinguish fully.

Stepping from the alley, Twain stopped. In front of him was a street, similar to the ones he was familiar with, but at the same time totally different. Moving along it like a school of salmon moving through a stream, were automobiles, the bodies smooth and rounded and so much that they resembled giant bullets. They were an array of colours, from blue, red, green, to grey, and white, and even, in one small automobile that looked like a dented bubble, aqua. Inside the vehicles sat men and women, singular or in groups, just as they walked along the streets, talking into small boxes in their hands, or with wires leading down from their ears and into their strange straight cut jackets or purses or bags. Other men and women did not dress the same, with some wearing simple, dark versions of suits that he was familiar with, and others appearing more casual, in blue and green and orange, among others. Sitting on the sidewalk, however, holding bags to them, were the dirty and poorly dressed homeless men and women that Twain knew anywhere, huddled within doorframes or the edges of alleys, and being stepped around by the walking crowd, who talked and beeped in a susurration of sound.

"You bought me all this way to show me another fantasy?" Twain asked, unimpressed. There were smells in the air, a mix of food and fumes and perfumes, that irritated his nose, and he reached into the pocket of his jacket. "You've really outdone yourself on the smells."

Next to him, Cadi had resumed his bony shape, with the man's eyes closed, his mouth compressed, and scars mapping his body. Clicking as it moved, the skull said, "This is not a fantasy of mine. None of them have been."

Twain wiped his nose, and gazed outwards: buildings stretched out like a steel valley, running as far as he could see. It was as he gazed at the building that he experienced a flash of recognition.

"This is Sydney?" he asked.

"In the twenty-first century," Cadi acknowledged. "We are standing in Kings Cross."

"I've never heard of such a street," Twain replied, walking down the path and gazing through a glass window. Inside, rows and rows of brightly coloured plastic items sat, but he could not, for the life of him, understand what they were for.

"It is not a street," Cadi said from behind him. "It is the heart of Sydney. In your time, it is known as Queens Cross, but it will be changed."

Twain looked into the reflection of the glass, but neither he nor Cadi was there. Accepting it as he did everything, he said, "They don't say good things about the Cross in Sydney, which I'm sure you're aware of."

"And with good reason." The Aborigine began walking down the path, weaving between the people, leaving him to follow. "The Cross, as it is so known, pumps life into Sydney straight from the English authority that founded it. The name tells anyone walking into Sydney this, yet most of its citizens instead choose to accept it, to treat the Cross as a dark novelty that they can enjoy on a weekend basis. But they shouldn't. It is not an amusement ride for the masses."

Twain's gaze ran from man to woman that he passed, each of them unaware of his presence. Listening with half an ear, he said, "We've places like this back home, and they never hurt no one."

Cadi stopped, and gazed intently at him.

Twain shrugged. "It's true."

"So naïve, Mark Twain." Cadi swept his hand along the storefronts beside them, and pointed down the street, where buildings ran in an endless line. "Why is it that nobody asks what fuels the city? Where is its heart, and what marked it? In Sydney, Kings Cross feeds off an act of violence that took place in 1788, shortly after the First Fleet arrived. Six convicts raped five Eora women in the swamp that was once here. It was here that what the English delivered in its fleet sunk into the ground, into the fabric of the land, and connected with the rotten umbilical cord that wormed out from its mother country. It killed the land. I saw this, and I could do nothing in response to it, until I learned to . . ."

He held up his bony hands, and his skull opened in an attempt of an expression, smile or frown he did not know.

Twain said, "It's not a good thing, and it shouldn't happen to anyone, but it doesn't have to be like this."

"But it is."

"Are you—"

Without warning, Twain was thrown to the ground, and a boot cracked into his temple, sending him reeling.

Struggling, Twain felt his feet grabbed, and he was dragged to the side of the street. Legs passed him, people walking, uncaring, while the dark, bony legs of Cadi were just at the edge of his consciousness. He struggled, crying out, and in response, he was slung around, his head smacking loudly into the brick wall.

A rough, white, young face shot into his view, and snarled, "Money!"

Twain shook his head. How to explain that this wasn't real, that he wasn't here, and that he was *Mark Twain!*

"Fucker!"

Twain's head exploded in pain, and he felt a second punch plunge wetly into his face. He sagged, and once again the boot caught him in the temple. He should have lost consciousness, should have faded into nothing, or perhaps another scene, but he didn't; instead he saw the young man furiously search his pockets, ripping the wallet and money out, and then, glancing down at his boots, tore them off too.

Without a backward glance, the boy turned, and ran down the street, the flow of people continuing past the fallen Twain.

"This is real," Cadi said from above him. "It is happening right now. It happens every day in Sydney. The dark amusement ride that is the beat of the city spreads itself out in acts like daylight robbery, sold drugs that kill, underage prostitution, and worse. You could not imagine what is worse. And it is kept alive not by the people, but by the scarred heart that beats here, in Kings Cross."

Cadi's bony arms reached down, and helped Twain to his feet. Glancing behind him, he saw a young, dark haired Asian man lying on the ground, blood pouring from his face, his skull split open.

"He will die," Cadi said flatly.

Twain did not respond. He felt sick and wanted to vomit, but knew that he would not, knew that there was more to be shown to him. In response to his silent acceptance of continuing, Cadi led him to a green door in the side of a building.

1802.

Pemulwy had begun, after the battle of Burramatta, to think of the land around the Harbour as Sydney Cove.

It pained him to think of the Eora land in such as manner, but as he made his way through the darkness, he realized that it was not incorrect of him to think that way. The land no longer resembled anything from his youth: the stingrays were dwindling, the bush had been cut away, trees were replaced with crude buildings of wood and other, more sturdy buildings made from yellow sandstone. Nothing about the land he made his way through resembled the Eora land, with the exception of the Harbour itself, somehow retaining its purity, its strength that cut a dark mark through the English land.

Pausing at the top of a hill, the Eora warrior dropped into a crouch and gazed at the ragged ugliness of Sydney Cove.

According to the English, it had been named after a man who had never seen it, and who would never do so. One young Eora had told him that Sydney was a genteel man—though he had been unable to explain to him just what made such a man—a friend of the white beeàna, but that he was a man who held the land, and everything upon it, in contempt. It was not an uncommon opinion, and after so many years of fighting the English, Pemulwy had grudgingly accepted that the only native born Englishmen who did not hold the land in contempt were the Rum Corps[7], who he hated with a passion. He had learned, too late it appeared, that there were divisions as wide as the Harbour between the English here and those in England, and despite his animosity towards them, he believed that if he had known this years before, he would have exploited it.

But of course, he had not.

I have *lost my taste for the war*, Pemulwy whispered, rising from his crouch, his muscles complaining. *I don't want it anymore. I have watched my friends and family die and walk into the towns, yet the English living here no longer appears as the crime I once thought it was.*

Time had, he realized, defeated him. And yet, as he gazed down at the town, he realized that he would not be able to turn away from his current actions: he would still kill King. But it was not for hatred that he would do it, or for the Eora way of life, or even the land. In truth, he did not know why he would do it.

He felt no anger or fear as he made his way quietly down the hill. His hard feet left only the barest hint of a track in their wake, and when he skirted around a pair of Redcoats in the street, he did not attack them. They were young men, and ugly like all the English were to him, but that was not why he stayed his hand. Part of him wanted to believe that he did so because he did not want to alert others to his presence, and in a small way that was true; but mainly, his refusal to step into the street with his spear was the physical manifestation of his unwillingness to continue the war.

He wondered, briefly, if a new Spirit had settled upon him. When the land had belonged to the Eora, the Elders had told Pemulwy that the Spirit of the land demanded protection, that it was angry if he allowed any tribe to take the land, and it was this that had fuelled him in the first years of

---

7. In 1808, the Rum Corps would depose of King's successor, Governor Bligh, and rule the colony for two years while treating it as their own bank to become rich, landed gentry. When removed from power, none of the Corps would be executed or severely punished; their leader, John MacArthur, a common born Englishman, would instead be remembered as the man who laid Australia's financial backbone with the wool industry he begun.

his war. But he did not feel it anymore, and indeed, admitted that there was a different feel to the land now. Was it possible that it rose out of the quiet houses of the English that he passed, dark with sleep, and with dogs chained to the back doors for protection? Pemulwy did not know, but it was entirely possible.

King lived in a two-story sandstone building in the middle of Sydney Cove. It was where all the Governors had lived, and was surrounded by large lawns, and vegetable gardens that were beginning to show produce. Pemulwy had seen similar gardens around the houses throughout the settlement, but their vegetables had showed sagging green tops, while at King's dwelling there was more life, the promise of things to come.

Pemulwy slipped over the surrounding fence, and made his way quietly and silently to the back of the sandstone building. Coldness was seeping into his fingers, and he flexed them as he scanned the garden slowly. Once, he had been able to scan the surrounding ground quickly, but now, even with the aid of moonlight, he needed more time. Time to distinguish the shapes, such as the fence palings to the left, and the firewood next to it.

When he was sure that the yard was empty, Pemulwy continued to the back of the house. There were no lights coming from the house, but on the second floor the Eora could make out the hint of something, either movement or a candle. The windows that the English had placed in the building were too thick for him to see through properly.

His hard feet lead him quietly to the back door, which, when he pushed upon, swung open with a faint creak.

Warmth still had its fading grip on the house, and emanated from the sandstone bricks of the narrow hallway that Pemulwy made his way along. Doors were to his left and right, and when he gazed into them, he found a small kitchen, followed by even smaller rooms that were packed like an overflowing parcel with couches and tables, and in the case of one, a piano.

Pemulwy had seen a piano once, pushed into a ravine, and almost on its side, the wood cracked and broken. The dirty keys had still produced a sound when he tapped them, however, and, despite himself, he had straightened the broken instrument and tapped sounds out of it in the midday sun.

Afterwards, he had been angry with himself for indulging in such an English thing. The Eora had instruments of their own, traditional ones that he enjoyed, and ones that he *should* use. But seeing the piano brought back the memory, and as he made his way quietly up the steps, he felt a faint twinge that he could not go and tap on it to produce sounds again.

On the second floor he was presented with two doors. In the first, he found a large, spacious room with two occupants: a white English baby, lying in its crib, and a large, meaty woman, asleep on the couch that lay next to the crib. Around them were thick curtains, and drawers, and plush toys. Pemulwy, easing the door shut, knew the two to be King's wife and child.

He truly had lost the taste for the war. Years ago, he would have thought nothing of killing the woman and child, just as the English thought nothing of killing Eora women and children. It would not have been difficult to turn around and kill them still, Pemulwy knew, even as he made his way to the second door that emitted a hint of light, but even thinking of the women he had known and who had died at English hands, he could not find the anger or will to do it.

He would kill King, and that was all. After King, he would find a different way to battle the English.

But why not now?

With a faint sigh, Pemulwy realized that he could not return to the tribe and face James, and the other young Eora, without having accomplished what he said he would. Besides, didn't King deserve it? Wouldn't it be a fine warning for the future governors that they sent in his place?

His fingers tightening against his spear, Pemulwy pushed open the door.

In the room, holding a long muzzled rifle, was King. The aging, tall, grey haired man regarded Pemulwy with his bright blue eyes, and then said, quietly, "You're a disease upon this land."

Before Pemulwy could react, King fired.

The lead tore into his chest, punching him out of the door, throwing him to the floor. His hands searched for his spear, but he could not find it, and his breath came in harsh gasps. His mind spun, and, in the darkness above him, a figure emerged. But it was not King. Instead, it was the young, smooth featured black face of James.

"If only you had learned to ride a horse," the young Eora said coldly and levelled a pistol at him. "But no, not the great Pemulwy. It was beneath you."

Hatred flared in Pemulwy, and he roared. In response, James' pistol bucked, and the world exploded in blood and pain that he would not walk away from.

Introduction to *A Walking Tour Through the Dreaming City*.

The Cross (once known as Queens Cross and briefly as Kings Cross before common vernacular was made permanent) in Twain's day was no different to the Cross of today. As Vella said in his history, it was, is, and always will be 'a centre-point for low gunmen, violent pimps, prostitution of all kinds, drugs, artists, musicians, crusaders, bent cops, and the best dressed transvestites the world has ever known.'

Twain's theory was that the Cross was undeniably linked to the English authority that landed in Sydney. 'It does not matter who you are,' he said in one lecture, 'but no one in the streets of [the] Cross is an Australian. Instead, you are nothing more than the pawns of a decaying Empire.' It was a harsh statement, and as Vella explains, untrue, especially in the light of the fact that the Cross has not changed one iota since Twain made that proclamation.

But there is no denying the influence Twain's words had. It can be linked directly to the rise of the Democratic Party and Arthur Butler, and, from them, the Republic that we live in now. Through Twain's words, Butler took control of the voting power of the blue collar working man and organized rallies, demonstrations, and, in the historical protest of 1901, a strike that shut down Sydney entirely.

Of course, Twain couldn't have known that Butler would make the same mistakes America did in search of the national identity to go along with the new Republic. (At any rate, Twain was busy with other political concerns. Having returned to America, he was accused of lacking patriotism as he publicly questioned the American policy regarding the Philippines.) In his search, Butler and the Republic of Australia were responsible for evil acts, many of which ignored what Twain spoke out on. It is therefore nothing short of a tragedy that we witnessed the Australian Government steal an entire generation of Aboriginal children from their parents and give them to white 'Australian' families to raise; we witnessed the Asian immigration made illegal, and a mob mentality encouraged that saw established Asian families beaten and driven out of Sydney; and, perhaps most pedantically xenophobic, we saw schools begin teaching the 'Australian' language.

The result led to decades of confused culture, where men and women who did not fit into Butler's description of an Australian ('standing by your mates, working a hard day, enjoying a cold beer, and a swim in the ocean') were culturally shunned and often targeted by hard line 'patriots'. All of this began to change around the sixties, with the influx of American drug culture that was brought into prominence by American movies and cinema, but it left its scars deeply within the nation, and especially, Sydney.

To walk down Sydney today is to walk in the shadows of the political past (it is in the buildings, the street signs, and the statues that link our cultural understanding together) and to watch a Government, whose history is responsible for the near genocide of the Aboriginal race and culture, refuse to make amends. It cannot but force one to question what Mark Twain brought to Sydney. A few have labeled him the man who broke Sydney, but I think that is an ignorant suggestion. Twain is not responsible for the actions of our politicians, just as the transported English before him were not. Rather, he was responsible for bringing to our attention the idea that we were in control of what we made of our city, and indeed our country.

'Sydney is the heart of Australia, and it is from here that everything flows,' Mark Twain said in his final performance, and he was correct. It is a heart we control, that we, with our presence, force the beat of, and which, like a mirror, reveals the best and worse that we, as Australians, bring.

Darrell Barton
Kings Cross,
Sydney.

1803.

....

Beyond the green door was a cool, dark room. As Twain's eyes grew accustomed to the dimness, he was able to make out the shapes of shelves, filled with books, and a large oak desk, with a high-backed chair behind it. In the middle of the table, in a large glass jar, was the head of an Aborigine, his mouth and eyes stitched shut, his head floating gently in light brown alcohol.

"The poor devil," Twain said quietly, approaching the desk. "What'd he do to deserve this?"

"This is my first revolutionary," Cadi whispered from the darkness around him. "The Eora warrior you saw earlier."

"Where are you?" Twain said, scanning the room.

"I am here." Cadi stood behind the desk, the darkness making his bones more prominent, as if there was no skin at all behind them. With his bony hands, the Aborigine stroked the glass jar of the head, as if it were a child that he could pick up and hold close to his chest. "After he had been killed, King had his head removed, to make sure that he would not rise again. He did it that very night, in his backyard."

Twain shuddered. "Where are we?"

"We are in London, in Joseph Banks study. King had the head sent here afterwards, to study, to learn what it was that made him hate them so much. In doing so, he took everything I had given the warrior, and isolated it from the Aboriginal people, destroying the last remains of his power."

"Surely something could have been done?" Twain asked, approaching the desk.

"No," Cadi replied coldly. "The warrior himself was the symbol. I realized the mistake afterwards, and rectified it with my Irishman, but in this case, the Eora's skin, his entire body, was the symbol that could unite them."

Twain stared at the floating head. After everything he had seen, everything he had been forced through, he wanted the head to leave an impression on him, to suggest to him the quality of the Aboriginal people who lived in Sydney and the white men and women that lived in the city too. But mostly, he wanted the head to explain the figure that had taken him along this journey with intensity that bordered on fanaticism. But the longer he stared, the more it resembled but a simple head.

"Do you understand why Sydney needs a new heart?" Cadi asked, passing through the table to stand before him. The head of the Eora warrior appeared to float in his stomach, part of the spirit.

"Yeah," Twain said uncomfortably, wanting to step back, but unable too. "I understand why you want one, but maybe you've looked at it wrong. Maybe things aren't as bad as you say. At any rate, there's nothing I can do about that."

"That's untrue," the other replied quietly, an underlying menace in his voice. "You bring with you a culture that can be embraced. A symbol for a revolution that can wash away the old hatred, and bring a new beat to the city."

"But—"

Cadi's bony hand plunged into Twain's chest before he could finish. The pain was immense: it spread through every fibre of his body, terrible, and inescapable. It was death. He knew that. He would never see his wife or daughters again, never write another word; it was all over . . . and then, through the pain, he felt the beat of his heart fill his body like the sound of a drum, beating the tempo of his life . . .

It stopped.

Cadi pulled his bony arm out of his chest, the flesh and bone parting until it released the still beating heart of Mark Twain.

Seeing it, Twain's consciousness failed, his legs went weak, and he began to fall.

"I will not let the English win," said Cadi without remorse, his voice reaching through the pain and shock.

The ground rushed up to Twain. Black and solid, he could not avoid it, he could not escape it, and he did not want to escape. Let it be over, let it finish, let him go. He could still feel his heart beating, but it was no longer his own: it was stolen, ripped from him to be placed into a city he barely knew. It would do no good. The spirit was wrong: revolutions were not done with symbols and stolen cultures, they were seeded from within, grown from what was the land and people, created anew. Change would rise in Sydney only when the city was its own creature, when the people in it embraced it, when they understood all that had happened. Change could not be forced; to do so would result only in a cosmetic, shallow, tainted beast—the exact kind Cadi fought against. Realizing this, Twain wanted to cry it out, to tell Cadi that it was futile, that he was *wrong*, that he had to acknowledge the past, that he had to accept it and resolve the issues that arose from it; that only by doing this could he destroy the rotten hands that held Sydney in its stranglehold; but he could not cry out.

The black slab of the ground raced up. Mark Twain dreamed no more.

Johnny Cash
(A Tale in Questionnaire Results)

1. Benjamin Li.

2. 12/8/56.

3. China.

4. Between Seattle and Beijing.

5. Divorced, two children, one dog, seven tropical fish.

6. I ran the Occult Research Division of BrandyCorp.

7. Eight years.

8. Before that I was primarily a freelance contractor, but I spent seven years in the employ of the Reagan Administration and, later, three in Fox Networks.

9. Nick Carlton was the owner of BrandyCorp.

10. Rarely.

11. I reported to the managing director, Amanda Tae.

12. As I said previously, I had very little contact with him, but it was obvious that Mr. Carlton was a Magician. I do not know what God or Goddess he took his power from, if any.

13. No. I watched Ronald Reagan cut the wet, bloody heart out of a living,

virginal thirteen-year-old girl to feed an Astoteele demon at dinner. At the end of the night, the President had formed a pack with the demon's family to ensure that a low-grade hypnotic suggestion would be processed through his voice whenever it was electronically played. So in comparison, *no*, I did not have any moral objection to Mr. Carlton.

14. BrandyCorp did not sanction any religion.

15. *Supposed* Son of God.

16. Well, three days after I dissected him, he did not get up.

17. Why would I want to eat the flesh of a fake messiah? Don't be stupid.

18. John Doe (he refused to give his real name) was still alive when he was bought to me. He had a broken leg and bruises from the plastic bullets that had been used to incapacitate him. Otherwise, he was a healthy thirty-two-year-old Caucasian male.

19. Angry. We had stopped him from attending a sold-out faith healing event in Florida that had been organized to by the Republicans.

20. Mr. Carlton did visit him. Twice, in fact.

21. Their first conversation was about Johnny Cash. They shared a cigarette through the bars of Doe's cell, and discussed the line in the song 'the Man in Black' about Jesus, Love, and Charity, and how Mr. Carlton thought it was out of place in a song he otherwise agreed with. But yet, he said, flicking the tobacco off his fingers after he rolled a cigarette, he still wore the black. The second conversation, a week later, was private, and ended with Mr. Carlton ordering his execution.

22. Only speculation.

23. Lethal injection.

24. Before his death, John Doe said quietly, "I have done so much wrong."

25. The demon attacks began shortly after that. Employees of BrandyCorp were issued with various talismans: chicken feet charms, demon-touched crosses, braids made from the hair of murder victims, and hands of glory.

26. A memo from Mr. Carlton on the 19th was the last I heard from him, but Amanda Tae claimed to be in contact with him until the end.

27. The memo talked primarily about the goals of the Republican Administration, but also made a reference to the Johnny Cash music that was being piped into the building. I believe it was his entire oeuvre, including rare live covers, and on continual repeat. I read the memo while listening to Johnny Cash sing 'Wanted Man'.

28. Amanda Tae instructed us to stay away from Texas and Washington.

29. No. She sent me to Texas.

30. It was the 20th of May, around two weeks before Reagan's death.

31. Empty. There wasn't a soul there.

32. I was sent to deal with the previously mentioned Astoteele demon family. The family was well kept and living in a fortified compound: two days later, with only three fingers remaining on my left hand, an empty bag of charms, every spell I knew used, and favours owing to a swamp witch, the demons were killed. Not banished, but killed: every black ounce of their family removed from *every* plane of existence. The result was that for the first time since Reagan, a President spoke to the country without a hypnotic suggestion in the back of his voice.

33. Redemption.

34. The White House retaliated with Reagan's death.

35. It wasn't a very subtle reaction. The Reagan funeral procession was so heavy handed that my eight-year-old son could taste the blood sacrifices tied to the body and coffin in Beijing. Still, it stopped a nation from paying too much attention to what the President said, and the fact that everyone in Texas was dead. I suspect that the funeral speeches from the remaining living Presidents would have ensured that whatever spell or summoning had been conducted would last.

36. I did not know that Mr. Carlton planned to visit the coffin, but in hindsight, I shouldn't have been surprised.

37. Initially, there were no spells. He used a grenade.

38. At the time I was enchanting chicken feet and listening to Johnny Cash's 'Ring of Fire.'

39. That video was the last I saw of Mr. Carlton.

40. No.

41. I do not know where he is, but I doubt that he is dead. When the guards rushed him, you can see that he was smiling. He lifted those silver pistols, began firing, and smiled. In my experience, no man dies smiling.

42. The guns *were* the spell.

43. When you try to picture the events of that day, the two pistols are more important than anything else. That's all you ever hear about in press releases or news reports, as there is no mention of a body. Just those American guns, speaking to an American audience.

44. No.

45. It was only a matter of time until BrandyCorp defenses were broken. Amanda Tae and I had been organizing the slow evacuation of the staff since my return from Texas. We replaced workers and families with flesh replicas, though the replicas were only good for six weeks after being taken from their plastic wrapping. They decompose like real flesh, eventually.

46. It was decided that Amanda Tae and I would be the last to leave. Captain of a ship, that sort of thing, though if I were to be honest, there was more to it. A loyalty. However, we planned to have the remaining staff out within three days, but then, mid-week, our defenses broke. The walls cracked. The smell of rotting flesh grew. Johnny Cash stopped singing.

47. I told you: Redemption.

48. I knew the girl that Reagan crouched over.

49. It's an election year. Mr. Carlton was, I think, one of those men who believed in the people. You listen to enough Johnny Cash, and you begin to see it.

50. There was no success in the end. We failed.

Possession

Three days before Eliana Stein found the girl made from bronze, the stocky Botanist noted the passing of her twelfth year living in the Aremika Shaft, though she did not celebrate it. That was the kind of woman she was: pragmatic because she lived alone, modest because her vanity did not extend to her celebrating her own successes, and fatalistic because surviving the passage of time, she believed, was an act of submission, not rebellion.

The Shaft (so shortened by all who lived in it) was best described by what it was not: an immense absence of soil. On the yearly journeys Eliana made outside the Shaft and into the low, sprawling, ash-stained Aremika City that circled the Shaft, she told those few who asked that she could not describe the huge emptiness of the Shaft. Rather, she could explain only by its horrific absence. The Shaft, she said, was a deep, burnt scar, and was like the woman who had lost an arm: you did not describe the missing limb to friends, but instead noted its loss, and the way in which that loss cast a shadow over the remaining parts of the individual and rendered them out of harmony with the whole. That is what Eliana felt when she stood in the dark, endless, windy hole that dove through the Earth. The pressure of the disfigurement was always present in the hole: it was the walls, the ground, and the wide emptiness before her. She could feel it constantly, and knew if any part of the Shaft broke, that it would collapse and smother her. There would be nothing that she could do in that eventuality. Even the shifting collection of faint, glowing dots that were scattered further up along the Shaft—the dots that signalled other Botanists who, like herself, wore the luminous clothing of the trade so not to be lost or forgotten by the Botanist Counters outside—even they were nothing against the deep wound that was the Shaft.

For her part, Eliana felt it more than other Botanists did, since she had gone deeper than any other had. It had not been asked of her to do this, but she had chosen the depth through some not yet fully self-explained reason. Still, without knowing the reason, she performed her job of monitoring the soil and helping it heal and grow in density and strength with the pellets that she planted. At her depth, the soil around her alternated between dark, brittle burns and thick, healing brown of varying types; but if she could have gone down further, where there was less life and the soil was hard and brittle like tightly packed blocks of cinder, she would have. The Department of Botany had told her it was simply not safe to go beyond her depth, however, and that they could not lower the unit for her to live in or hook up a cable for her to leave, not until the soil further up was stronger.

On the day that Eliana found the girl made from bronze, thick black ash had fallen into the Shaft during the night. Smoke rose from the factories outside Aremika City daily, and it was perpetually in the sky and ground, but the ash was thick enough to bother her only when all these elements combined. When they did, the ash fell so prodigiously that when Eliana awoke, she found the pathway around her slim, bronze unit coated in black, and the pale fungi that grew across the walls, and which served as the only natural light, was dim beneath it.

It was the ash, however, that led her to the girl.

When Eliana stepped from the unit, she did so holding a thick-headed broom. A brass track ran around the Shaft's circumference like a tarnished halo. Her unit was mounted on it, and from inside, a gear system allowed her to move manually along the track. However, at the moment, she walked and swept the paths with the broom. If she didn't clean straight away, the ash would contaminate the soil and leave a horrid stink, especially since it took her a day to walk the circumference of the Shaft. She had no complaints, however, and dutifully followed the path that ran to a bronze plate that anchored a thick, taunt cable into the ground. The cable led up into the dark, joining hundreds of others that disappeared in thin lines up to the surface and the hint of a scabbed red sky that sat at the start of the Shaft. Through the cables, a Botanist received mail and food and, in a swaying, narrow bar that served as a chair, was raised out of the Shaft. Eliana had no mail, left the Shaft only once a year, and was not due a food drop for another two weeks, so it was only by her attention to the detail of sweeping that she found the girl, who had fallen next to the cable. The truth of it was, if the ash fall had not been so heavy, the girl might not have been found alive at all.

But she was.

The girl made from bronze—the Returned, since she was not a real girl—this artificial girl had a loud, irregular moan in her chest: a broken machine whine that announced itself in a grinding of gears. It was loud and troublesome to the woman who held her and every now and then it stopped, as if in death.

When Eliana, holding the heavy, broken figure, first experienced the pause, she did indeed think of it as death, so long and final did the lack of life seem. She stepped to the uneven edge of her path in the Shaft, ready to release the body. To dump the refuse. But with a ragged howl that gargled and coughed life back in a spasm through the girl's body, her heart returned to its stuttering, moaning journey. Still holding her, Eliana watched as the girl's eyes flickered open, met the Botanist's, and then drifted shut.

She was pretty, Eliana thought as she turned, and continued down the rough path, even now. It was a created beauty, however, for Eliana doubted that she had been born with such a cute face, and such smooth, white skin and large, dark eyes. The girl's short black hair did not feel right against her skin, either: it was too dry, too hard to be real hair, even if it was tangled and dirty, and a patch on the back of her head had been torn away to reveal the bronze skull underneath. There were cuts down her pale face and neck and her clothing was torn, though neither cuts nor clothes showed sign of blood. Not all the Returned bled, however, and in this case, Eliana was pleased. The girl had lost her legs in the fall: they had splintered and broke upon landing, leaving a sharp, twisting mess of jagged bronze, and internal silver and bronze wiring dangled out of her open thighs. Eliana had left a single, preserved foot back at the cable. There was no way to reattach it, and the girl weighed so much already that there was no point in bringing it. In addition to the loss of her legs, the girl had also lost her left hand. It had been torn off from just above the wrist, perhaps as she had grabbed at something, perhaps the cable that ran down to Eliana's level, the cable that the girl frantically reached for as she fell, as the desperation forced her to struggle to touch it, to grab it, but where the speed of her descent—

Well, who knew?

A cold fluid from the girl was staining the Botanist's hands, but Eliana ignored it. Worse had touched her hands in her life, but still, she hoped it was not urine. There was no smell to the girl, but the Returned ate, drank, pissed, and shat, simulating the life that they had once been born into, so it would be only a matter of time before the internal parts of her body began to fail if they were as broken as the external parts.

Ahead of her, the slim, pale-lit outline of her unit drew closer. Eliana thanked the God That Could Not See Her that she knew the narrow tracks of the Shaft's circumference so well that she need not look down, that she did not need her gaze to direct every step. Though she did wish, squat, and strong as she was, that she had not aged so much in the Shaft; that she still had the strength of the thirty year old woman who had descended so long ago and who could have carried the girl without the strain she felt.

In the end, Eliana was forced to set the girl down to gain her strength before continuing. She sat for a few minutes on the path, in the pale glow of her uniform and a brighter cluster of fungi. She was used to seeing things in that eerie glow, but even so, the girl did not look healthy, or functional, or whatever other term you might use for a made person. Did a Return die? Did they go pale and cold? Well, perhaps not cold. The Returned were always cold to touch. With a grunt, Eliana resumed her sure walk with the girl. If she had not been so close to the tarnished, bronze door of her unit when the strain began to tell again, she would have had to rest a second time. Instead, her muscles burning, the Botanist shouldered her way into the narrow unit and, thankful for once that she did not keep her bed upstairs, placed the girl down on the dark blue sheets.

In the bright, yellow light inside the unit, Eliana could see that the girl was made, not just from bronze, but brass as well. The darker and lighter colouring that shone through the tattered remains of skin around her arms and legs suggested imperfection and sickness that had existed long before her fall. The girl's clothes, which were made from red and brown, likewise hinted at blood and defecation. As if listening to her morbid thoughts, the sick machine moan of the girl's heart grew louder, as if threatening to burst from its casing, struggling, pushing . . . and then silent, silent, *silent*, before with a spasm and a cough, it started again.

Though her arms still ached from carrying the girl, Eliana descended to the bottom level of her unit. It was, like all single Botanist units, made from three narrow floors, linked by a set of rungs down the middle. The centre floor was where she slept: there were tall, narrow closets and a comfortable chair that she sat and read in. The top floor held a small kitchen and the single, narrow table that she ate at. The knives and forks and cooking utensils were suspended from the ceiling and dangled like a pit of spikes reversed. When strong winds buffeted the unit, they swayed dangerously and occasionally fell—she had been hit more than once, though thankfully she sheathed all the blades. There was an opening up there that she could push to release smoke and odours from cooking. On the bottom floor was the workbench where she kept her samples, notes, and where she could manufacture pellets. There was also a tiny shower and toilet, the drains of which opened out into the Shaft in what she considered a small contradiction to her work of healing. In the opposite corner was a large cage that ran from floor to floor and which held a single, medium sized crow, all black and smooth, and who watched her with cold glass eyes.

Under those eyes, she sat at her workstation and pulled free a piece of paper. In a thick, bold script, she wrote to the Department of Botany and explained what had happened. In her opinion, Eliana stated, she did not believe the Returned had much time left. She did not ask how the girl had come to be at the Shaft, or how she fell, though she might have, since it was difficult to do either without help; but she did not ask because she was afraid of upsetting someone, which would result in aid not being sent. In her own mind, Eliana had decided that a Botanist had let her through, and the resulting theories of murder and mystery flowered in her mind. Who knew if they were true?

Once she had finished the letter, she placed the note in a small brass case and walked over to the cage. The crow slipped out and perched on her arm with cold claws. It waited patiently as she attached the case to its leg. Once that was done, she climbed up a floor, and released it into the dark of the Shaft.

When Eliana could no longer see the crow, she turned and regarded the girl who lay on her bed, slowly staining her sheets. A smell had begun to emerge: an oil machine mix of urine and shit and something as equally unpleasant. The girl's body was still moaning, though it reminded her of growling, now, as if it was fighting for life while the rest of it lay dying.

When the girl made from bronze awoke that night, she did not scream.

Eliana had expected her to. She spent the evening in her narrow kitchen, expecting the cry at any moment. Returned or not, the Botanist believed that the sight of shattered limbs and torn skin would be reason enough for horror. At the very least, she had expected tears. But the girl gave neither. Instead, she pushed herself into a sitting position and waited, quietly, until Eliana descended from the kitchen. Having placed her flowing, luminous Botanist uniform in the closet, she now wore a blue shirt and a pair of comfortable, faded black pants. Her tattoos, words and patterns made from red and black ink, twisted along her thick left arm, and around the exposed left-hand side of her neck and foot. It was not until that foot, with its slightly crooked toes, and the nail missing from the smallest, touched the cool bronze floor of the unit, that the girl spoke:

"I appear to be broken."

Her voice was faint, but purposefully so, rendering it a pampered girl's voice, the quality of which instantly annoyed the other woman. "Yes," Eliana replied, curt where she had not planned to be. "You fell."

"This—this is the—"

"Shaft, yes."

The girl spoke slowly, each word a chore, the stuttering moan in her chest causing her to pause after every short sentence. "Yes, I fell."

"You remember falling?"

"Yes."

"Landing?"

"No."

Eliana approached the bed. The noxious odour grew, and she struggled to keep it from showing on her face. Folding her thick arms in front of her, Eliana gazed down at the girl, but the latter did not return her gaze. Finally, she said, "I have sent a bird to my department, telling them of you—"

"What? *No!*"

It was her turn to be cut off now, her turn to pause. Her thick eyebrows rose in her only hint of surprise. Before her, the girl, the fragile, lost girl who had fallen, and who had sat before Eliana in a confused haze, disappeared. Evaporated like water beneath the hot red sun. In response, the pity that Eliana had meant to be feeling, but which she could not for reasons she had not been given time to explore, was no longer required, and her dislike, her hostility, which she had been ashamed of, had sudden reason for purchase inside her.

The girl spat out, "Why did you do that?"

"Who are you?"

"*Why?*"

"You're dying."

"Ha!"

"You are."

"Of course I am!"

Eliana had no reply, had not expected that.

The girl made from bronze gave a coughing splutter of a laugh. It was caught between self-pity, self-hate, and desperation, and it ended raggedly as the struggling moan in her chest choked it off. Finally, pushing her single good hand through the tattered remains of her hair, she said, "I won't be thanking you for this."

"I think," Eliana said slowly, out of her depth, trying to find a way to understand the situation. "I think you best explain to me what is going on here."

"As if I would explain anything to someone marked like you are!"

The tattoos. Of course, it was the tattoos that spoke of Eliana's religion, of where she had been born. The clean skin of the Returned did as much for her as the tattoos did for Eliana. The intricate words and designs that ran across the Botanist's body recorded the forty-two years she had been alive. Parents, siblings, her growth into adulthood, her failed jobs and relationships: the words of each ran beneath her clothes and spent most of the time on the left-hand side of her body, before crossing at her shoulders and neck and descending down her right side. Once a year she left the Shaft for those markings. Once a year a Mortician's needle and ink set down her life so that when she died, God would be able to read her body, her life, and judge her, for Life, for Heaven, for Damnation, for Obliteration.

"There is no God in the Shaft," Eliana said, finally. "Have you not heard that?"

The girl laughed again, but this time it was forced, angry, and each broken movement she made in the laughter stripped the appearance of youth from her. Finally, when she could force no more out, the woman-- the woman who was much, much older than Eliana, and who smelled of decay--lowered her head. With her very real eyes staring at the woman who looked her senior, she said, "I need a drink. Do you have one?"

She did.

It was cheap wine that Eliana brought down for the Returned. The bottle was green, the label plain and simple, and she had used a quarter of it some weeks back in a meal that had not been improved by its inclusion. It was not an act of friendship, nor was it an act of trust, but it was a signal that the Botanist was, at the very least, understanding of the situation. No woman was at her best while dying. When the Returned took the bottle with her one good hand, she did so quickly, snatching it, ripping it from Eliana's strong, blunt fingers, before taking a long drink—and that helped too with her decision.

"How old are you?" Eliana asked, watching. She held a second, unopened, good bottle of wine in her hand, and did not bother to hide it.

The Returned swallowed, then said, "This is like vinegar."

"You didn't answer my question," Eliana repeated.

"No, I did not." Her good hand placed the bottle between the shattered stumps of her legs. Loose silver wiring was reflected dully against it. "My name is Rachel, by the way."

"I didn't ask that."

"No." Her dark eyes met Eliana's. "You're too busy trying to figure out *what* I am, rather than who."

The Botanist pulled the cork off her wine bottle, said nothing.

"I'm one hundred and twenty-eight," the Returned said, a hint of defiance in her tone. "Happy?"

"Yes."

Eliana didn't say it, but the Returned's—*Rachel's*—words had affected her. The Botanist knew that she had been treating the woman as a thing. She thought that she had left that kind of prejudice behind when she had entered the Shaft, but Rachel's words suggested that she had not.

Grabbing her orange chair that had a colourful array of patches over it, Eliana swung it round and dragged it near the bed. Once it was close enough, but not so close that the stink of the girl assaulted her overly, she sank into it, propped her feet up on the edge of the bed, and took a long drink in front of the other woman.

"I bet yours tastes better," Rachel said.

"Let that be a lesson." Shame had not made her more sympathetic. "Politeness has its rewards."

At that, the Returned laughed: a short burst, different from the earlier laughter, natural this time. A faint, unwilling smile creased Eliana's face in response.

"This is going well, don't you think?" Rachel asked. Her broken arm lifted, paused. She grunted and her good hand picked up the bottle. "When I was standing on the edge of the Shaft, Joseph—do you know Joseph?"

"Callagary?"

"Yes."

A tall, thin, white, clean skinned man on the Department of Botany's Board of Directors. He had a stylish bronze eyepiece that recorded everything. "I know him," Eliana said, and not kindly.

"Yes, that was my response, too." Rachel lifted the bottle, drank. Around the stumps of her legs and the torn parts of her genitals, the stain was refreshed in both wetness and odour. "I've known worse, mind. Much worse. He showed me the Shaft when I asked, at least. Was more than happy too. I was his student for a little while. It turned him on, I think. He told me the Shaft had been made by lava—that the centre of the Earth had ruptured, leaving the heat nowhere to go. So it burst out. It scarred the world, he said. Such a dramatic boy. I still remember that little drop in his voice. *Scarred the world.*"

"That's the theory," she said.

"Believe it?"

"No one has seen the centre."

"No." She fell silent. Then, "No, he said that. He said that some had journeyed down. He said that they never returned."

"And you?" Eliana pulled her legs off the bed, leaned forward.

"What?"

"What was your plan? Were you running from Joseph?"

Rachel let out a breath, half a laugh, half a grunt, and rubbed her chest as if it were in pain. Perhaps it was. "Joseph was just a man for the night."

She frowned. "You're a prostitute?"

"Yes." The Returned lifted the bottle, regarded her with the defiance she had shown earlier. "I'm a prostitute. A dirty *whore*. Are you morally outraged, now?"

"I've known whores."

The other woman stared at her.

"Just not Returned whores," Eliana finished. "I've never heard of it before."

"You live in a giant hole in the ground." Rachel took a long drink and the dark stain across the bed sheet increased. The wine was going right through her—her thirst, her need, would never be sated by it. Seemingly unaware, she added, "In this case, however, I do admit: there aren't many of us. It's expensive. Being Returned is expensive. You have a body partly carved and partly found. It has to look real. That's not cheap, so to buy us is not cheap. No."

Eliana did not know how to respond. She was not, and never had been, a woman who could connect with others quickly. She responded better to situations, and was able to meet a moment with the appropriate emotional response without difficulty. But sitting in front of Rachel, watching the wine stain her bed, trying to hide her growing revulsion at the smell that was growing stronger, and aware that the woman's voice was not really focused on her, Eliana was being asked not to react to the moment, but to the person; and here, she did not know what to say. Fortunately, she did not need too:

"I have over a hundred years of being fucked," Rachel said. Her good hand tightened around the neck of the bottle and a faint cracking followed. "In eight days, I will have been a Return for a hundred years. Another month, and I'll have been working for a hundred and seven years. Working! Do you know what that means? Do you have any idea? How many men and women have fucked me? How many have looked at me as if I was nothing—as if I was an object!

"My boss looks at me just like that. She organizes who sees me. She keeps me in drugs. She makes sure I get what I need to live. She's surely a lot better than some of the pimps I've seen, but she doesn't see me. She doesn't talk to me. She talks *about* me. She talks around me." She stopped, gave a faint *ha*, and then fell silent.

"I don't—"

"She's my eleventh boss," Rachel said, not even noticing that she interrupted the other woman. "My eleventh *pimp*. I hate that old term. But she's my number eleven. I have watched ten others get old. I have watched clients get old. I've watched them all go grey and small. It doesn't matter how rich, how intelligent, how whatever they were. They each faded, they—

"I had worked for two years before I was Returned." The woman switched topics without pause, her mind erratic. "I wanted money. I had plans—

plans. The world—this world—I wanted to see it. With the money I had left I could buy a house. I wouldn't owe anything to anyone. But there was a problem. I got sick. I had a hole in my heart. A *hole*. Surgeons told me I wouldn't live past twenty-eight unless I got it fixed. And you can earn a lot of money on your back, but it's not enough to get a new heart. No. You need help for that.

"The man who paid for my Return ran *The Brothel of Exotics*. That's what he called it. He was a Returned himself: Baron De'Mediala. His real name was Gregory. I—I didn't want to die. Twenty-eight is too young to die. He sat me down in his office. It was filled with statues of birds: flamingos, cockatoos, seagulls, and dozens of other birds, coloured yellow and green and pink—every colour but black and red. If there was a hint of black or red in it, it wasn't there. I later learned that he had a strange obsession with bright colours. Bright colours meant life. He had even dyed his hair a shocking lemon.

"He said to me, 'The price, it is great.' He had that way of talking. A theatrical way. I heard a rumour that he had once been a stage magician. I told him that no price was too high, that I would pay it. Even if it meant a hundred years on my back, I would pay. He told me that I would probably never be free from the debt. He said, 'M'dear, m'dear, each year a repair must be done, a part of you fixed. Each year you will have to fix your appearance. Each year your living tissue will require ointments. Each year the wires in you will need to be cleaned. Each year your look and fashion will need updating.' Each year, he said. But it didn't matter—I told him it didn't matter. I was so afraid. I didn't see endless service as a problem. I thought, 'What's so different about that to the life I currently live?'

"I learned. The Baron—that's what I called him, *the Baron*—he knew. He had Returned himself. He knew the cost. He kept himself free with our servitude and—and—" Rachel's voice trailed off for a moment.

Eliana, having not moved once during her speech, shifted her bottle, but did not drink. Opposite her, the Returned lifted the bottle, took a short, sharp drink, and then said, "He was killed for bodysnatching. They caught him one night standing in an open grave. That's what I heard. There were eight of them and they burnt the skin from him. When he didn't die, they removed his organs. You only need the heart—" she tapped her chest, rubbed the spot where the moan gurgled "—that mechanical heart to live. I don't know how long it took them to get to that. I know you can live without everything else. I once had lungs. A liver. I had all my organs, and they worked—but now? Now I have supplements. I can't afford real livers, real replacements. I have fakes. I have simulations for sensations. I simulate. I—

"The Baron was right. There's no end to your debt. The debt—it's to a Surgeon, or a Hospital, but it's not just for one job. Not just for the Return. It's for every day of living you do after it. Every day is debt. My debt would be passed from boss to boss, and I would work to pay it off, and I would work to make sure that I was kept alive.

"It wasn't such a bad life in the start. There is an attraction to be exotic. A power. *Ha*. A power. I've wanted to stop so many times. One boss even let me. She was a terribly obese woman, caught in her own addictions. I think she understood it. I had been working for fifty-six years, by then. I—there are no jobs that will pay a Returned what she needs. I was free for two weeks before I went back to her. When I got back, I decided I would train myself. I enrolled in a college, but I never finished any course. I kept telling myself I would. I kept telling myself I could. I said it for forty years. I said it in four different cities. I said it with five different bosses. Eventually, I just—I had to just admit that I couldn't change. I hated that.

"It was simple, really. I told Joseph I wanted to see the Shaft—I used my best girl's voice." The last of the bottle was tipped into her throat. She did it roughly, angrily, and wiped her mouth with the back of her good hand after. When she spoke, there was only self-loathing in her voice, "It's hard to kill yourself when you've already died once. A girl I—a girl I was *friends* with did it. Not so long ago. A month. We'd—we had known each other for sixty years. The night before, we got drunk and talked about how we would do it. You couldn't cut veins, we said. You couldn't poison yourself. You couldn't drown. You couldn't suffocate. There was only the heart and the head. It was like a nursery rhyme. Do you know what she did?"

There was a pause, but not long enough for Eliana to answer.

"She paid a man to cave her head in with a hammer. A hammer! *A hammer!* I—I saw her the day after. She had had the man chain her to a chair. He had left her in the basement—and—and—

"I figured the Shaft would be a good choice. That was my idea. The Shaft. All you had to do was jump. I could never sit there and let a man cave my head in. That waiting, that—no. *No*. All I had to do was push Joseph back—let him get me in close, first, tell him I wanted to stand on the edge, tell him it excited me. That was all. Then I could just push him back. Then I could just jump. Then—then—I would be free."

Rachel stopped, her good hand releasing its hold on the bottle.

In the silence that followed, it occurred to Eliana that it was now her turn to speak, that she should say something. She should offer sympathy. Understanding. At the very least she should acknowledge the other woman. But she couldn't. The silence between the two stretched until it was taut and Rachel's eyes closed slowly and her head sank and Eliana looked down at the smooth floor and tried to find words . . . and had almost succeeded when a faint scratching at the door interrupted her.

It was the crow: its sharp, glass beak was pecking against the door.

When Eliana opened the door, it flapped through to the cushioned armchair silently and sat, shaking flakes of ash out of its black feathers. They fell over the fabric, over the floor, the residue of its journey outside the Shaft and beneath the red sun. Once it had done that, it waited, patiently, for the Botanist to open the brass casing on its leg.

Across from it, Rachel gazed at the crow in what Eliana considered a sudden lucidity that was inspired by apprehension and fear. There was no resignation in her gaze, however, no sense that she had accepted her fate, or even knew it; though it was impossible that she could have imagined that the tiny scrawl on the tiny note on the crow's leg brought her any news that she would want to hear. The Department of Botany would send a man or woman to repair her. At the very least they would stabilize her before she was taken out of the Shaft.

Surely, she could not hope.

Surely.

"I don't want to hear," Rachel said. "If they are coming for me, don't tell me."

Eliana picked up her bottle of wine from next to the couch, ignored the crow, and passed it to her.

"Don't waste it," the other said, quietly. Her gaze never left the bird. "It just goes right through me."

"Take it, anyway."

Silence.

"Go on."

"I want to—"

"They're coming."

"—You haven't—"

"They were always coming." She thrust the bottle a little. "Take it."

"Okay." Rachel's voice was quiet with submission. Instinctively, her broken arm reached up—she must have been left handed—but a moment later, her good one found the bottle. The first one, made from cheap glass, lay on the bed, the neck splintered in a web of cracks. When Rachel took the bottle, her eyes, the eyes she had not been born with, but which had been born to someone else, those dark, dark eyes, held Eliana's with a terrible fragility. "Please read the note to me."

Eliana approached the crow. It scratched gently at her hand and she rubbed its cold, bronze head through its feathers. The crow had been in the Shaft as long as she had—had, in fact, come down when the unit was lowered and put into place. It had been her only companion for the years, but she had never named it; nor did she know if it was male or female. The crow was, as Rachel had said of herself, an object, a thing. It responded to Eliana's touch only because it had been taught to do so when it was alive. At least, that is what she told herself, though she was unable to fully believe it.

"What does it say?" Rachel said, her voice still quiet, still soft.

"It is from Callagary," she began, but then stopped. She had her back to the other woman and, conscious of it, she could not continue. She turned. "Joseph. He wrote this. He said that there was an accident on the top. That they had feared the worse. A Surgeon is on his way down as he writes."

"A Surgeon?"

"Yes." Silence. The crow's cold claws pulled at the fabric of the chair. Awkwardly, Eliana added, "I'm sorry."

Still, Rachel did not reply.

"I—"

"How do you live here?"

"What?" Rachel had spoken hard and quick, as if she was accusing her, and it caught Eliana off guard. "What are—"

"It's awful down here." Rachel's voice softened and took on, once again, the tone that a woman might use when she talked to herself, and did not require an answer. In her hand, the bottle lay still, drank by only Eliana; but the stain, still growing in size and accompanied by an ever growing sharp odour, had finally begun to drop faint traces of discoloured red wine on the bronze floor. "There's no fresh air. It's so dark. Your light—it's not like the light up there. It's harder. Brittle. Everything feels like it is burning. How can you stand it?"

"No one watches down here." Eliana hesitated. Rachel's eyes were not focused on her: they wandered about the narrow unit, as if everything was new, and slippery, and she could not grasp any of it. Her good hand no longer gripped the bottle, but rested on it. Quite clearly, the strength, strangely for a body made, and without muscle, was gone. *She's dying. She might not be alive by the time the Surgeon arrives.* Quietly, Eliana said, "On the surface, all we worry about is life. Who comes back. Who has what rights. Who is dominant. We fight, because we think God is watching. Or God isn't watching. The world is dying around us and we fight and we try to make people live a certain way never understanding that it doesn't matter. That the world we live on is—"

Rachel's eyes focused, suddenly, on her, and Eliana's voice faltered, the last word unspoken on her lips.

"Don't let them take me," the dying woman said.

A single luminescent dot was descending towards her.

Eliana shifted. In her straining arms, Rachel was heavy, and the stuttering, gurgling moan of her chest was the only sign that she was still alive. She spoke softly, now, a continual murmur as if she were speaking to a mother, or an older sister, and her cold, hard head was pressed against Eliana's neck and shoulder, as if she were a child. Because of this, the Botanist did not tell her of the figure that rode the thin bar down her cable, and who, in an hour or so, would be upon her unit. She wondered if he—it would be a he, she decided, on instinct—she wondered if he could see her, standing bare foot in her faded black and blue, her hard, bare feet walking off the dirt trail and to the edge of the path. The pale glow of the fungus around her did light the area, if poorly, and yellow light did fall out of the unit's doorway. It was possible that he could see her, if he was looking.

It didn't matter. It simply didn't. A stone stabbed into the sole of her foot, and she grunted from the pain, but kept walking. The moan in Rachel's chest began to grow louder. It rattled as if she was empty. As if all she was could be described by a heart that had been made from bronze. Perhaps, even, that was true, as the sharp, putrid smell that had been about her in the unit when Eliana picked her up had all but disappeared in the Shaft. Perhaps all that was left of her was a struggling, dying heart.

The Shaft was before her. Its emptiness yawned wide and full, and she could see the track that ran its circumference like a giant, fallen halo; a broken halo, for she could not see the wall on the opposite side. It was as if, on her ledge, she stood at the very edge of a burnt, broken world, and that there was nothing, an absolute nothingness before her.

"It's okay."

Rachel's whisper barely rose over the sound of her heart. If her cold lips had not been so close to Eliana's ear, the dark wind of the Shaft would have stolen it, the now grinding growl of her heart smothered it. When Eliana met her gaze, she found Rachel's eyes open, partly lucid, partly aware, but not fully. She was not gone, but she was going.

"It's okay," Rachel repeated. "It's okay—God is not watching, not down here."

"No. He never is."

And she let go.

The Souls of Dead Soldiers are for Blackbirds, Not Little Boys

When I was twelve, my mother took me to see a doctor at the Samohshiir Medical Clinic. We could not afford a private Doctor and this was the closest public one, so we left early, and walked the two hours from our home to the clinic, and waited in the dim morning light with a dozen others who had travelled early and on foot, like us. I did not particularly care about seeing the doctor, for at this point, my illness was not considered serious, but above the clinic there were thousands of lights in the roof of the world. They were the most lights that I had seen anywhere before, and I was content to sit on the stony ground and watched them brighten. To my gaze, the white stones sitting in the roof of the world were like tiny, misshapen eyes, and looked as if the ground herself was watching us living inside her. My father, a miner, had laughed when I told him this, once. The light was made from the empty world outside, he explained, and the red sun's light filtering through long shafts of crystal and quartz to us.

The doctor that I eventually saw was named Osamu Makino. He was a small man with a thin, sad-eyed, lined face beneath disintegrating grey-white hair. When he stepped out of his office and into the waiting room to call out my name, he was dressed in the doctor's black pants, black jacket, the black gloves, and the doctor's white closed-collared and buttoned shirt. Under the bright white light of the room—the hospital had been built around a huge triangular eye shaft that flooded the room with light—he appeared as if he were falling apart; that it was not only his hair, but his entire person, that was crumbling into nothing before us.

He examined me in his bright surgery, dripping ointments over my hairless chest, placing cold coins on my eyes, and pressing down on me with warm, powdered fingers. Eventually, he began rubbing a slender bone across my arms. While he did this, he dropped powder onto my left arm. Finally, he said, "Does your skin hurt?"

"Sometimes," I replied, quietly, for I had always been a quiet child. "It feels as if something is pulling at it. At night, mostly."

My mother had brought me to the clinic after she and my father had found me walking around our house two nights earlier. I had never walked in my sleep before and, when they had stopped me and asked me what I was doing, I spoke about a life that I had not experienced, about things that I could not have known. I remembered none of what I said in the morning, but when they asked me if anything was wrong, I did not speak of the pulling on my skin. We could not afford for me to get ill, even with the public clinics. But after consulting the family history and agreeing that there was no lingering ancestor in me who could be the cause, my parents felt it best to take me to a doctor, anyway. So, when the doctor asked me about the pain in my skin, and I responded, my mother shifted her thick, heavy body in her worker browns and pursed her thick lips together in a frown.

"You should have told me," she said, finally.

I nodded.

"It doesn't matter now," Doctor Makino said. He stood and brushed flakes of powder from his black pants "There's no harm, so long as he doesn't lie now. Tell me, do you have other pains?"

I shook my head. "No," I said, for emphasis.

"No strange dreams that reoccur?"

"My parents say that I walk in my sleep."

His lips curved into a sad, disintegrating smile. "I was not asking what your parents told you, but what you experienced. Do you dream?"

"No."

"Why are you asking him this?" my mother asked.

"Your son's skeleton is distorted." Doctor Makino sighed and rubbed at the left side of his face with his black gloved hand, as if to erase himself. "There is a second shadow around his—the skeleton that is naturally his, I mean. It is the first stages of soul infection, I am afraid, but you need not worry. It is early. We can remove the infection—"

"Infection?" Mother interrupted.

"Yes." Doctor Makino's sad dark eyes never met mine, only hers. "Infected is probably not the best word to use. A soul is not meant to be an aggressive thing, but in the situation your son finds himself, the soul cannot stop itself. It is a lost soul from the war; there are more than a few in our city now, though the Queen and her department never speaks of it. The war—the attacks against us continue, despite our successes, and soldiers do die. The souls infecting our young are those Aajnnese men and women who have lost their soulcatchers, or who have had their catchers broken by the enemy after their death, thus leaving their soul lost and scared."

I had a soulcatcher around my neck—my fourth. My father and I had made it from pieces of bone and silver on my eleventh birthday. He had shown me how to bond the silver with the bones of a blackbird we had purchased at the market, but it was I who had made most of it, and I who had killed the bird. I still remembered the blackbird watching me silently with its white eyes as Father and I had walked through the narrow, crowded streets of our neighbourhood that evening. The roof of the world was lit with a weak scattering of eyes, and so most of our light had to come from the blue and green mushrooms people planted on the sides of the road. The blackbird did not utter a sound when, at home the following day, I had reached in with my hands and snapped its neck.

It bothered me, that last part, as if it knew what I was to do, and was allowing me.

"Who . . ." I hesitated.

"What is it, Mi?" Mother asked.

I asked, "Who is it?"

"I don't know," Doctor Makino said. "The problem is that these souls are falling into the bodies of our young and their identities are completely unknown. Without knowing who they are, it is difficult to draw them out, and no one has yet been able to explain why it is happening. It is becoming more and more frequent, that much I know, however. Just last week a young girl was bought in with three souls—three, would you believe! She was in agony, poor girl. Souls pulling at every part of her. She had already gone blind, the poor girl—"

"It can be removed, yes?" Mother asked. "This soul. We can remove it?"

"Not by me, no," he said. "I am sorry. It is beyond me. You will have to write to the Queen and request a soulbird. I will provide you with a letter to accompany it."

"What will happen if, if the Queen says no?" I asked.

"She won't," my mother said sharply. "The Queen protects us, remember."

The doctor's disintegrating smile was less comfort. "The soul in you has died violently, I am afraid. It was not ready for death. Few of those fighting are, I suppose. But it is important for you to understand that the soul is trying to live again—that it wants to live! It is trying to make you into itself so that it can have that life. Because of your youth it will eventually be able to dominate your own soul, to rule it, if you like. When it has done this, your skin and bones will begin to grow into this old memory at an accelerated rate. It is happening now; that is why your skin aches."

I did not fully comprehend the danger of the doctor's words by the time he had finished speaking. I had not yet seen the boys and girls whose souls had been overtaken by lost souls—who would be called the *Infected*—and whose bodies were now monstrosities. I had not seen the extended arms, the twisted faces, and in some cases, limbs that they had removed in brutal, ugly fashions to fit the phantom memory of injuries that had been sustained before death. My mother's face when she stood, however, was pale and grim in a way that I had never seen before, and so I knew, then, and knew again as the doctor gave his private address to her "just in case," that there was some danger. I had the sense then to be frightened and to realize that the words Mother spoke on the way home were hollow comforts, meant to assure both her and myself.

When we arrived home, the blackbirds were waiting with letters.

Satomi

I want to go home. It's cold. So cold. I've never been this cold. The wind pierces the thick army greys I am wearing, ignores my gloves, sinks into my bones. Kyo tells me that I will get used to it, that my duty will warm me, but I don't believe him. I can't. Everything around me is dark and damp. Everything is heavy with ash that is turning the ground an ugly black-brown.

This ugly empty world spreads out beneath the stilts of our watchtower like a stain. If not for the thin, stilted shadows of other watchtowers around us, I would think us alone and dead. I have not seen Aajnn for over a month. I am here beneath the empty red sky with a musket Kyo assures me I will never have to fire. Fire! As if it will in this damp! The powder for it is useless. I tell him this, teeth chattering, but he shrugs and tells me the Queen will never allow the enemy to come close to us, anyway.

I am writing in the fading light of the red sun. The sun—the sun is worse than we were ever told. It fills the emptiness day and night. At night, the sky turns an ugly brown black, never truly dark. To think, our clear, beautiful white light is drawn from this!

The sky reminds me of how much I have left behind, how much I loved the narrow, twisting passages of our home. How much I miss the cool, clean smells. Everything is so mixed up here. Ash and meat. Meat and trees. Trees and waste. Why did I come here? Why did I just not ignore the Queen's conscription and go further down, to the deeper towns, to where the lights are blue and green, and it draws nothing from this awful, awful red sun?

My only pleasure comes in watching the blackbirds. Day or night, they pass through the red sky. They settle on our towers. They scratch. They look for food. Later, they fly away, either behind or in front, to Aajnn or towards the thin, thin plumes of ash that signal the approaching enemy. The birds, at least, are free.

Yoshio

It is wrong of me to write that the blackbirds were simply *there* when my mother and I returned from the public clinic. In truth, they were there for the entire walk home. The dark feathered birds sat alone on the sloping roofs of houses, sat on the wires across the roof of the world in twos and threes as they often did, and landed on the sidewalk, to peck at the glowing mushrooms, or in the cracks of the road. They were silent, as always, but there was never anything strange or untoward about these birds until we emerged from the narrow tunnel and into our neighbourhood. It was there, with hundreds of blackbirds perched silently, always silently, always watching silently, that my statement that the birds were waiting for us was born.

I was born in the neighbourhood called Yokto. For most of its existence, it was beneath the notice of anyone who did not live in it. It had been built only seventy years ago in a small cavern that could hold fifty families comfortably, but which held more than two hundred, now, in cramped, narrow streets. In Yokto, the roof of the world hung so low that none of the houses could ever grow beyond one storey, and those at the corners of the neighbourhood had to do without the steepled roofs that were in fashion, and which blackbirds favoured. The poorest of the poor lived in flat roof houses. Yokto was a dim, chill neighbourhood in comparison to others far across the roof of the world with the lightest scattering of eyes, a hundred and thirteen, none of them bigger than my fist at the age of twelve. We relied upon fungi and portable stones for light, and it served, but with only so many lights in the roof of the world, Yokto also kept a certain chill, as it never drew enough of the red sun's warmth for us.

By the time of our return, the blackbirds had covered the neighbourhood to such a point that their presence was noticeable, but not the curiosity that it would eventually become. My father, who had returned from the mines at midday, said that the blackbirds had migrated one at a time. They emerged from the tunnel's black like an inky drop of water falling from a tap. As he was illiterate, he did not use such language, but you will forgive an old man this quirk in his own memoirs. Yet still, emerge the blackbirds did, and they came with scraps of paper in claws and beak, and they dropped them on the streets and the houses of Yokto. Burnt and dirty and caked in dried blood, these letters lay, unmoving, until the soul-infected children of Aajnn arrived to retrieve them.

Satomi

An order today. An order? I don't know if I could call it such. They've told us to capture blackbirds. As many as we can. Any way we can. Alive or dead. It matters not. The musket in the tower up from us lets out a crack every so often, proof that they have the same order, for there is no enemy to shoot at. No birds fall from the sky, however, and there is no sense that they have hit anything, so far. And why should they? You don't catch blackbirds, Kyo said after the order was delivered. If they're wild, you just don't. It's the Queen's law.

Our musket has proved useless, but we are trying despite ourselves. Orders are orders. We are using a blanket. When one of the birds lands before us, we throw it, trying to toss it over the bird to catch it alive. So far, we have succeeded only in throwing the blanket off the tower and into the ash and mud below.

Yoshio

My mother wrote a letter to the Queen, asking for a soulcatcher. She included Doctor Makino's letter, but there was no immediate response, which my father said was unsurprising. No one in Yokto could afford a soulcatcher, and the Queen's mercy was not as infinite as it had once been. My mother ignored him and more blackbirds arrived, and more paper filled the streets. Stories of people trying to pick up the letters reached everyone, and my father tried it himself, to know if it was true. Like the stories, my father found his hands pecked by a sharp beak, but it could have been worse, as there were stories of a sudden murder of blackbirds falling upon individuals, their black wings beating and claws scratching in their faces silently.

"There is over three thousand now," my father said, staring out the window, a bandage around his left hand. He was a short, stocky, unshaven man in worker browns. He could not read, it is true, but he could gauge numbers and lengths and widths with a glance better than anyone I knew, and no one disputed his estimation now. "There's no sign that they're going to stop, either."

"The Queen will send somebody," Mother replied from the small dinner table. She was writing a third letter requesting a soulcatcher, and had a third letter from Doctor Makino, who supplied them each time she went. A blackbird's feather scratched across paper. She did not look up when she added, "It will be explained soon enough."

From my position on the floor, I saw my father's back straighten, the thick muscles around his neck tighten at the mention of the Queen's name. The war had changed my father's relationship with the Queen. He had mined before for new neighbourhoods, to find minerals, to help advance Aajnn, to help it grow. But with the war, his job had changed, and now he mined for metals and minerals that could be turned into weapons. His job, he said, was not to kill, or to aid in the construction of weapons that would, but when he complained, he was told that all resources in Aajnn were being directed to the war. He could work or starve.

The argument, however, was an old one between my parents. The more pressing concern was the need for a soulcatcher. During the week since my return from the doctor, I had not slept well, and needed to be drugged after the second night. It happened, on that night, just as I was drifting off to sleep, that I felt my bones and skin moving. At first, I thought that the doctor's words had come back to frighten me, that it was just the lingering hint of a nightmare; but when I touched my right arm, the skin shifted, and phantom fingers pushed up against it. I screamed. It was not, perhaps, the most masculine response, but it felt—I remember it now as clearly as that moment when I first felt it—as if a hand had been trapped beneath my skin. That it was caught in the meat and the muscle and the veins. That it was tangled against the bone. That it was struggling for freedom, trying to force my body into the right size and shape so that it might be able to move freely.

My only response was to scream. When Doctor Makino arrived in his doctor's blacks, appearing from the dim night light as if he had been waiting in the dark for this to happen, he wasted no time in sedating me. I was to be sedated, likewise, each night, and in that haze I was only dimly aware of the second body pushing against my skin. But in the morning, I was sick and groggy, and unable to attend school, but there was no presence of this soul, except in my mind. I followed my mother on her errands, or sat in the main room, or worked at some other task, but at no point did I stop thinking about whose soul was inside me.

Satomi

They tell us that the enemy makes blackbirds from brass. That beneath the black feathers, beneath the beak, beneath the hard skin of claws, there is nothing but brass machinery. That there is no blood. That there is no soul. That the birds are nothing but the machines a man made. The machines a woman made. The machines that have been sent to spy upon us, to tell the enemy who we are, where we are, and how to kill us.

The plumes of smoke draw closer and I ask myself, "Will the enemy be of blood and bones?"

Yoshio

My left arm, to this day, is longer than my right. I am right handed, and so my right hand and arm is used more, yet my left is thicker, stronger, the arm of a man who would always be more active than I. It is not something that you will notice upon first meeting me, but it is the physical reminder of my infection, of being Infected, and it is the only way by which I can now gauge what the owner of the soul inside me once looked like. Yet, in comparison to many other children in Aajnn who were Infected, my deformity is not even worth mentioning.

The Infected came into Yokto in the second week after my visit to Doctor Makino. It was they who picked up the burnt and bloody letters off the streets.

The first who I saw was a girl, no older than six. She was walking down the narrow lane that my parents' house was on, following a blackbird. The bird was jumping from letter to letter, occasionally flying, but clearly leading her, and she was hurrying along after it. Behind her came Doctor

Makino in his doctor blacks and a tall woman in worker browns that, I assumed, was the girl's mother.

When the girl was outside our house, I walked down to her. The right side of her face was lopsided and still to the point that even her right eye did not move. Through her worker browns, I could make out the swell of a breast on her right side; it was an ugly thing, too big for her, and made more prominent next to the flatness of the rest of her chest. As she saw me approach, she did not speak, but remained still and quiet, a sullen girl.

Before I could speak, her blackbird leapt, and flew down the lane. The girl ran in a limping run, one leg larger than the other. Her mother moved quickly behind her, but Doctor Makino turned to me, his dark fading gaze resting on me, and then over my shoulder. When I turned to follow his gaze, a black blur startled me. Looking back, I saw that a young blackbird had dropped to the lane and stood on a narrow letter, watching me intently.

"I think this one wants you to follow it," Doctor Makino said.

"How can you be certain?" I still remembered the dark blood down my father's hand. I would not risk that.

The doctor, however, sighed and rubbed at the right side of his face with a black gloved hand. He looked tired, and sounded tired when he spoke: "The letters are meant for those like you, Michio. The Infected. At least, that is what we think, and certainly the birds are only allowing those like you to pick up certain letters."

It didn't take much to make the connection between the letters and the soul inside me. Would it really tell me the identity of the person inside me? Would it help? Before I could talk myself out of it, I stepped out into the street, picked up the letter the blackbird had moments before been on. Tearing its dirty envelope open, I read quickly. "It is from a man called Yoshio."

"Is the next?"

I followed the bird, picked up a second letter, opened. "Yes."

At the end of the lane, the blackbird stood on a third letter, waiting. The narrow buildings and dim light from the roof of the world made it seem as if I would be following it into the unknown, and I suppose I was, though I did not feel frightened. The doctor said, "Follow it and collect your letters quickly. The more you have, the more you will know about this Yoshio, and the easier he will be to remove when—*if* a soulcatcher arrives." He paused, then added, "*Quickly*, Mi. Do you understand?"

I didn't, and said so.

"The queen will not like this," he explained. "The letters of dead soldiers are problematic enough, I imagine, for the secrets that they will reveal about the war. You hear rumours—you are too young for these rumours—but I hear them. The Queen and those around her deny them, but they have been busy telling us all that we are winning the war for years now, and cannot say otherwise. What if these letters say otherwise?"

I had no answer, but the doctor did not expect one. He thrust his black gloved hands into his black jacket pockets, and began walking down the street in the direction of the young girl and her mother from before. It was in the opposite direction of where my blackbird waited, and when I turned to see him again, he appeared only as a dim outline, lit by the light of the mushrooms beneath his feet.

Heeding Doctor Makino's words, I collected the letters that the blackbird landed upon. Even in my haste it took me all morning. Once, I tried to collect a letter that the bird did not land on, but for that, I received a sharp peck in the hand. It did not draw blood like the bird attacking my father, but I did not touch any letter other than those my bird landed on afterwards.

When I returned home, it was late in the afternoon, and my mother had been looking for me. I was scolded, but not harshly, for she had seen the streets fill with children who had been infected, and watched as they picked up the letters, and had been able to deduce what had happened to me. But also, in her hand, she held a fresh green envelope that also lightened her mood. It was a letter from the Queen, informing her that a soulcatcher would be arriving in two days time, and that we would not have to pay for its services.

Satomi

The enemy is made from brass. It sounds insane, but it's true. I saw it with my own eyes. Commander Takahashi showed me. Well, not me, not personally. I have never spoken with him personally. He won't speak to any of us individually. No, he told us all, together. He called all of us on the Northern Line into the Forward Command so that he could show us the enemy.

It had been laid in the middle of the tent, its skin sliced open, and we could clearly see that it had been built from tarnished pieces of bronze. It was a man, though, no matter what anyone says. A man. We could clearly see that. A pale man. A man with brown hair and deep set eyes. A man who had once lived and breathed, you could believe, but he was now a man made with brass.

The Commander did not give him a name. He was the enemy. Just the enemy. A man from The Shibtri Isles. Not even a man, if it could be helped. A thing. A thing from the Shibtri Isles, the Commander said, more often than not. He compared him to the birds we shot. Told us that they were not our blackbirds, just as this was not a man like us. They were both things. Things made by the enemy to be our enemy.

We had expected men and women of blood and bone, just as the Queen said, but no. They, the Commander told us, will not fight. They will send these machines, these replicas of men and women to fight, and leave the casualties as a burden for us.

We were silent after that. Shocked. Confused. Offended? A little, but it did not matter. There was only silence. Silence in which we all heard, clearly, the click, and then the faint hum of the brass machinery starting. A gentle sound almost. A humming.

And then the thing—the man thing—sat up.

The soulcatcher wore the catcher's dark blue pants, blue jacket and blue gloves, and, like Doctor Makino, the soulcatcher wore the white, high collared shirt that her occupation demanded she wear beneath these. To my twelve-year-old gaze, however, the soulcatcher was much more attractive than the doctor had ever been. She was a woman and I was immediately besotted, though in hindsight, I imagine that it is more correct for me to write that she was a girl, no more than six years older than me, and having only recently been appointed to her position. No family in Yokto warranted a veteran soulcatcher and experienced soulbird.

My soulcatcher's name was Mariko Ohara. She was a small, dark haired girl, and curved in ways that I could not keep my gaze from noticing. My staring was no doubt made worse when she had removed her jacket and placed it on the steel chair in my bedroom. It is, therefore, with some amusement that I write that her first words, after the courtesy of saying hello, were spoken to me with a knowing smile on her lips and amused light in the dark eyes that were behind her thin, silver glasses; those words caused in me such utter shock that my immediate response was to blush like I had never blushed before, and to tell her that she couldn't possibly mean that.

"I'm sorry, but I do. You have to take your clothes off." She was trying to be firm but failing. "I'm sorry, Michio, but my bird cannot search you if you're wearing your clothes."

"Must he take off all of them?" Mother asked.

She was making the situation much worse and it took all the willpower that I had, then, at twelve, not to spin around and shout at her.

My distress, however, must have been plain to Mariko, for she said, "He can wear shorts, of course. Of course. He just needs to leave his chest, arms and legs free, so that my bird can search you. You'll need to take off your soulcatcher too, I'm afraid. The birds do not like them."

Her soulbird was the biggest blackbird that I had ever seen. It was easily twice the size of those that had made Yokto their home. It—I could never think of it as a he, or even a she—was both wider and taller than those, and it had a thick barrel chest. Its black feathers, usually so sleek on blackbirds, were shaggy, as if to suggest a wildness to the bird that could not be tamed. Its long, dark slash of a beak did not leave one with a feeling that this was not the case, either. Yet, despite its appearance, the soulbird was perched in its narrow cage quietly, drawing easy breaths. It was not bothered by the fact that it had no movement and that the black bars of its cell pressed in like a fist against it.

Once I had changed in my parents' room, Mariko told me to lie on my back upon the narrow, single bed that dominated my room. Once I had done this, the soulcatcher and my mother tied my arms and legs down with heavy leather straps. It was while they did this that I felt, for a moment, ashamed of the room that I occupied. It was the first time that I had ever felt ashamed, and that, indeed, ashamed me. Compared to others in Yokto, I was not suffering: One of my parents worked, I did not share my room, I had a table and chair at which to do my homework, and I even had a few books and toys. I could even read. My own father could not do that. Yet, in this position, I was able to compare my mother's faded brown worker clothing and Mariko's new, thick white shirt, and the silver studs in her ears—three in the left, five in the right—and the glasses she wore. My family could afford none of these things, I realized. Even the bed sheets I lay upon were old and threadbare and had been mended more than once. It caused in me a sudden bout of self-consciousness in relation to the poorness of my family that I had never felt before, a poorness that if I could have hidden from this beautiful girl before me, I would have.

There was nothing I could do about these thoughts. Indeed, when Mariko lifted the soulbird's cage above me, her slender fingers opening the door, those evaporated quickly. The soulbird stuck its black head out.

Mariko bent down, and placed her mouth next to it: "We are looking for the soul of Yoshio—he does not belong."

The soulbird's white gaze fell upon me. It was an oddly empty gaze, one that I did not like. In its cage, the big black bird shifted. Its feathers ruffled. Its long sharp beak opened and closed in silence. Then, slowly, it's body scrapping against the bars, feathers falling off as it pushed itself out, it dropped lightly onto my naked stomach. Its cold claws pinched my skin. Its white gaze returned to mine. The emptiness in there was slowly becoming frightening but it was not something that I could look away from—

Its sharp beak plunged into my skin.

There was pain, but worse, I realized, was that it had ripped a piece of skin off my stomach.

He sat up!

I did not move. No one did. The brass man's brown eyes were wide open. In the moment that they glanced over me I knew, knew, that he was alive. Alive as you or I. But it was only for a moment that I could think that. The next, shouting, screams, and chaos. The brass man had leapt off the table.

In the confusion round him, he had no trouble reaching Commander Takahashi. Men in soldier's grey stepped back from him. Men that were meant to fight him. To stop him. Men who had been assured that the brass man was dead. They stepped back. They yelled for him to stop. But they were frightened and confused and did not think to stop the brass man's thick, mechanical hands from grabbing the Commander by the throat.

We attacked him, then. Men threw themselves at him. Others smashed chairs. Anything. But it was not enough. Not nearly. Commander Takahashi's neck splintered. We heard nothing, but when the brass man tossed him away, the Commander landed in a bent angle that no living man could make.

I do not think the brass man expected to live. Whoever had sent him, whoever gave the order for him to die and come back to life, must have told him that there was no way to survive. And so he made no attempt to do so. Instead, he attacked the officers. He attacked only those with rank. He ignored anyone else. Even as we attacked him, he ignored those of us in simple grey.

I broke one of his arms off. I had a hammer. A big, long hammer that they use in mining pits to break rock open. The tools were outside the tent. They are giving new recruits hammers, Kyo and I had joked when we saw them. We made jokes about how we would apply for them, for they were weaponry we were both more capable of using. And when the brass man was attacking, we had no choice but to run for them. Yet with that hammer I took an arm off. With another Kyo smashed open the brass man's leg. Together we broke open his head. Together we killed it. We could not have done this with a musket. Yet still, even having done this, the brass man had killed five of our officers with his own hands.

We are back in the watchtower now. They sent us afterwards. Send us back to watch the lines of ash draw closer. To shoot blackbirds. To await this enemy.

Yoshio

"It is not Yoshio."

Mariko's voice. It was faint, however, as if it was being smothered or pushed away, and could be heard only from a distance. I struggled to hear as she continued to speak, straining as much as I could, but her words were simply incoherent to me. I wanted to open my eyes and look at her, to assure myself that she was there, that she was a person I could recognize, but another voice told me not too. *Don't open your eyes*, it said. Why, it did not explain, but the voice sounded like mine in all but the subtlest of tones, and it had such an unquestionable authority that I did not dare disobey it. Not yet. Not until I knew more.

"But the letters are from him." My mother's voice spoke this time; it was loud and clear, as her voice always was. "How do you explain them, then?"

"A lie, maybe."

"There are over ten thousand blackbirds in Aajnn. What kind of enemy could send so many?"

Mariko's voice was still faint: "An enemy winning."

"The Queen says otherwise."

"I do not wish to disagree with the Queen."

"You just did," my mother said. "Your soulbird is not helping my son. You tell me that these letters are wrong. That this Yoshio is not in him. You are even suggesting to me that the blackbirds in our neighbourhood—in our entire city, even—are not real. The only way that this could be true is if the Queen has lied to us for the last two years about this war. That is what you are telling me, is it not?"

"The Queen—"

"The Queen protects us!" Mother interrupted.

Don't open your eyes. I wanted to, needed to. I could feel the silence around me, thick and angry now, and opening my eyes, I knew, would diffuse it. I would prove to them that it was Yoshio inside me. That the birds were right.

"Mu."

It was my father's voice, distant as Mariko's was.

"She is a guest, Mu," he continued. "More than that, she is trying to help our son. It's been three days. It's as she says—this Yoshio is not in him."

Don't open your eyes.

My mother's breath was heavy and ragged. "I know. It's just—No, I am—I am sorry." Her tone was rigid, angry, but the anger was directed at herself, not Mariko. I could not hear the soulcatcher's voice reply, but my mother said, "No, please, I shouldn't have said that. I have believed in the Queen since I was born. She sent you, you must understand. She sent you for our son. She has never—to think that she might be lying . . ."

"She's just tired." My father's voice grew stronger, clearer. "Mu, you need your rest. You can't be with him all the time."

Don't—

"What if he wakes up?"

—open—

"That's why Mariko is here. You've barely slept in three days."

—your—

"I want to be here for him."

—eyes—

"You need rest."

I opened my eyes. There was no one in the room. There was no room. Rather, there was only whiteness and a faint, faint pecking, coming from all directions about me. I tried to sit up, but I could not move. The pecking grew. It sounded as if it were coming from a sharp beak that was being scraped across hard stones. My arms and legs were immobile. I could feel straps holding me down. The pecking continued, steady, coming from all around me. I struggled to raise my head. I felt a stab of pain. Then another. I looked down and saw, standing on my stomach, its claws a wet red, the shaggy, wild soulbird. Its long, sharp beak had just pierced my stomach and plunged into the bloody mess that already existed. As I watched, it drew back, ripping the wet, raw contents of my intestines with it. As it raised its head, the soulbird's white eyes met mine and I realized, with horror, that they were no longer a clean, crisp white, but rather they were stained red.

Its beak opened, and in a voice that was mine, it said, "I told you not to open your eyes."

99

Satomi

The tower to the North exploded today.

One moment, it was there. The next, its thin legs were all that remained, and its broken wreckage smoldering beneath the morning's red sky. I had been on watch when it happened. Kyo was sleeping. I had gotten us dry powder for the musket and so I had it sitting on the rail of the tower. Sitting ready. Kyo had helped me, even, after what happened with the Commander, though as we stood and looked at the wreckage, I knew that our new musket was useless.

The explosion began in raining fire. It's the only way to explain it. A soft sprinkle of fire began to fall and then, suddenly, the tower exploded! It burst apart. Ripped apart. It was shredded. I don't—I can't explain it to you. The fire rained down and then, suddenly, the slowly bleeding mid morning had opened up like a wound, and there was a broken tower on the horizon and no sign of the enemy. No brass men. No brass animals. Just the plumes of ash, drawing closer. Ever closer.

I know more fear, every day.

Yoshio

When I awoke, Mariko was sitting in my room. Her blue jacket was hanging off the back of my chair and she was sitting at my table, reading the dirty, burnt letters that I had collected. I was no longer strapped down, though my limbs felt sluggish, as if they had not been used for some time, and I was tired. There was a thin white blanket covering me and, before I said a word to Mariko, I lifted it. I was completely naked, but to my relief, there was no other mark upon me.

"How do you feel?" Mariko picked up a stone pitcher from the floor and poured a cup of water, then came over to me. "If your throat hurts, drink."

I did and, after watching me take my first hesitant sips, she said, "It took five days. You've been in a sleep, of sorts, for five days, but you won't feel rested."

"Where—where is your bird?" I asked, my voice soft, scratchy.

"At home. He finished yesterday, so there was no need to make him sit in the cage as I travelled here. Are you sure you're fine? Five days is a long time to be under, so if you're feeling nauseous, or your hurt, you should tell me."

I shook my head. "Just tired."

"Good."

"Where is . . ." I hesitated, the memory of what I heard while under still fresh in my mind. "Was it Yoshio?"

"No."

"Who was it?"

Mariko sat on the edge of my bed. "That took a little while to figure. You're only my third patient, Mi, and I still have much to learn. Forgive me. My soulbird had found something, but it was difficult to remove. It wasn't Yoshio, as I said, but that does not account for five days. Even an unknown soul should be able to be removed within two. But still he worked by a third and fourth. Only a suicide is so difficult."

"Kyo," I whispered.

"Yes, Kyo. It took him five days to pull Kyo out—if I had read the letters, it would have taken less, perhaps. But I thought they were fake. I've only just read them now. In fact, I was just reading Yoshio's final letter now, where he finds Kyo." She stood, and picked the dirty piece of paper off the table. Aloud, she read, "I found him this morning. He had done it in his watch. In the time when he was meant to have his gaze on the dark red sky. When he was meant to be watching the plumes of ash. To report if they came closer. When he was meant to be watching for the first touches of flame falling through the sky at our outpost. But he hadn't been doing any of those things. He hadn't been watching. His eyes were open, but he would not see anything. Kyo had done it early in his shift. He was stiff when I touched him. Cold. So cold. Colder than the wind that cut through my clothes."

She stopped, but I knew how the rest of it went.

He lay against the wooden wall with the musket next to him. The musket that was now stained with his blood. The musket that we had been given to defend with. To share, one between two. The musket we had just only gotten dry powder for. That musket that he had used, finally. The musket that he had used to crush his soulcatcher so that his soul could return home to Aajnn, so that it could find a sanctuary that he could not here.

And I wondered, as I helped the doctor take Kyo away, how it is that I will return home?

Yoshio

I never saw my soulcatcher again, but we only remained in Yokto for another month, so it was to be expected. As Yoshio wrote in his first letter, he should have gone deeper into the world rather than taken part in the Queen's War; he should have gone into the cities that were lit in blues and greens and, I learned later, purples and yellows and much, much more, and where the red sun and the Queen were not known. It was into these cities that my parents took me.

I remember well the morning that they told me of their decision. For weeks, we had heard rumours that cities neighbouring Aajnn had fallen. That they had fallen as much as six to eight months ago. But it was not until a Queen's messenger, wearing the pale green that signalled his service, came around and spoke in Yokto that it was finally confirmed. The letters the birds brought, he said, were from real soldiers. The Queen was now attempting to establish a peace with the forces for the Shibtri Isles and we need not panic. Or words to those affect. On the morning after that, I awoke in my bed, chilled, the lights on the roof the world dimmer than usual. Outside, blackbirds sat quietly, as they always did. Yokto was a neighbourhood of blackbirds now, and Aajnn a city of them. Climbing out of bed, I walked down the cold hallway to the living room, where my mother sat at the small, stone, dining table, crying.

I had never heard my mother cry before and so I approached her quietly. As I drew closer, I could see the outspread wings of a blackbird on the table. They were still. As still as the wings of the blackbird on my eleventh birthday. My hand drifted up to my soulcatcher, to feel the warm bone and cold silver. I hoped that I would stay in it after I died. That I wouldn't become lost like some many others. Gently, I placed my hand on my mother's shoulder.

"Mother?" I asked. "Is everything fine? Why are you crying?"

In response, her hand reached up and clutched mine. She did not speak, but her answer was in blood on her hands. The blood from the blackbird she had killed that very morning.

The Funeral, Ruined

It was the weight that woke Linette. Her weight. The weight of herself.

The flat red sky above Issuer was waiting when she opened her eyes. Five hours before, when she had closed her eyes, it had been a dark, ugly brown-red: the middle of the night. Now it was the clear early morning red, and a thick, muggy warmth was seeping through her open window with the new light. There would be no rain today. Just the heat. Just the sweat. Just that uncomfortable, hot awareness of herself that both brought. The worst was Linette's short dark hair, dirty with sweat and ash. The ash that had come through the open window during the night. It had streaked her face and settled in her mouth and she could taste it, dry and burnt in her gums. Her left arm, with its thick, straight scars across the forearm, felt heavy and ached; but it always ached. It was a dull lazy ache in the heat, and a sharp, pointed pain in the cold, as if, with the latter, the brittle weather was digging into her fractured bone to snap it. Her feet, tangled at the bottom of her coarse, ash-stained brown sheets, sweated uncomfortably, and her long, straight back could feel the sweaty outline of the bronze frame beneath the thin mattress that she lay on. There was no end to herself, Linette thought, and she would never be able to sleep again, so aware of it was she.

Her dreams, however, had not been a sanctuary. In them, Linette had lived under a different part of the red sun, wrapped in heavy brown clothes, wearing pieces of light bronze armour, and holding a short, wide-nosed gun. Around her, clouds of black ash spewed from the back of bronze, grey and silver coloured machines. Cages of crows peppered the ground and, inside, the black birds sat silently, waiting. They were not real, she knew. They never had been. The ground the fake birds lay on was mud and ash and the waste of brown and red trees that had been torn down to make the circular camp she lived in. The wastage clung to her boots, leaving a trail to its centre behind her. There was a man beside her, but she couldn't make him out. He had been asking her when she planned to read the letter, but she had responded by telling him to be quiet. Two men had escaped, she said. They could be anywhere. They could be watching—

They were, but she had awoken before that.

It didn't matter: she knew the outcome, had lived it, and didn't need to experience it again.

The letter, however, was not part of the memory. The letter was part of her muggy, hot life in Issuer. It was sitting in her tiny kitchen, leaning against an old bronze kettle: thin, straight, pristine and white. A perfect set of teeth to speak with. Her name was printed in messy letters on the front, and though a young, clean-skinned man she didn't know had delivered it, she knew the author.

Slowly, Linette pushed herself up with her good arm. Her left was a dead weight in her lap. It would take a shower and exercise for it to gain full movement. Two months out of the hospital, out of the army, and a month living in Issuer and her arm had only just begun to improve to the point that she could use it properly. But it took time, still. She slid across the bed that was big enough for two—but held only one—and placed her feet down on the cool stone floor of a room so bare that a visitor would have thought no one lived in it.

The room's possessions lay in the hallway in a jumble. Linette had thrown them there last night. The large, bronze framed mirror that had once sat on the far wall to give the room size now leaned against the wall with cracks around the top. Near it lay a brass clock, and next to that a stocky bronze fan with bent blades, followed by a dozen tiny mechanical devices that she had been unable to stomach the thought of having near her as she slept. The way that each simulated a natural event, or imposed an artificial meaning . . . they disgusted her, just as the easy familiarity with which she had treated them at one stage in her life did. In anger, she had thrown them from the room and opened the window so that the muggy, ash-stained breeze could enter.

She had not yet opened the letter.

My Dear Linette—

I do not know how to begin, but I do know that there is little time left for me to write. In half an hour, the operation will begin. I am apprehensive. My hand trembles. I have always prided myself on clean, simple letters, but look at them now. They cross lines. They mix against each other. They slope one way, then another. They fall outside the neat order that I have cherished so much. I suppose, given what is about to happen, it's the way things should be. Nothing in life is neat and contained.

She tried to eat, but the taste of ash lingered in her mouth, even after she had rinsed.

From her chair at the kitchen table, Linette swallowed her half-chewed piece of apple, and then tossed the remaining half into the bin next to her sink. The apple was small, brown, and made an unpleasant, soggy slap as it hit the brass bottom of the bin. Silence followed. A tall woman, now wearing black pants and a long sleeved, black, buttoned shirt, Linette had not allowed a sound to escape her mouth since waking up. She had left the bedroom rubbing the scars on her arm, disgusted by the way sweat gathered around the thick, puckered flesh. She had stepped around the mess in the hall, entered the toilet, pissed, showered, scrubbed herself with hard movements, worked her arm until it moved like the other, then dressed and picked up the apple. The only noise had been her feet on the slowly warming concrete floor.

Not so long ago, the mornings had been filled with sound: men and women she knew in smoky, hazy camps, talking about bad food, operations, people back home, and those they knew now. Before she had left, and when she had lived in Ledornn, there had been conversations about what kind of toast she would prefer, and who would come up with dinner. Insignificant, shallow, domestic conversations . . . .

Linette gazed through the dirty window of the kitchen. The tall, dark shadows of windmills lined Issuer's morning skyline, a few turning slowly, but most were still. The empty red sky hung above them regardless, still and oppressive.

She did not think consciously for the half hour that she sat at the table, her fingernails clicking on the bronze top every now and then. Her mind had drifted and, in a mix of conversation fragments, bits of song, parts from books, and even scenes from plays that she had seen, her mind turned itself over until, finally, she began to focus on a man. He was blond, slim, and his teeth were crooked, and he had been an unlikely lover for her as much as she had been for him. She did not want to think of him, and when her arm began to throb again, either with real or symbolic pain, she knew that she had to stop before her thoughts turned into a morbidity that would crumble her resolve for the day.

Quietly, Linette entered the small, pale grey painted living room. There was a long brown couch in the middle, and a slim bronze table in the corner with a brass and silver lined radio on top of it. A box of outside opinions pushed aside. On the floor, however, were a pair of old, scuffed black boots, which Linette picked up. Holding them, she sat down upon the couch, and there, paused again.

In the kitchen, the letter sat, still, against the kettle.

"I have been to too many funerals," she said, as if it could reply to her.

It could not, of course, but the fact that she had spoken to it both frustrated and upset her. With hard yanks, she tightly wound the frayed black laces of her boots up. On the right boot she missed a hole, and on the left, two. She ground her teeth together harshly both times, but retied carefully, wiping her hands free from sweat.

Finished, she rose and crossed the tiny kitchen, to the back door. Her strides were quick and purposeful: the walk of a woman who had an unpleasant task ahead of her, but who would meet it without flinching.

Are you angry?

That day when I first met you, you were angry. Nearly two years and that is what I remember about you most. It is not your beauty, not your smile, not your habits . . . .No, for over the years, I have realized that these do not define you. They are secondary to your anger—that brilliant, burning anger that exists because the world is not right. The anger that exists because you must fix it, somehow. The first time I saw you was from afar, standing beneath a bronze parasol, while you stood at the front of the Anti-War rally in Ledornn, and it was there that I saw that anger. You demanded to know why Aajnn mattered so much to the Shibtri Isles? Why the Queen and her Children were such a threat?

You told us that they lived in cramped cities beneath the earth, away from our red sun, and with the bones of crows around their necks to catch their souls when they died. They were full of superstition that made the men and women who had Morticians tattoo their life into their skin for God seem at the forefront of science and logic.

What impressed me most (and everyone else, I imagine) was that you were not a person off the street, but a career soldier. You stood in front of us in the straight light brown pants and suit of the army, your medals and rank displayed for all. You were proud of who you were. You were proud of what you had done for the Isles. You were proud to be in service.

But now, you were angry, and that anger would not allow you to be silent, no matter the consequences. It was an anger to fear and, I am afraid to say, I did—and do—fear it.

The pear shaped Ovens of Issuer dominated the city's horizon, though they were easily an hour away by carriage.

Lately, the twin Ovens had a tendency to blur around the edges for Linette, but even with the beginning of her deteriorating eyesight in her thirty-eighth year, the immense girth and height of the creations meant that they were unable to be passed over when she looked at Issuer's skyline. In contrast, the hundreds of long, bronze windmills that rose out of the city could—and did—fade from her awareness. The Ovens, however, lurked on the horizon like a pair of dark, hunched watchers outside the city, covered in a layer of soot as a disguise. If you managed to forget them (and Linette doubted she ever could) then you would be reminded each Friday when they belched tart-smelling ash, and plumes rose out of each to signal the burning of the weekly dead.

Outside of her house, Linette spent a moment in morbid contemplation of the Ovens. It was where she would finish her mortal journey, she knew: a friend, a family member, perhaps even a Mortician, would take her body wrapped in white sheets up to the silent monks who lived beneath the Ovens. There, she would be bathed, cleaned, and finally placed in the giant pits that never fully cooled, and which would ignite at the end of the week, consuming her. There was nowhere else that she would prefer to end. She would not be buried in the ground, not given—or sold or stolen—to a Surgeon's workshop . . . what was left of her would be burnt away. She would be given freedom.

Her small house sat at the end of Issuer, surrounded by other small, cheap, red brick houses. Packed dirt worked as a road around them, but within minutes, she had stepped onto the paved streets of Issuer proper. There, the tall windmills turned at a variety of paces, powered by electricity that was strung from house to house. Issuer had never been big: it was a transient's city, organized in an ordered grid, with street names that indicated purpose. Everything in it was designed to make it easy for the visitor, of which Issuer saw many. It was a city—more a town, really—where men and women arrived for a few days, a week, and after they had seen the Ovens burn and their duty was done to family and loved ones, they left.

The windows to the private houses Linette passed were shut, the boards pulled closed. Inside, bronze fans circulated the air, but the impression of personal lives being closed off was not an illusion. The people who lived in Issuer mostly kept to themselves, and it was only when you entered the middle of the city that openness existed. There, the public stores, hotels, and other places of business kept their windows unbolted. There, fans sat on the streets, blowing, while larger windmills—the largest in the city—turned above them. There, men and women, mostly young, presented the smiling, happy face of Issuer to visitors. Everywhere—and everyone—else, Linette believed, looked like a coffin: closed in, quiet, and still.

Death was the commodity of Issuer. Alan Pierre, a black man who had come to the Isles as a child and made a fortune as a body snatcher, had founded it. When age had finally driven him into looking for a way to settle, he had looked at the makeshift tent city that had existed outside the Ovens and sunk his considerable, ill-gained fortune into turning it into something more lasting. It wasn't long until hotels were built, and then Surgeons and Morticians arrived, as did the other trades that had attached themselves to the industry of death. The people, like Linette, who drifted into the town, drawn by their own morbid frame of mind and their internal struggles, had always been part of it.

Linette herself did not know, exactly, what it was that drew her to Issuer. Her pension provided enough for rent, food, but very little else. In another city, she might find work and earn more, but while her life was mean, she did not dislike it. The heat bothered her, but it was not as bad as the cold. She was lonely, but—

No.

No, that was wrong: she was not lonely.

She had not been lonely since she moved here and had been able to gaze upon the Ovens daily.

I am not a soldier, and I do not pretend to know what you went through, or why, indeed, Issuer allows you to sleep more calmly than you did in Ledornn;

but I like to think I have been supportive of all your needs. That I have tried, as much as I possibly can, to be supportive of you.

It has not been easy, Linette. It is true, yes, that I have not been in the best health, but your hatred towards the advancements in our society have made our lives—our illnesses and injuries—more difficult than they should be. Neither of us can heal with your attitude.

For you, it is your arm that bothers you. Why would it not? The machete of an escaped prisoner splintered the bone and it is now held together by steel rods. It will take years to heal, if ever it does, and it bothers you greatly. The obvious solution to your injury was a replacement, which was offered by the army Surgeons, but you rejected this—and you have since rejected anything that the Surgeons have been able to offer that takes away what you are born with. You tell them (and you tell me) that it is unnatural, that it is not right.

But what is right, I ask? Tattooing your body for God? Wearing a charm around your neck to capture your soul? To believe the Ocean is a living God? To believe the hundreds of other, unexplainable things in this world? Are these somehow more acceptable to you now than the science that has been developed, the advancements that will allow us to live long, healthy lives?

Though Linette did not believe in a God, she made her way to the men and women who traded in that belief on the Morticians Avenue. Specifically, she made her way to the long, straight building of the Mortician Yvelt Fraé, which was made from caramel-coloured bricks. It had a dark, brown tiled roof, and was the largest building in the street, lying curled between a dozen smaller houses of varying brick colour. Yvelt's building had three bronze windmills around it, two on the roof, and one larger piece cemented at the back, which towered over all others on the street.

At the bronze door, Mrs. Fraé, whose hair, it appeared, had been freshly dyed a red-brown, greeted Linette. Her skin, however, sagged around her jaw, wrinkled over her face, and continued to do so down her neck until it was covered by the brown gown she wore. Beneath the tattoos across her body there was no tautness of youth, and so the illusion created by dying her hair seemed ridiculous and nothing more than a vanity.

"Linette, it is a pleasure to see you." Mrs. Fraé's deep voice sounded as if it should emerge from a larger women. "Linette? Are you—"

"He's dead."

"Ah." A pause, then, "I'm very sorry."

"There was a letter." Her voice was short, clipped. She could feel the emotion in the back of her mouth, threatening to spill out over her words. "He—he wasn't there yesterday."

"Come in, come in," Mrs. Fraé murmured, stepping back from the door to allow her entry.

The inside of the house was lit in a warm orange and divided by a set of thick, bronze doors. Over each panel of the door was a pattern of angels and devils at war, naked and carrying weapons. The figures on it were ridiculous: sexless for angel, sexual for devil, and posed in mid action. Behind the twisting battle, Linette knew, lay the private residence of Mrs. Fraé and her family, who were also part of the Mortician trade. She had never seen behind the doors, and never would, but expected it to be different from what she saw now. The side of the house she stood on was plain, but expensively decorated with a floor covered in wooden boards and cushioned lounges made from pale brown leather. There was a real, ash-wood table at the end of the room, with a ledger that was used for appointments and payments. A feathered quill lay on it. It looked as if one of Mrs. Fraé's angels had made a table out of the dead for her, and left one of its own feathers to write with.

"Would you like a drink?" the elderly Mortician asked.

"No, I—" The emotions from before welled up, threatened her, and she swallowed. "I'm fine. I would just like to start, if possible."

"Of course."

Linette had known that there would not be a problem. She had left early, before Issuer fully awoke, and arrived when she knew that Mrs. Fraé would be awake with the early morning vitality of the elderly. Had she arrived later, and the woman had been engaged, she would have had to wait, for once a Mortician left his or her mark on you, another would not touch you until the first had died. Linette knew that she did not have the patience to wait today.

Mrs. Fraé led her to a small room where, with a click, white electric light flooded its darkness. In the middle lay a chair made from bronze with thick cushions on it. The bolts and screws and dials in it ensured that, while the chair was ugly, it could be folded into a number of positions. Mrs. Fraé flattened the chair into a board before turning to the trays that lined the side of the room, filled with needles and pots of ink.

Linette had received her first tattoo shortly after she had moved to Issuer, when her arm had been mostly useless, but it was the memories of the war that damaged her most. She had been in the army for twenty-one years and had seen men and women die, just as she had killed, by her reckoning, more than thirty in various battles. Psychologically, death was nothing new to her. She had always been able to rationalize it, to make it part of her job . . . at least until the campaign against the Empress and her Children began, and she found herself fighting men—always men—armed with mining equipment and rusted machetes and muskets so old they wouldn't hurt anyone but the owner. It was impossible to look at those men and see a threat. After she left the army with her injury, she had struggled with that awareness, and how to deal with it.

On her back were one hundred and thirteen names in the neat, elegant script of Mrs. Fraé. They were the names of soldiers: friends, some, but a large portion were men and women who she had fought with, peers and comrades before friends. Each one of them, however, had died fighting the Empress and her Children. Each one of them had died needlessly. Died for nothing but the greed of their own country.

"Do you still want this outside the others?" Mrs. Fraé asked, referring to the new tattoo. "On the small of your back?"

Linette nodded.

She did not need to speak his name, and for that, she was grateful. Climbing on to the bench, Linette pulled her shirt up, then curled her arms beneath her chin, and waited. The puckered flesh of her bad arm was uncomfortably warm against her and she could feel her muscles tensing in anticipation for the moment when her skin was pierced—

"So."

A voice. *His* voice.

"So," he said, repeating it, drawing it out, letting his very familiar voice sink into her. "This is my funeral."

I am dying.

Soon, I will be taken into a chamber where two giant tubes hang from the ceiling, and I will be submersed in a green liquid. There, I will die. There, I will be put into a new body. There, I will return. I will return without these weak lungs I was born with; without the holes in my heart; without the pains that stop me from being able to travel this world of ours without having oxygen next to me. When I awake, I will be, for the first time that I can remember, without pain.

You would rather me die. You said that to me, only a week ago, stroking my hair as I lay in our bed, exhausted by the muggy heat, and unable to draw a good breath. You would rather me die than return a man made from bronze and silver and skin. You would rather mourn me than celebrate me.

You defend the right for the Empress and her Children to worship and live as they wish, but it strikes me that their beliefs are not so different than mine. For them, they return in a new body, reborn into their family by a sister, brother, daughter, or son. Perhaps even their own parents. The men and women who believe in God, and who we share our cities with, believe they will be reborn too—given a new life in Heaven (or Hell), after their life has been judged by God. So why is it that I cannot return?

You will be angry, I know, when you read this. You will see it as betrayal. I do not wish for you to do so, but you will.

If I—

I will find you, Linette. I will talk to you—the Surgeon is in front of me right now, and she is urging me to finish, so I must. But I will find you, after—I will.

For a moment, he looked just like the man she remembered: slender, pale, blond, with a blade of a smile that revealed his crooked, yellow teeth. Except, of course, that they were not crooked, and therein the truth was told. They were straight, and white, and he was, she knew, dead.

The room was quiet with the pause between words and action. Linette (and, she assumed, Mrs. Fraé) could hear the faint murmur of machinery that surrounded the man before her, much in the way that insects create a susurration of noise in the evening. If allowed, it would slip into the background, become a familiar, normal buzz; if it could be allowed, that is. To Linette, the sound served only to remind her of the fact that, beneath his pale skin, he was no longer bones, no longer blood, no longer all the things that she was. Instead, he was bronze and brass bones circled by copper and silver wiring with a complex motor in the centre of his chest. The skin, like the pale red pants and black shirt he wore, was just another piece of clothing—a piece of fashion, to allow him to look as if he were part of the world.

"Nothing to say?" he said, finally. He remained standing in the doorway to the room, the orange light behind him bathing him in an artificial warmth. "I came all this way—"

"You should leave." Her voice was hard. "I don't want you here."

"Linette—"

"No."

"I—"

"Mrs. Fraé, please." Linette turned to the elderly Mortician, who had been watching the exchange calmly. "Can you do nothing?"

"Don't look to her," he said, a hint of smugness in his voice. "How do you think I am here? She left the door open. She agreed to my plan to meet you here."

Mrs. Fraé smiled faintly, apologetically, and Linette felt the betrayal deeply. It was true that she did not follow the same faith as the Mortician, and that her tattoos were about grief, not God. Her words were a closure she could not get elsewhere in life, but she had begun to trust the older woman as she trusted few. As the work on her back drew to an end, Linette had felt a bond with Mrs. Fraé, and to feel that connection severed so sharply, so quickly, so instantly, hurt her more than she would have ever considered.

"I thought seeing him would help," Mrs. Fraé explained. "You have an irrational—"

Linette jumped off the table and stalked towards the door. Her body was tense as she approached him, but her gaze held his, and she knew, *knew*, that if he touched her, she would lash out.

"Linette, please, listen—" The murmur of his body grew louder when he opened his mouth. "Please. Stop. Listen to us."

His hand moved to her, but she reacted quickly, slapping it aside. "Don't touch me," she hissed. She could feel her grief and anger mixing, close to hysteria, and she fought it back as best she could to retain her control. "Don't ever touch me. Never. Do you understand? *Never*. Don't come anywhere near me. I know your kind and you may think you're someone I know, but you are not. You're not him. He's *dead*. You're just the copy of him. You're nothing but a tool—an object. Something to be used. Something to be sent in to kill men with. Something that can pretend that its dead so that you can sneak in like an assassin and kill them without remorse. Something that can switch off every emotion because it is just a wire. Something that lets me switch off my emotions. Something that lets me kill one, kill ten—kill fifty! Something that allows me to kill as many people as I please because—"

"*Linette.*"

"*Because* you make death meaningless."

Silence. His mouth opened, the hint of growling mechanics growing into an artificial shout, but she shouldered out, bashed past him, threw him off balance with his new, heavy weight, and his voice did not emerge. Her damaged arm throbbed in a sharp, renewed pain. Good, she thought. Good. She wanted to feel the pain. The pain would stop the tears, would hide the hurt, the betrayal, and if, perhaps, while she stalked along the streets of Issuer back to her house . . . if perhaps tears slipped out from the corners of her eyes, then she would know it was the pain in her arm, and nothing else.

For all the differences we have, for all the difficulties that we have faced since your return, Linette, I want you to know that I am still dedicated to us. To preserving us.

Antony.

The tears had stopped by the time Linette reached her house, but her body was covered in a sheen of sweat, as if it had begun to weep silently now that her eyes were dry.

She was conscious of the twin shapes of the Ovens behind her, and the finality that they represented. It was a small comfort, and as she stood at the side of her house and gazed back at Issuer, with its barely populated streets that were threaded together by shadowy lines of electricity and punctuated by bronze windmills, she took that comfort for as much as she could. Even though the city had betrayed her—no, not Issuer itself, but a part of the city, part of its trade, its life—the Ovens sat, unmoving, waiting, a period that put everything into perspective for her. A period that gave her security. She took from the Ovens everything that she could, and when she entered the house finally and saw *his* letter, leaning against the kettle just as it had before, her previous anger and hurt failed to rise.

She could throw it away, and knew, perhaps that she should. She could rip it, cut it up, drown it, burn it . . .

And yet, despite herself, she did not.

Under the Red Sun

1.

....

The Surgeon arrived atop an old cart drawn by crystal-headed horses.

Mother insisted that we bury her daughter in the dirt and so we did, though we were unable to protect the barren soil she lay in.

On the day of her burial, I stood with my brother, Henry, beneath the red midday sky and dug into the dirt with one of the shovels that he had made. Neither of us had our Mother's faith, but we worked as diligently as if we did. The air was still and humid and the blades hit the ground with hard, blunt punches. Mother sat in her mechanical wheelchair beneath the shade of a bronze parasol, her thin, pale skin marked with faded words that were tattooed across her in a history of unshed, blue tears. I could read the words, vaguely, as they were words that had been shrunk and combined with others, to the point where, untrained as I was, I became lost in the words that were not the names of my siblings and I. Through her cancer ravaged vocal cords, Mother whispered to the expensive cherry-red wooden coffin beside her and, though she could not raise her voice anymore, her manner of hunching and hand movements suggested a privacy of words that I could only imagine all parents said to their children once they had passed on. Words that are kinder, gentler, and perhaps more wise and knowing in this conversation than any they had had in life. At least, I hoped those words were being passed. Mother's conversations were without haste as it took Henry and I five hours to dig a grave deep enough for her, but shallow enough for us so that when we returned in the evening, we would not spend the entire night re-digging. My mother, as I said, had faith in a God, a faith that was dying in her, yes, and a faith that Henry and I wished had died before our sister, Fiona. Pragmatists, we knew that dirt burial meant that she would be dug up by body snatchers and sold to Surgeons for body parts. Fiona's skin, like Henry's and mine, was unmarked. That meant she had no history. She was clean, but for the wasting that had killed her. It would take a day for a snatcher to arrive. Maybe two. She would be stolen before the week was over, certainly. Yet we did not wish to upset Mother, frail as she was, so we dug according to her wishes, knowing that we would return in the evening to take Fiona's body down to the Ovens in Issuer, two days away. Afterwards Henry and I would sit outside the soot-encrusted monoliths and watch as the fat ashes of the weekly dead spilled out across the dry, cracked riverbeds that lay in the shadows behind.

The sky was red when we finished, red like freshly spilled blood as we lowered the coffin down, said our words, and wheeled Mother over the dust-stained trails out of the graveyard. And it was red like dried blood when we returned in the night without her.

Henry and I navigated the cemetery silently, the electric brass lamp that I held a weak yellow eye to guide us. My Brother, jingling metal with every step, carried the shovels and stretcher over his broad, muscular back without complaint. My own body ached from the unaccustomed work. In addition to the digging we were about to return to, I had, just before, bribed the man at the gate. He was covered in blue tattoos stronger than Mother's and had a mechanical monocle over his left eye. My bribe had been to close that eye while we came and left. We did not fear the authorities, but we had no desire to upset Mother should it be reported to her. With the eye closed, she would never know.

That bribe, I was to learn quickly, was not necessary. In the artificial light, and with tombstones stretched like paid mourners around us, we came upon the already opened and violated grave of our sister.

"She's gone." Henry spat in disgust and dumped the shovels and stretcher on the hard ground. "She wasn't here more than a handful of hours."

I approached the edge of the grave, looked down: the wooden cover had been broken half off and Fiona was truly gone.

"Bastards," Henry repeated behind me. "Bloody bastards. What're you looking at?"

Quietly, I said, "Her clothes."

"What do you mean? Her clothes are still there?"

They lay half in the shadows of the coffin and half beneath the loose dirt. I swung the lamp down and my eye caught the flash of a bracelet.

"She's naked," Henry said. His voice had been drained of its anger and in its place was a bewildered, almost naïve sense of disbelief. "What kind of man would want a naked girl who died of starvation?"

I eased my way down into the hole. "Snatchers do not care about the way one has died."

"Why strip her?"

I could not begin to understand it. I picked up the bracelet. Beneath it was a necklace, the chain broken. "They did not take the jewellery, either."

"Do you think they've sold her?"

Beneath the necklace a ring with a piece of jade in it.

"*William*," Henry demanded.

"I do not know." I pulled myself out of the grave with Fiona's jewellery deep within my pockets. The three pieces that she had loved most stabbed at my thighs. If they had drawn blood, I would have understood. "She has been dead for three days. In another seven she'll be useless to them."

"Ten days." He rubbed his thick hands over his face, trying to push away the grief and concern and anger that ran across him like spilled blood. Lowering his hands, he said, "How will we even be able to find her? I've no idea where to begin."

"We will need a Mortician."

"We're not their people. They only look for marked people. They won't help us."

Staring into the empty grave, I replied quietly, "I know of one that will."

2.

....

He erected pavilions beneath the red sky while we marvelled at the sight of the horses' brains, clear as our hands in their heads.

Henry and I parted outside the bronze gates of the graveyard. He climbed into a passing carriage, the shovels wrapped in the empty stretcher, and disappeared into the sound of gears and the smell of oil as two mechanical horses pulled his carriage down the paved road. Atop, the driver slowly diminished in a black and greasy smear.

Despite my weariness, I was pleased to see Henry leave. He was my brother, but while we were family, we lived very different lives, and there were parts of mine I did not wish for him to learn about. Henry had earned a fine reputation as a metal artist, his skills in demand more than ever as the population of Ledornn grew and the industrialization of the country rose with it. He was serious and dedicated to his profession and had even bought a small factory to produce his work. I, on the other hand, had none of these traits. I was frequently unemployed, had no real marketable skills outside the odd book review I wrote, and relied, as even I will admit, too readily on Mother's money for survival. However, unlike Henry, I was a man with weaknesses and loves not supported by society, most of which I had kept private for the family's sake, and wished to continue to do so. I did not want Henry to meet Jonas, the Mortician, and learn about the aspects of my life that had introduced me to him. He would be able to guess at the first of those reasons, even now, but I did not want him to know how I planned to force Jonas into doing what I wanted.

Jonas lived in a large flat in the City of Ledornn, which, from the graveyard gates, was marked on the horizon by a sharp tangle of fiery red light that sat like a jewel in an uneven black crown. It was a long walk from the gates, but I found a second carriage before long. The short, greying driver nodded at my directions, and pulled his tattered black coat tightly around his thin, tattooed frame. He jammed his foot down on the accelerator and the mechanical horses took off in a burst of steam while he hugged the long steering wheel. Inside the sparse carriage, I dozed off. It was uncomfortable on the flat, ripped cushions and did nothing to improve my physical disposition by the time I had reached my destination, but I did feel somewhat rested. After paying the driver, I stood on the street and stretched and twisted my body, trying to bring it back to shape. Drunken men and women passed me and one of the latter shouted a greeting. I waved, despite not knowing her. Once they had left, I crossed the street and entered a narrow alley.

On either side, soot covered buildings reached up seven floors. Scars of light shone feebly from the wounds. Within minutes I had stepped into a narrow stairwell and was deep inside the building on my left. The railings of the stairwell gave me the impression that I was climbing through a mouth of broken teeth—though if I was climbing out of danger or into it, I was not yet sure, but for Fiona it did not matter. I had shared everything with her—including my relationship with Jonas.

Finally, I reached the fifth floor and a door with the number 86 on it. I knocked. It was late, but I knew Jonas would be awake.

The door cracked open a moment later. A single, dark green eye stared out. "William?"

"Yes. Can I come in?"

A pause.

"It is urgent, Jonas."

The door swung open.

Jonas was a big man: tall, and made from bones too sizeable for his skin, which had left his body with the taut, stretched impression of undernourishment. He was not wearing a shirt, but even had he been, I would have been able to tell anyone who asked that his whole body was as bony and thin as his arms suggested, for it was a body that I knew intimately. Jonas' face was similarly formed, and it did not suggest a kind man: it was defined by slashes: cuts made to signal a mouth that was pressed into a straight line, and dark eyes that squinted beneath heavy black eyebrows. He had thick hair that was never combed and a thin, scratchy beard that he was unable to grow into fully, and which he shaved with a straight razor every fourth or fifth day. The cold impassiveness that was in his face was not only contained there, but spread through his entire body, as if the black tattoos that ran across his arms and chest had been burned into his skin as a brand by his parents when he was a child. Certainly it was how the first had been done.

"What do you want, William?" Without waiting for my answer, he turned his back on me and walked down the dark hall and into the pale blue light of the main room. "It's been three months. I wasn't expecting to see you again. If you've come to buy—"

"No." I closed the door, followed. "I have not. I did not expect to return."

He sat down carefully on one of the two old, brown cloth chairs that were in the spartan room. It smelled of antiseptic and dried flowers. The door leading into his workroom was closed. Next to the chair was a small pile of books—his reading for the evening, for Jonas was not a man who slept much. "So," he said, "we agree. You weren't meant to return."

"You are a violent man, Jonas. My mistake was that I did not see it earlier." I sat on a chair opposite. "But I am not here because of you and I."

"No?"

"My sister has died."

Jonas did not react with sympathy or disinterest. Instead, he waited, his green eyes still in patient knowledge that there was more to come. Beneath that gaze, I told him what had happened. At the end, I said, "I will not see her used by Surgeons, Jonas. I will not have her turned into the clothing for someone too rich to know when to die."

"That's always been a strange belief for you," he said. "You're too rich and too clean to hate it, but yet, like your kind, you are an atheist."

"I have no desire to live in a body of bronze organs."

"So you have always said."

"So I have," I replied evenly. "Will you find her body?"

"It's easier to find a body that I have tattooed, or a body that has returned."

"Is it beyond you?"

His dark eyes disappeared in a slow, thoughtful blink, and then he said, "No."

"I want you to find her." I tried to keep the desperation from my voice. "Please, Jonas. I can't let her be used. She feared it more than death. Name your price."

"No."

I continued, "The things that were done—"

"Stop." The coldness of Jonas' gaze fractured with thin cracks of an emotion I had not thought to see; but it was mixed with resentment and anger, emotions that were more expected. "I will find her, William. I am not a cruel man, no matter what you've thought. I know I treated you badly. I know that I hurt you—hurt you physically. I am not proud of it. But, at the same time, it gives me no pleasure to know that you would use it against me."

"She was my sister," I explained. "There is nothing I wouldn't do for her."

3.

But before long, he called us inside, where he revealed veins of silver and hearts and lungs of bronze and blades that pierced skin in shapes and sizes that we had never seen before.

I returned to Mother's house shortly after. There was nothing for me to do, Jonas said, though I suspected that he did not want me around. He talked of regret, but neither of us had touched, and though we had passed close enough to smell each other (he in that blend of oil and chemicals and sharp after shave) the distance between us was indefinable. We stood at opposite ends of the world. We stood as strangers. We stood behind walls. When Mother's dark house appeared before me, I had listed more than a hundred ways in which we were apart, but it was the barren gardens and barred windows and smooth, soot stained brown stone that sat beneath the red-brown sky that gave my thoughts form. One of us was that house. With a faint sigh, I entered and walked through darkness to my bedroom, but stopped at the bottom of the stairs as Ellie, Mother's maid, approached. A slim girl, dark haired, olive skinned. She had thin, delicate black words tattooed up her left arm, which disappeared beneath her black shirt. Her bare feet skimmed across the tiles, clean beneath the cuffs of brown pants.

"It's late," I said. In her hand she held a glass of water with a faint orange tint to it. "Is Mother fine?"

"She does not sleep well," Ellie replied. "This will help her."

We began walking up the stairs. "I want her to have every comfort. She's—I cannot lose more of my family." I paused, the emotion embarrassing me. Ellie did not appear to notice. I said, "What is that?"

"A sleeping draught of sorts," she replied. "A herbalist brought it over yesterday."

Mother's room was stuffy and dark. Leaving the pale light of the hall, it took me a moment to find her, lying on her side with a thin blanket over her. I could hear her heavy breathing and her whispered words—a thank you, I believe—to Ellie. The young maid nodded and beckoned me over before leaving with the now empty glass. I sat down next to the bed and gazed at Mother's old, wrinkled face, slightly slack from fatigue and, perhaps, the beginning of the drugs in her drink.

"Out late," Mother whispered.

"Yes. Sorry."

Her tiny fingers fluttered in dismissal. "I cannot judge you."

"Mother?"

"I cannot." A sharp intake of breath. "I cannot judge any of my children. No more. I have. I have judged too much."

I could not reply. Her breathing settled into the pattern of sleep, but I continued to sit in the shadows. If Mother had said that earlier to Fiona

. . . but no, it did not pay to think that way. I had to deal with realities. With what had happened. Slowly, I rose and left the room, my own fatigue crashing in on me. By the time I arrived in my room, I could only barely remove my clothes. I slept quickly, but it was a fitful, restless sleep. In the morning, I remembered only that I had dreamed of Fiona's stiff fingers being massaged in oil by warm hands and, later, painted an old sky blue by brushes made from bone.

4.

The Surgeon was white-skinned and white-haired; and he had eyes such a pale blue that they were ice; and his clothes, a black suit, top hat and shoes, with a white shirt beneath, looked as if they had once belonged to a mortician and not a surgeon.

Fiona was born ten years after me, my father's last child, his only daughter: a dark-haired girl that took after him in looks and personality in the ways that his sons had never done. Partly due to his inability to understand Henry and me, and partly because she was so much like him, he had loved Fiona the most; and it was for her, and her alone, that he enlisted the skills of a Surgeon when he fell ill.

She had not understood that at the time, but in the years after Mother made sure that the knowledge was used in the cruellest way. Neither Henry nor I could stop her, for she hoarded her pain as proof that she had wasted her youth on a man who had not returned for her. In addition, she had been as horrified as all her children when her husband had returned to the house wearing the body of another man—his birth body so ravaged by cancers that nothing new could be made from it—and his chest humming the faint machine growl defiance to mortality. Mother could see nothing but betrayal in his pale skin and veins of silver, and worse, it was Fiona whom he first approached, Fiona whom he first scooped up and held close to his chest . . . and Fiona who had, of course, responded by screaming, horrified by the sound, the coldness of his touch, and the perversity of her father's words emerging in a new voice.

On the Wednesday two weeks after his return, the servants found Father's body lying in the entrance of the house, his mechanical heart ripped out.

Not for the first time, I let my thoughts drift in circles about the symbolic nature that the position of his suicide occupied, as I sat outside *The Baroque Moon* waiting for Jonas. It was a small café, made from red brick and with wide, open glass windows, and a series of small bronze and glass tables out front. Above me, the sky was a dull, flat red, and the wind still, just as it had been for the entire season. It was uncomfortable, but that meant that no ash had been blown into the city, and that the sky was not covered in fumes. I would tolerate the heat to breathe an air that did not clog in my throat, as I had with Fiona before the wasting had forced her to her room. Even then, she had kept a set of bent postcards that showed the old sky, and which she pasted to the walls of her room to show a world that didn't exist, but a world that even if it did, she could not have walked out into. Beneath that sky of this old world, the seasons had been on show. Browns and yellows and greens: each card held a different combination, a mix of colour that signalled an entirely different world to the one that any of us had been born into. At the time she placed them up, Mother had told Fiona that the cards were a silly fancy, a child's thing, but she kept them at her side as her diseases slowly murdered her.

Her death was a lot more difficult on Mother than Henry and I had imagined. Fiona's withering was the physical manifestation of what Mother had done mentally and, as Henry had said afterwards, but quietly and only once, Fiona's death was more a kindness than cruelty. But the death had caused in Mother a sudden realization of her own mortality coupled with the responsibility of what she had done, and it had sent her into a black depression. It had altered all of us, I guess. I had changed, certainly, a sudden awareness of my responsibility—responsibility that Henry had, perhaps, always been aware.

Before he left in the morning, Henry had informed me that Mother wished to visit Fiona's grave today and that it was all she wished to do; but he had managed to convince her otherwise, telling her that she needed her rest, and that she should wait a day at least. The truth of it, however, was that we had left the grave ripped open, and he planned to return to fill the hole before she did. He had briefly asked about my night, and I had told him that the investigation had begun, though when he pressed for more details, I only shrugged.

Jonas arrived at the café shortly after I did. He was wearing scuffed red and black boots, old, patchwork brown pants, and a dark red shirt, the cuffs of which had frayed and were open; they revealed the black tattoos that ran down his arms and traced around the back of his hands in circling patterns. With one of those hands he pulled back a bronze chair and sat, smoothly, across from me. Without waiting, I poured him a glass of water. Then I asked him how the night had been.

"Difficult," he replied, his voice carrying a hint of weariness. "A lot more difficult than I had imagined."

"Is it impossible?" I asked, unable to keep my concern from showing. "If it is impossible, please tell me. We will find other means."

Jonas' long fingers wrapped around the glass lightly, tapping against the clean surface with his black nails. "No, it's not impossible. Just difficult. I've never had to find a clean body before. I've found men and women in new bodies, and I've found marked bodies. There's a reason behind both of those—a set of rules I can follow to find each. The Returned go back to their families, their old routines, for a while at least, and marked bodies are stolen to change histories, to be taken to another Mortician who is willing to rewrite the original inks for God. Clean bodies are rare. Rarely buried, rarely stolen. Still, I found a Surgeon who was willing to help us."

"He was sympathetic?"

"No," Jonas said shortly.

I had no reply, so he continued speaking: "The Surgeon was a woman who operates a small but expensive theatre on the edge of Ledornn. When I first approached it, I didn't think of it as anything special. From the outside it was a small, white walled building with a bronze, mechanical garden to keep it clean. Dull flowers shined and tarnished dots slipped from leaf to leaf. One of the first creations of a Surgeon, as you know, and hardly an indication of success. On the inside, however, the floors and walls were polished wood, and there was an elaborate pond set into the far left of the floor. Fat silver and bronze mechanics swam in it. A young Returned sat to the right at a desk, waiting for patients."

"How did you pass him?"

"I am, as you say, a violent man." Jonas' fingers tightened around the glass. "Since it was early and no one else was in the clinic, I found the Surgeon in a workshop out the back. Her name was Catherine. She was a large, clean skinned woman with blonde hair and was not surprised when I entered. She continued her work, soldering wires into the bones of the glass-plated hand before her. As I approached, she explained that the hand was nothing more than a fashion piece—something a client wanted to wear at functions. 'An expensive accessory,' she said.

"'You're fairly calm,' I told her. 'Most Surgeons aren't around me.'

"'You've made quite the impression on my colleagues in the last few hours. Most were quite terrified to find a Mortician standing in their workshops, having broken through doors and destroyed mechanical eyes. News like that passes around. It passes quicker when it's reported that you're looking for a clean body. A young woman's clean body, at that.'

"'Do you have it?'

"'No.' She withdrew the soldering needle and blew dirt from the end. There was the smell of burnt bone in the room. 'No, I'm too small a clinic for her.'

"'But you know her?'

"'I know the body.' She placed the needle down on the table, and it let out a small hiss as it touched the wooden stand. 'A man approached me three, four days ago. He was a young man who wanted the body of a girl who had died of the wasting disease—the same girl you are looking for, I imagine. He had the location of the grave and burial time noted. There was quite a lot of money offered for the body, but it was beyond me in this clinic. I would need another five bodies of the same age to replenish what had been damaged in her death, at the very least, and the equipment to return the skin to a healthy cleanness—I don't have that equipment. I told him so.'"

"Who was he?" I interrupted.

"She wasn't given his name." Jonas finished his glass of water, placed it down, refilled. "Since she didn't ask my name, I'm inclined to believe her. Besides which, she gave me the name of the snatcher who had been responsible for stealing the body."

"How did she know him?"

Jonas shrugged. "News travels, I suppose."

"You don't think it's a lie?"

"No. I know him."

I hesitated, then said, "When are you going to find him?"

"After this."

"I want to go with you."

He shook his head, said, "It's better not to know."

"I must." I leaned forward and touched his hand—a calculated gesture, a piece of forced intimacy.

Jonas jerked away.

"I must know," I said quietly.

"It'll do you no good."

"I *must* know—*please*." The desperation in my voice was quite real. "This cannot be kept from me!"

"You will regret it," he said.

"There's nothing I don't regret already." My hands fell into my lap, heavy and useless weights. "Nothing."

5.

"Look at the sky," he cried out from within his tent. "See its colour? It is the sign that we have been abandoned by that which loved us. That we have been left to rot in the dirt."

Jonas and I left *The Baroque Moon* and headed into the slums of Ledornn. The streets that we walked shrank and the buildings shuffled closer together, a mouth filled with too many discoloured teeth, with each tooth overlapping another. Lines were strung out between each building, leaving a network of coloured washing and sun faded banners hanging limply over us. The deeper we went, the more the noise of the city increased, with people shouting from windows and children running through the streets. There was a marionette play on one corner. The painted background was of an elaborate building on fire and the sky a slow red stain. On the ground stood The First Surgeon: he held broken bones and rotten meat and tried, desperately, to mash the two together, while telling the crowd in a stuttering voice that they need not fear death, that they need not fear anything anymore.

I was self-conscious as I walked down the streets, aware that my skin was too clean for the neighbourhood, and that I had progressed further into the slums of Ledornn than ever before. Jonas had always lived on the edge, the border where people with money and people without could reach him equally. I had naively believed that it would be no different here than there. Still, I had to know who the man was that was looking for Fiona. I trusted no repetition of the words. The memory of my father's mechanical heart, her disgust with her body, and the self abuse that she put herself through due to our mother's words . . . all of this weighed on her when men made advances. And while she had not been unattractive when she was healthy, the wasting of her body did not add to the complexion.

Following Jonas, I walked down narrow alleys, through a small market filled with the sound of voices and cooking meat and the air was saturated in a mix of food and spices. As we continued walking, the spices that I could at first identify disappeared, lost beneath others as we passed new stalls and vendors. Finally, Jonas stopped outside a large hotel made from yellow bricks. It was called *Black Rock*, and was covered in thick, heavy black soot blemishes like dirty handprints. It had a paint-peeling veranda attached to the front that was occupied by three elderly men, each with faded tattoos of blue, black and red that ran up and down their bare arms and around their necks. The strongest patterns ran across their faces and skulls.

The inside of the building was defined by a low wooden ceiling. Beneath it were a dozen round tables, half of them full, and there was a long bar on the far wall. A tall woman with red hair and red and black tattooed hands stood behind it. When she met my gaze, she did so with a hint of curiosity, but it did not linger. It drifted to Jonas, and she nodded respectfully at him. He spoke to her quietly—I stood in the doorway, feeling uninvited, the gaze of every figure in the room on me—and she responded with nods and points and by placing an item in his hand. After that, he turned and motioned for me to follow him up the stairs.

The hallway we entered was narrow and stained with shadows. Jonas indicated that I should be silent as he made his way to the door numbered 6. Gently, he inserted the key into the lock and pushed it open. A tiny room lay behind, barely big enough for the narrow double bed and the chest of drawers next to it, much less for the large man that lay on his back on the bed. He was dressed in thick brown pants and a white shirt, and his feet, which stuck out, were covered in blue and black patterns. His tattoos ran across his thick neck and left cheek in flowing script, and though I could read only little of what was recorded, it suggested that for a middle-aged man he had lived interestingly.

With a swift movement, Jonas stepped up onto the bed. Curiously, the man did not stir. Reaching beneath his shirt, Jonas pulled out a thin bladed knife and then dropped into a crouch above the man, the blade held outwards and pressing lightly against his throat. Still, the man did not stir.

Jonas whispered, "Wake up, Ves."

The man's eyes shot open and his body tensed, hands curling into fists, feet digging into the mattress for grip . . . but he did not attack. Slowly, his mouth working around the two syllables of the name, he said, "Jonas."

"Yes. Close the door, William."

Gently, I eased the door shut.

"You're on me," Ves said. "Why you on me? There's no need for the knife."

"Don't lie."

"I wouldn't hurt you."

A tiny smile stole across Jonas' face.

"I wouldn't," Ves repeated.

"You've been stealing bodies." The knife pressed against his throat, enough to crease the skin. In response, I pressed myself against the wall, though I doubted that either man knew I was in the room anymore. "You've been working for Surgeons. I told you that it was unacceptable to do their work, didn't I?"

"Ye—yeah." Quiet. Barely audible. "But I—but I haven't been—"

"Don't lie." Jonas' voice remained at a whisper. "I know you stole a body last night."

"It weren't marked."

"So?"

"*So?*"

"So I told you no more."

"You." Ves' voice cracked. He swallowed against the knife's blade. "You can't tell me how to live. I just took the body. Unmarked body. I left everything that was buried with her. You ain't got *no right* to punish me for this."

"The dead are sacred, Ves."

The man was silent.

"I told you if you did this again, I would stop marking you."

The man didn't respond.

"Ves?"

"Yeah?"

"Do you want that?"

"God'll not judge me proper, Jonas."

A thin bead of blood ran down the blade. "Who paid you?"

"A—a Surgeon from the Academy on Baker Street." Ves' dark eyes began to water. "It was just money for a clean girl. I didn't see no harm in it."

"Who's the Surgeon?"

"Frances Dillon."

"Why does he want the body?"

"He said it was a job. Payment." The blood slipped off the edge of the blade, stronger now. "I—I won't ever do it again."

I opened my mouth, ready to press for more details, but Jonas' free hand shot up, palm flat, stopping me before I could speak. His gaze, however, never left the man beneath him. "There are no more warnings, Ves. If I hear that you have snatched another body, your history will end. God will judge you on the recorded mess of life. There is no more patience in me for you. Do you understand?"

"Yes." The knife slipped away. "Thank you."

Jonas rose above him, a tall, cold man who, given his position, could easily have been flung to the side and attacked. But Ves didn't react. The man above him had marked his skin, had inherited the job from his Father and would pass him to his apprentice, and no one other than those three would mark him. Ves, his body limp, the life drained out of it, knew this; knew the threat, felt it more keenly than I could ever imagine. It was a threat against the soul. To do anything but agree to Jonas' demands would be to damn himself.

6.

"I have come today to show you life that makes us equal," the Surgeon said. "I have come to show you that you need not fear a thing."

Outside the hotel, Jonas said that he needed to sleep. I wanted to go straight to the Academy, but he told me, rightly, that it would be easier to find Fiona, or the Surgeon, Dillon, without crowds. We wouldn't be able to take her body out of the grounds in the middle of the day, he said, and added that I should also rest if I wished to come in the evening.

At Mother's house, the inside was still, the air stale. I found Ellie in the kitchen, standing in the open back door. I asked her why the house was so closed.

"Your mother told me to shut everything," she said, without turning to face me. The red sky stretched out beneath her gaze. "She grows frail, William. She turns the house into a coffin."

I could not argue. Instead, I turned and made my way through the stuffy rooms to Mother. Her room smelled of apple, but too thickly, and she lay on her back, her breathing shallow. Quietly, I walked to the window, but she stopped me before I could open it.

"It is not good for you," I said.

"Nothing is good for me. Not anymore."

"That's not true." I sat on the edge of her bed. "You must look after yourself."

"I am damaged." Her pale blue eyes opened. "You know that. I am damaged and have damaged everything around me."

"Mother—"

"I damaged what he loved!" The strain on her vocal cords sent her into a coughing fit, rolling onto her side. I poured her a glass of the pale orange water, and she drank it down quickly. Once she had finished, she sighed deeply, and sank into the bed. "He loved her," she whispered. "He loved her more than me."

"Mother—"

"Go." Her hand lifted, fell down. "Please. Go."

Frustrated, unable to find any words to explain how important she was, how I needed her to be strong, I did as she asked. In my own room, I dug through my drawer of pills and vials until I found a bottle of sleeping pills. They were white, not orange, and I wondered what Mother was taking. Did it matter? Sighing, I washed down two pills and fell asleep beneath the afternoon's red sky.

7.

He revealed a tiny cage with a mouse in it. It was a brown mouse, docile as he took it in his hands, docile as the Surgeon suffocated it. Then, after showing it to us to prove that it was dead, the Surgeon lifted a small metal box up. Wires fell from its sides and, efficiently, he hooked them to the mouse's body. Then there was a hum, a shock, a second shock, and the mouse twitched and returned to life.

"William."

I had bought the sleeping pills from Jonas. Drugs were how I was introduced to him, originally. It was through a friend, a simple exchange of cash for pleasure. Just another way to pass the time. It wasn't uncommon work for Morticians, and Jonas made the various pills and powers and fluids that he sold in his workshop, mixing the chemicals next to the pots that he mixed the ink he used to mark men and women with history for God. In my childhood, a lean, grey haired Mortician would visit Mother; I still had memories of his long hands pouring dark blue ink into glass vials, and the red cuts those needles made in my Mother . . . but after

Father's second death, she stopped having herself inked. Her history, she said, was finished. God could judge her on the fact that she had brought herself out of poverty, married well, and had three children. We nodded, humoured her, but didn't understand it fully. In the years after, her faith returned in parts—a response to her own sickness—but no needle ever pierced her skin again.

"William."

Jonas' voice.

"Wake up, William."

My eyes opened slowly. "What are you doing here?"

"I came to find you." His hand was resting heavily on my chest, a familiar weight, a comfortable one, a weight that, despite myself, I missed. "The door was open," he continued. "I came in. I'm sorry, William, something has happened downstairs."

"What do you mean?"

He shook his head gently. "Get dressed first."

The pressure of his hand lifted and, immediately after, I felt its absence most keenly. But then Jonas' words returned to me, spoken in a soft, gentle tone, a tone I had never heard, not even when I had laid beside him. *The door was open*. It was never open. Mother made the servants lock it. She made her children lock it. If the door was open then—then what? My thoughts were blocked. The reality would be much worse. Quickly, I pulled on a pair of pants and, shirtless and bootless, stepped out of my room.

Jonas was waiting for me on the balcony. In the white tiling of Mother's house, his brown and red colouring cast him as an intrusion, a stain; with that thought in my mind, his strong, patterned hand pulled me to the railing. His face, usually so cold, so impersonal, was etched with sympathy like lines of silvered age.

I looked down:

And in the middle of the white tiles, my brother lay face first, the back of his skull broken open. The blood around him had spilled into an anonymous pattern, his body having expelled all that it wished to signal his end. It was such a trifle amount, in consideration.

"He has been dead for about two hours," Jonas said. "Stiffness has begun to set into the joints. His skin is changing. The blood does not flow."

No. It was dark and still.

"There is another body in the kitchen."

Around him were dry, blood stained footsteps.

"Mother?" I asked hoarsely.

"No. Ellie."

Was that relief? It was difficult to know staring at Henry.

Quietly, Jonas added, "I was marking her. She was one of mine."

I faced him. "Where's my mother?"

Jonas's gaze narrowed, a still green growing cold.

"Tell me," I asked, my hand squeezing his. "Please. She's important."

"She's not here."

"What do you mean?"

With a deliberately slow movement, he lifted my hand from his. When he spoke next, his voice was empty of the sympathy he had previously shown, each word now sharply pronounced, a tiny knife that he meant to drive into me. "She's gone, William. She's not here. Your brother has been murdered. Ellie has been murdered. Your Mother has not. Instead, she is absent. Her wheelchair is gone, and if you look back down closely, you'll see a tire track through your brother's blood. A tiny rail at the edge crossing over it."

"I don't understand," I said, reaching for him, but he stepped back. "What is going on?"

"I thought it was your father." Turning, he began walking down the stairs. "You talked about him so much, William. About his death, about how he loved his daughter. I asked myself, *Who else would have interest her*? Is it possible that your father didn't kill himself? That it was simply staged. An elaborate lie to leave the family that rejected him? I've seen it before. And who else, when you think about it, would want the body of a girl who had wasted away? She had no lover. Your mother hated her. Your brother barely knew her. There was only you, and you—you would not do this to her."

"Jonas—please—don't—"

"Most snatches are done by family members. Just like any other crime, William." Jonas stepped around the stairwell and approached Henry's body. "To hear you speak of your Father and Fiona is to hear the hint of a second story. A not unusual one, true, but one that would explain why a Returned man would want to bring the body of his daughter back to life." He stopped next to Henry's corpse. "But there are faults in the story. There's no soul in an empty body. It doesn't matter if you have faith or not, William. You can't bring back what was there. And why would your father have someone else in her body? But the bigger problem to my logic is that your father is dead. He has been dead for six years now. Dead since he ripped his heart out. The Surgeon that performed his initial return told me this. Under your mother's angry eye, he came to this house and checked every part of the body, but there was nothing left. Nothing that he could salvage."

"Why are you telling me this?" I cried out.

"There is a dead girl in your kitchen, William."

"I know!"

"But you do not care."

"I just want to know where my mother is!"

"She's at the Academy of Surgeons," Jonas replied, his voice like bladed ice. "That's where she went after killing your brother and Ellie."

8.

"He has lived and died and lived again. For him, death is empty. It is nothing. We do not need it. I know this intimately, for I too have lived and died and lived again."

"Jonas!"

I ran down the stairs, calling his name, but he paid me no heed as he stalked out. By the time I reached the doorway, he had disappeared into the deepening shadows of the night and houses in my neighbourhood. It did not matter, however, for I knew where he was going. I did not understand nearly enough of what he had said: that Mother had stolen Fiona's body, that she had killed Henry, that she had hired a Surgeon . . . it was ridiculous. We were family. She would not do this. She *could* not. Mother had not been able to lift herself out of her wheelchair for nearly two years and was dependent on servants to prepare her food. But Jonas believed that she was at the Academy of Surgeons and, logically, that was where he was going. I quickly pulled on a shirt and boots and, avoiding the sight of my brother, left the house in pursuit.

I caught a carriage to the Academy and sat in the back, my hands twisted into one lump of flesh, and my pulse refusing to slow even when the sharp towers appeared before me.

While not the geographical centre of Ledornn, the Academy of Surgeons had been known as the heart of the city for hundreds of years. A designed, built, and cared for heart. It had begun as an institution where Surgeons were trained and returns were performed, but in the years since its initial opening it had expanded in both size and concept. Returns were still handled on the campus, but its expanding dark bricked form had sprawled into yellow pavements and courses on math and science and disease as well as others. Henry had attended the three years of his apprenticeship within its walls, a mark of prestige for even Mother.

Henry . . .

I stepped out of the carriage outside the Academy's bronze gates. It was closed, but in the centre was a silver crest of two galloping horses. On the left was an open gate that led me onto the hard red-brown stones of the campus, my footsteps echoing in the empty, stained night.

As I drew closer to the main building, my approach was smothered by sounds of boots hitting the ground, of grunts, and unclear words. The centre of the campus was dominated by a large building shaped like an obelisk and scattered with bright yellow lights across its form like weeping sores. It was in the light of that building that I saw three men fighting across the pavement. The first was Jonas, and he moved with a quick fluidity, ducking beneath attacks from two clean skinned men holding blunt nightsticks. I slowed as I approached, but my arrival caused the two men fighting Jonas to pause and, using that, Jonas drove his fist into the head of the man to his right. He stumbled, and Jonas kicked his feet out from under him. The second man hit Jonas across the side of the face.

There followed, suddenly—as if it were the physical manifestation of Jonas' rage—a glint. Then the man that had hit him stumbled backwards, clutching at his throat, trying to stop blood that was spraying from his neck. Once he had fallen, Jonas walked back to the second man and stomped viciously on his head until he went limp.

Without turning to me, he said, "You shouldn't be here. Go home, William."

"I don't understand what is going on," I said. "Mother didn't do the things you said she did. I know that."

"You don't know."

"Neither do you!"

He shrugged and began walking up the stairs into the main building.

I followed, trying to speak to him again, but he ignored me. His bruised face, which had once turned cold and impassive to shut me out, was no longer so. Now, it showed me nothing. It was as if I did not exist. As if I had never walked my fingers up and down his spine. As if he had never shaved me in the mornings. Around us the electric lamps of the building burned in thick buttery light, stripping back the emotions on each of us, allowing us, for the first time, the ability to see the other as we truly were. I saw the pride, the kindness, the ruthlessness, and he saw the hurt and pain and whatever else I revealed, but unlike me, Jonas was not moved. He kept walking until finally he began to descend into the bowels of the building where the operating theatres were kept.

I hesitated, but followed.

Until I left that narrow hallway, I had never seen a Surgeon's theatre. My father had no faith, my mother more than enough, but the one thing they shared was a moral objection to returning, in your own body or another's, made more so by our family history. Most returns were fashioned out of two or three bodies, with the skin being taken and preserved by those who had not died from disease. I grew up in a house that did not support returns, an anomaly, certainly, and one further raised due to the fact that Father home schooled all his children. So it was that when I stepped into the dim operating theatre, I did not know what I would truly encounter.

Jonas had already entered, shoving the double doors open, and stalking through the dim green light of the room.

On the ground lay an elderly Surgeon. He was tall and silver haired and wore the white and black edged gown of a Surgeon. And he was quite dead, his neck having been twisted sharply so that bones had pierced the skin.

I had seen too much death by then to let this anonymous corpse bother me at all. Instead, my attention was drawn to the hum in the room.

It was a background noise at first, a susurration, almost hypnotic once it was noticed. It was caused by the three large silver boxes on the wall. They were discoloured by the green light emitted from the two long tubes suspended in the air. Each tube was filled with bubbles—bubbles that obscured the inside as if a person had breathed into each. The two tubes were attached to a metal framework above that also kept the power boxes, hanging like pendulums, in place. From each pendulum, like thick tentacled hands, emerged black coils that pushed deeply into the tubes, deep into the green fluid that filled each.

To the right of the room sat Mother's wheelchair, empty, but with her purse and Fiona's postcards sitting on the seat.

"William."

Fiona.

"William."

Fiona's voice, but my mother's words, coming out of speakers on the ground.

Beneath the tubes, Jonas turned towards me. Above him the bubbles dissipated slowly but surely to reveal Mother and Fiona. Around each head was a crown of thin, black wires. Both their eyes were open and watching me. Each movement they made was in union. Two sets of eyes blinked. Two left arms twitched. Two sets of lips parted.

"I don't want to die," Mother's voice began.

Fiona's voice finished, "Don't let him kill me."

"Why have you done this?" I cried out.

"She can't reply!" Jonas yelled over the hum of the machinery. "She can see you, but she cannot hear you!"

"Why did she do this?"

"There's nothing but hate in her!"

I began to reply, but could not, and only shook my head.

"On the uniform of one of those men I fought was dried blood! William, who goes to work with dried blood splashed across their clothes?" Jonas reached up and grabbed one of the cables that connected the tubes, his long, black nailed fingers curling around it tightly in a grip that would not be broken. "Those are the men who came for your mother! Who killed your brother! Who killed Ellie! Those men who your mother had hired days ago—"

"Why are you saying this?"

"This cannot continue!"

"You have no right!"

"You would let this happen?" he shouted.

I hesitated. Would I? *Would I?* I heard again the faint murmur of her words emerging through Fiona's vocal cords, given sound by a fuzzy microphone in the tube with her. Giving her the chance to plead for her life, to tell her son that she needed him. How did Henry react? With anger, I was sure. And Fiona? What would she say? Did it matter? We were family. *Family.* You didn't do this to your family. Mother's voice whispered my name, again.

"*Would you?*" Jonas demanded.

"She's my mother!"

"It's not enough!"

9.

The Surgeon opened his shirt, revealing pale, pale skin and a long, jagged scar down his chest. Picking up an electric lamp, he shone the light onto himself, and revealed, in his chest, a network of gears and wires, each of them moving at a steady pace. Clicking, turning, powered in ways we could not comprehend, designed by a mind we could not know, but a gift to us. To all of us, should we want it.

In the morning, I left for Issuer with Mother, Henry, and Fiona wrapped tight in white burial sheets. I was taking all three to the Ovens. I would hand each of them over to the clean skinned men and women who operated them, who had a different kind of faith than I, again. No longer an atheist, unable to believe in God, no words to mark myself with, no faith. I was lost and after handing over the bodies in Issuer, I would sit alone and wait, until the end of the week, when the dead were burned. Afterwards, I did not know what I would do. For the journey there, Jonas sent a young, red haired Mortician to Mother's—my—house to prepare everything. Jonas would not come himself. I would never again see him, I knew. And so, in the morning, when the Mortician I did not know arrived in a carriage with my family, and sat there, waiting for me to step out, I did so with a feeling describable only as emptiness. I sat inside the carriage, surrounded by my silent family and own thoughts, while the Mortician drove us down an empty road beneath a red sky that had turned black.

Soon, ash would fall.

John Wayne

(As Written by a Non-American)

Autumn, New York, 1949.

John Wayne leaned casually against the Empire State Building. Six foot four, with large, blunt features, he looked as if he'd been shaped by the hand of God on the day that He had forgotten His tools. He wore an expensive, but plain, dark brown suit with a simple, long sleeved, white shirt beneath it. His feet were encased in a pair of creased leather boots and the wide brimmed leather hat that he wore was sun-faded, its rich brown texture leeched away by the ritual rise of the sun. Wayne wore the hat pulled low to obscure his features as he waited and watched the crowd shift and twist its elongated form around him.

He had been waiting for nearly sixteen minutes. The worn out stub of a cigarette staining his fingers with faint, decay-yellow nicotine measured the time. Once he had been the kind of smoker that burned through a smoke with impatience, but now, in his forties, Wayne had changed his style. He smoked slowly, tasting the tobacco, nursing the hot sensation into his throat, allowing it to soak into the flesh. It took him eight minutes to make his way down to the end of his cigarette, until he had nothing more than a tiny nub in his fingers to drop onto the pavement and squash beneath the front of his boot.

A second butt crushed: sixteen minutes exact.

When he returned his gaze to the world, he found his companion crossing the road: Orson Welles. Younger than Wayne, and pressing outwards in a fleshy smear, Welles was still an imposing figure. He was supporting a short goatee around the chin of his boyish face, and wore a bone-coloured suit, a red handkerchief in the left breast pocket, and a dark grey shirt beneath the jacket. In his pale hands, he carried a long cane. Much to the irritation of Wayne, he held it as an accessory, rather than a necessity, and spun it in a circle as he crossed the road.

Wayne said nothing about it. Instead, he pushed himself off the wall, tilted back his hat, and grasped Welles' hand in a friendly shake.

"I apologize for my lateness," Welles said with exaggerated politeness, waving his cane at the traffic. "You know how Manhattan is."

Wayne nodded and, without another word, the two men began walking, joining the pedestrian flesh that ran throughout the city in a long, sinuous vein.

In front of Wayne was a young, slowly fattening Indian couple who, when they glanced behind, began whispering quietly but excitedly to each other. On his right walked a black man in a green suit, holding a tiny blue radio (Wayne was sure it was a radio) up to his ear. To his left was Orson, and then the traffic, full of crawling yellow and black cabs.

"It's good to see you, John," Welles said, his cane taping out a disjointed rhythm.

"You too."

"You look good."

Wayne glanced at his companion slowly, then said, "You look like you've put a bit of weight on."

"It comes and goes."

Reaching into his jacket, Wayne pulled out a cigarette, followed by a box of matches. "Still, you ought to watch what it makes of you."

"Indeed."

Wayne followed Welles into a narrow alley. The buildings rose in a patchwork pattern of red and brown brick, laced with cement, while the pavement beneath was swept clean. At the end was a single door, without a sign, and through it a dimly lit anti-chamber. Welles nodded at the tall, lean black woman standing behind the counter in a tailored black suit, and Wayne expected her to speak in return, but she inclined her graceful neck and directed them to the door wordlessly. Beyond it was a long, dimly lit restaurant: the booths and seats were covered in rich crimson splotches of velvet, and down the middle was a line of black circular tables. In the dark, Wayne could not make out the patrons easily, though he could hear the scrape of their knives and forks and the inaudible whisper of their conversation.

A black man in a crimson jacket directed the two to their booth. He had an ethereal quality about him, suggesting that his station, dictated by the matching jacket, was more important than his personality. To Wayne, it was the nature of the service industry, though he was surprisingly irritated when the waiter tilted his head and smiled in his direction and, ignoring Welles, uttered the only words he would say throughout the entire meal, "I'm a big fan, sir. It's my pleasure to serve you."

Once seated, Wayne dragged the ashtray towards him and ground out his cigarette in the glass bowl, leaving black stains. "Strange place," he observed, removing his hat.

"Always the obvious statement, I see. But I like it," Welles replied. "It's unlisted, and very quiet about what one orders."

"Really?"

"The press is a pestilence."

"Has its uses when movies come out."

"Indeed it does, but we've had this conversation before, I think."

"True," Wayne replied. He fell silent as the waiter placed a menu in front of him. When he had left, Wayne said, "Guess we'll need a new topic."

Welles leaned forward and whispered, "How about the Soviet Union?"

"What?"

"Or Joseph Stalin?"

"Christ," Wayne muttered sourly. "That ain't funny, Orson."

Welles leaned back, smiling faintly but without mirth. "I've got to warn you, John. I've heard that Stalin himself has put a price on your head."

"Best of luck to him."

"It's not a joke. You've been quite public with your hate for communism."

"It ain't no democracy," Wayne replied, his voice rising. He hesitated, not wanting to speak politics, but gave in. "There ain't nothing right and decent in the way Stalin runs his people over there, and I ain't going to be quiet about it."

"You won't hear me defending Stalin. I've heard of awful things done in his name."

"Damn right," Wayne muttered. He reached into his jacket and pulled out a red and white cigarette packet, and a brown box of matches.

"*But*," Welles continued, "but he isn't to be taken lightly, either. The man *does* run a country."

"The man's a beast."

"He's just a man, John."

"No." Wayne flicked his match and brought the flame to the end of his cigarette where, after drawing in his first breath, he waved it out. Smoke trailed in a grey, indistinct wisp over Wayne's sun-browned face, then evaporated. He said, "No, he ain't. Maybe everyone who follows communism ain't bad. I'll allow that. But the face of it nowadays is that of a rabid beast, and the leader of that pack of beasts is Stalin."

"Still, you should watch yourself—"

"No," he replied shortly, cutting Welles off. "I know you say it out of friendship, Orson, really I do, but no. You're wrong. You can't be no coward 'bout what you believe, and a man has to say what is right when it is so. Especially men like you and me, since we got louder voices that most other folk. And one of them responsibilities of having that voice is exercising it. That's the notion this very country is built upon. That's what democracy *is*."

"This democracy is not perfect," the other replied. "Or are you forgetting that it stole this country from the natives?"

"It's two different things," Wayne replied angrily. "We didn't do anything wrong in taking this great country away from them. There were great numbers of people who needed new land, and them Indians were selfishly trying to keep it for themselves. Maybe we weren't right in the way that we did it, but without us, this land would've stayed nothing but mud and tents."

"It must be lovely to see everything so black and white."

"So long as you make sure you're on the white side. Now lets change the subject. I didn't come out all this way to argue with you."

They ordered. The food arrived and settled wordlessly. After the waiter had left, and in the dimness of their booth, Wayne tried to warm to his companion; but Welles' words had dug beneath his sun-browned skin and laid a tiny egg into his mind. No matter how he tried to brush it off, tried to smile that dismissive half smile of his, his thoughts kept returning to the egg and its suggestion that it *was* true.

After the meal, Wayne and Welles stepped out into the overcast afternoon. The city's fragile shadows fell over them like thin sticks of crumbling ash. Welles, leaning on his cane, said, "It was a pleasure, John."

"Yeah, it was nice," Wayne replied, pulling out his cigarettes.

Welles nodded, motioned to speak again, but stopped.

"What?"

"Remember what I said," he advised quietly, leaning forward. "A red menace is not to be taken lightly."

Wayne frowned around his cigarette, but before he could press Welles, the other man shook his hand and left. It was strange, but then Welles *was* strange. He had been ever since Wayne had first met him—it was a strangeness that resulted in people not wanting to work with the man, despite his talent. Still, it was not Wayne's problem.

By the time Wayne was on his second cigarette, he was on the Avenue of the Americas and behind three Korean men in identical dark blue suits. Behind him walked two black women, and their conversation, high pitched and full of unnecessary hyperbole, reached over him: one of their children had enrolled in the US Army, and was currently sending them postcards from France, telling them of a world they had never seen. It was beautiful, they said, though it took Wayne a moment to register that he heard *she* instead of he in relation to their child in the military—a mistake on his part no doubt.

He bumped into the Korean men.

"Sorry there," he began, the words dying in his throat as the three turned to face him.

Red. The first thing he noticed was the red handkerchief in their pockets; each folded just like the one before it. Then their eyes: dark still pools that reflected his frozen face back at him. With a hesitant step—why was he hesitant?—he tried to croak out his apology, to force it through the sudden chill that ran down his back and caused the Welles egg to crack ever so slightly open.

The middle Korean pointed a long finger at him and spoke sharply in his native language. Around him, the crowd stopped and swelled, bloated with curiosity.

Wayne took a second step back. "There ain't no need for that kind of language," he said quietly, holding up his hands in a show of peace. "It was just an accident."

The Koreans stared at him, their bodies still, their eyes never wavering, that hint of *red* in their breast pocket never evaporating—that red over their *hearts*.

"Christ," he muttered, anxiety rushing through him. He tried to push it away, but couldn't. The cracks in the Welles egg splintered, the shell parted, and tightness grew in his chest. His palms began to sweat. He glanced around him, but too quickly, and couldn't make out any of the features about the people around him.

Frantically, Wayne ploughed through the people to his right, bursting out of the flesh ring around him. Free, he stood isolated upon the footpath. Next to him was a large open window belonging to a florist, its display patterned in red, white and purple. The distortion of the final colour registered with a slither up his spine. It wasn't *right*. Something was *wrong*. People flowed around him in tiny isolated droplets, but he remained, he realized, out in the open, where anyone could see him. *Anyone.*

The thought was ridiculous. More, it was stupid. Wayne knew it. It was utterly stupid, but before he could cast the thought away—as if following some other directive than his own—his gaze followed the rim of his hat up into the grey sky and along the rooftops that were mapped out in a jagged line. *Some man could've made his way up the stairs. He'd want a fine perch, so he could pick his moment; he'd have to organize it so that there wasn't a crowd around me, he'd have to make sure that I was suddenly in the open and that his shot wouldn't be missed.*

Nonsense.

Yet he turned in fear.

His gaze ran over the crowd around him, catching a hint of red. The Koreans. They were quiet and still, watching him, stripping back his flesh with their gaze, squeezing the Welles egg and cracking it further . . .

The middle Korean stepped forward and slapped his hands together.

Wayne didn't wait to see what happened: he fled into a side street, away from the Avenue of the Americas.

As he ran, Wayne's mind fought to be rational. He pushed together the Welles egg, made the cracks tiny and indistinct, though he could not remove its foul presence entirely.

His run slowed, turned into a striding walk, and a new cigarette burnt away as he tried to orientate himself internally. Externally, he didn't recognize the narrow and empty street he was on. 43rd? 35th? The sky failed to reveal his position to him: the buildings looming around him were identical to hundreds of others throughout Manhattan.

There was only one difference to the streets he had just run through. It identified itself along the street with a bright splotch of neon red light that ran along the top of the building, spelling out *Wal-Mart*.

Wayne approached it slowly. A fractured voice in his subconscious questioned the presence of the store. It wasn't right. Yet, in contradiction to the tiny, isolated thought, the sign remained with its bright electric red and blue beacon. The glass windows were papered in advertisements from the inside, offering chocolate for ninety-nine cents, six rolls of toilet paper for two dollars, bourbon for seven, and an endless run of colourful items that Wayne had never seen before, their prices bursting out in red and yellow.

Dimly aware he was doing it—and without knowing why—Wayne dropped his cigarette to the ground and entered. Inside, the light was bright. So bright that it would have been in competition with the big spot lights used on movie sets; but unlike those, which worked with one huge, bright, hot focus, the lights in Wal-Mart ran along the roof and gained strength by reflecting off the white floor and ceiling. It gave the building's presence a hazy, indistinct quality as if it were constantly shifting in and out of focus until finally it did settle, and a sense of calm settled over Wayne.

Glancing to his left and right, he stared at the clothes on the racks: they were of a design he'd never seen, and made stranger by the fact that the colour had been washed out by the light, leaving what remained to look as if it had been made from watered down paints. Around him a characterless sweet toned murmur of music passed from unseen speaker to speaker in Chinese Whispers.

There was no need for him to be in the store, no reason for him to continue, but he did. The clothes shifted in the cool, artificial whisper of the air conditioning, and soon he came upon aisles of plastic boxes and saucepans and bicycles that looked space age. Food was also offered, and behind him, the entrance to Wal-Mart disappeared in a bright whiteness . . . but it didn't matter. Nothing mattered in the tranquility of the store.

The glass cabinets at the back of Wal-Mart were a beacon for him—it was possible that they had been calling ever since he had walked through the doors, and that their promise was a need that only his subconscious had been aware of and that, only now, he was recognizing.

When Wayne stepped around the corner, leaving the washed out blue and black of car repair kits and the brown of fishing rods behind, a smile unfolded across his face and he stopped. There, he took in the sight of each item in one long drinking glance.

Guns.

There were over fifty, and most were the length of his arm, and ended in polished wooden stocks.

Wayne approached them slowly. The voice of dissent that had raised itself earlier was gone, but it had left a faint tactile impression on his brain, suggesting that this wasn't right. But what could be wrong? How could it be wrong? The guns, neatly lined up, were soldiers: loyal and steadfast and unquestioning in their proposed service.

"See anything you like?"

Wayne blinked. He had believed he was alone, was sure of it, though he wasn't quite sure why he had been so confident of the fact. It was a store. Stores had employees, even without customers. Nevertheless, the young man had materialized as if God's pencil had suddenly sketched him into the world. There was nothing extraordinary about the young man: angular, bony, without muscle, and white. His skin much paler than Wayne's, and his hair was a short, spiky blonde that had been dyed in a fashion trend that Wayne was unaware of. He was wearing black pants and a blue and red Wal-Mart t-shirt with the name *Lincoln* printed upon it.

"Sorry to startle you," the young man said, offering his hand.

Wayne took it: loose and dry. He said, "Don't worry none about it."

"Cool." He retracted his hand. "See anything you like?"

"They all look good," Wayne replied, his gaze returning to the black metal shafts.

"They're great for protection—I mean, you've *got* to protect yourself, right?"

Without changing the focus of his gaze, Wayne nodded.

"It's an increasingly dangerous world out there. It's not what it used to be in the streets or in the world around us. A lot of people envy the kind of freedom we've got. Especially in some of those—in, you know, the *black*" —he whispered the word and it escaped his lips like a curse— "neighbourhoods."

"Black?" Wayne repeated, a sour expression crossing his face.

"Yeah, man. You got to watch for them, y'know? They make up around seventy percent of the jail population, most of them in their for armed robbery or murder or—"

"I have no problem with an *American*," he interrupted. "Don't matter their colour."

"Well, individually, yeah, some of my mates are black," Lincoln replied quickly. "But that's individually. As a group—as a group, you've got to admit it's something different. A lot of hate in those people as a group."

"We ain't done well by most of them."

"We've been more than fair."

"No," Wayne said, the word ringing out with a deep certainty. "We ain't been fair to them. The key to being an American is *free*dom—notice my emphasis. We got to make sure it's for everyone in America, not just those people born the so-called right colour. Black people have the exact same rights as me and you, and not respecting that, that was a thing that we've got to deal with, cause we've done wrong by them."

"I didn't do a thing to them!"

"You're American, right?"

"Damn straight," Lincoln shot back. "Proud of it, too."

"Then you got to accept that this fine country hasn't always had its finest moments when dealing with some other folks."

"But—"

"No," Wayne repeated sternly. "There's right and wrong, and we did wrong."

The young clerk stared at him, clearly not pleased. Then, with a slight smile, he ran his hand through his hair and said, "Well, I'm not going to argue with you, man. Never thought I'd hear that in here, though. Next you'll be saying we should give back the Native Americans their land."

Wayne shook his head. There was no humour in the situation. "Ain't been nothing wrong done there, boy, and don't let me hear you argue it like some folks I know."

"Course not."

"Good. Now, I've been looking over your guns here, and I reckon I fancy the look of that twelve gauge you've got there."

"The Browning, yeah?"

"Yeah."

"That's three ninety eight."

Kinda expensive, Wayne wanted to say, but the price was quite good. What was he thinking? "That's fine," he said, finally.

Lincoln pulled the key out of his pants, opened the glass cabinet, and removed the shotgun. Outside the glass, the barrel and wooden stock were darker, as if the entire shotgun had gained an extra weight in reality simply by being placed in Lincoln's pale hands. Reaching out, Wayne took the weapon into his own grasp as if it were a child. He had been around guns all his life, both real and fake, but there was a rare joy in holding a new gun for the first time, to become acquainted with its texture. He could tell that this shotgun was something special: a rib of the Earth that God had reached deeply into and pulled out.

"Yeah, this'll do," Wayne murmured, placing it down on the counter, his fingers never leaving the metal.

"Okay," Lincoln said, appearing on the other side of the counter. "It's pretty easy from this point onwards: all I need is two pieces of ID and for you to answer some questions for me. Then, well, then this'll all be for you."

Wayne nodded. He opened his wallet and pulled out his driver's license and credit card, and passed them to Lincoln.

The clerk examined them, nodded, and handed them back. "Okay, that's fine," he said. "Now you've just got to answer these questions—I'll just fill in your name and address here at the top.

"Okay," he said, having finished filling in the details. "First. Have you ever been convicted of a felony?"

"No."

"Are you, or have you ever been, homosexual?"

"No."

"Do you regularly wear black?"

"No."

"Are you black—ah, don't worry about that. It's just the next question, sorry."

Wayne grunted, his displeasure evident. "I don't like that question, boy. Colour ought to not have anything to do with it."

"It's just the question. I don't write the sheet. Anyhow, you've got one left, ready?"

"Yeah."

"Okay." Lincoln took a deep breath, and in a rush said, "Have you ever thought that your Government is lying to you? And that this lie exists to hide the truth about a political system that has ceased to be about democracy, but has become a Capitalist-orientated Government that runs the country not with the needs of the people in mind, but rather with the needs of its investors. These investors being the large companies that support the President during his campaign for office. Furthermore, has it ever occurred to you that this Capitalist Government is promoting a Right Wing Christian view throughout politics and economics on a global scale, which is ensuring that new technologies and theories that exist outside the Capitalist cannon are stunted in their growth?"

"I can honestly say," Wayne said slowly, "that I ain't never thought that in my entire life."

"Great," the other replied brightly. "I'll just call, get everything checked, and then, assuming there's no problems, the gun is yours."

Wayne waited while the young man called. It took five minutes for him to repeat the information, and another five to wait for conformation, and then he hung up. "Everything is fine," Lincoln said. "Just got to pay for it."

"Sure. Credit card is there. Don't suppose you mind giving me some bullets?"

"Sorry, it's against store policy."

"Sure?"

"Yeah, but there's a *K-Mart* a block down, and you can get some there."

"They ain't going say anything about me bringing in the shotgun, right?"

"Won't be a problem. You've got a receipt."

The bullets were easily obtained. Wayne placed them in the box next to the twelve Gauge, held both in his right hand and felt, for the first time since leaving Welles, safe. Safe enough that, when he figured out where he was (38th Street), he didn't hesitate to make his way back towards the Avenue of Americas, a stream of cigarette smoke trailing in smoky-grey victory.

Above him, the sky rumbled with thunder. The fragile shadows that had strained earlier across the ground finally broke and seeped into the concrete, washed away like dirt down a drain. Wayne didn't quicken his pace. *Let it rain!* He didn't care. Nothing bothered him. If it weren't for the people around him, he might have laughed at the fear he had felt earlier. A fear that did not bother him as he paused at the curb, waiting for the pedestrian light to change, and saw two Middle Eastern men step from a yellow and black checkered taxi.

Wayne didn't know from just where in the Middle East they originated. It could have been Afghanistan, Iran, or Pakistan; he wouldn't know unless they announced it. Identically shaped, they were thickset men just under six feet. The first man, wearing a blue turban, had a face that had been horribly scarred by acne. The second man, in a white turban, had thick eyebrows and moustache, and a short neck, as if he were missing vertebrae. Both wore grey suits, with red handkerchiefs in their pockets.

Red.

Nothing to worry about, Wayne told himself, his grip tightening on the box. *Nothing.*

Their gaze fell on Wayne.

He smiled politely in return. *Red*. Why did he care? He didn't. Yet Welles' egg sat in his brain, connecting with the colour as if it was an answer to a question that had plagued him since his birth.

The two men made their way up the street, their gaze never leaving him. Wayne told himself that he had nothing to worry about—nothing—but the Welles egg fractured and its fluid began to seep out, sending a small wet curling finger of fear through him. He tried to ignore it. He had the shotgun: its very design and purpose to protect its owner. There was nothing to worry about. Nothing at all.

The pedestrian light changed.

Crossing, Wayne quickened his pace. At the end of the road, glancing behind him, seeing them following—*redredredredred*—he dropped his cigarette and began weaving through people. His thick hands bent the corners of the shotgun box, as dampness began to trickle down his spine. Behind him, the two Middle Eastern men quickened their pace.

Ahead, the pedestrian light was red. *Red. Christ*. He knew that if he waited, it would bring the two Middle Eastern men up beside him. *Good*. No. No, it wasn't good. The shotgun box dug into his palm in demand. He wanted to rip the lid off and load it. But he wouldn't. He would feel safer if he did—he should—but he wouldn't. He *couldn't* open the box, not here, not in the middle of the street.

Wayne left the Avenue of Americas.

He turned sharply, making his way towards Park Avenue using 6th Street. Quickly, he worked his way through the people, pushing past them, telling himself—lying, he was lying—that he was heading down to the street early only because it was quicker to the Waldorf and it was going to rain. That was all. It had nothing to do with the two men. Nothing.

He glanced over his shoulder, searching for their turbans. Nothing.

He was a fool, an idiot. His grasp relaxed. He blamed Welles entirely, even though the fault lay within him. He had allowed the tiny doubts and fears to flood over him and force him to react in a fearful, suspicious way. An Un-American way.

Walking up to the front of the Waldorf, Wayne greeted the doorman in a short, terse greeting.

"Sir?" the short man said.

"Yeah?"

"There are two men waving at you, sir."

Bending the box with his grip, Wayne turned. There, at the bottom of the steps, were the two men, their red handkerchiefs brightly displayed. The colour was all that he could focus on, all that mattered, and his hand, bending the box, came into contact with the stock of the shotgun . . . Then, and only then, did Wayne realize that they were holding a pad of paper out to him.

"Please," the blue turbaned man said. "We were told we could find you here."

Wordlessly, grinding his teeth, Wayne laid the pad across the crushed shotgun box, and signed his name.

He wanted to call Welles and attack him over the phone, but he didn't. He knew that if he did, the other man would simply deny it and chuckle down the line at the success of his private joke. But the next time he saw Welles . . . well, that was another question, and another time.

Placing the shotgun box on the coffee table, Wayne kicked off his boots, and dropped his hat down on the chair. A moment later, he picked it up and tossed it onto the table with the shotgun, then sat down and pulled the phone towards him. There was a line of lightening outside the window, followed by the sound of rain smacking against the glass in a hard rhythm. At least he had avoided the storm. That was one thing. Dialling room service, he ordered a steak and potatoes dinner, then hung up, picked up the receiver again, and called his wife.

Esperanza answered on the third ring. Her sweet voice reached him with the faint trace of static, "Hola."

"Howdy."

"*John*! Es tan bueno oír de usted. He estado preocupado."

"Worried?" Wayne frowned into the phone. "What've you got to be worried 'bout?"

"Oí ese Joseph Stalin—"

"You ain't been talking to Welles have you?"

"Orson? No. No, un periodista llamó esta mañana, lo buscando."

"Reporters," Wayne repeated sourly. He pulled out his cigarette packet and shook one of the slender white sticks into his mouth. "There ain't nothing to worry about, love. Welles is just playing some sort of joke. Probably like that radio play stunt of his."

"Ah, bien. El periodista no pensó era un chiste. Quizá debe ser usted un poco más cuidadoso?"

Tiny spark of fire, a burst of smoke around the mouthpiece. "I'm always careful."

"Bien, quizá usted puede ser un poco menos crítico del Comunismo?"

"I ain't going to be quiet with my opinion just cause of some story," he replied immediately. "This is America and I got the freedom to say whatever I want."

"*John.*"

"Don't *John* me like that. I'm right, and you know it." He drew a long, satisfied lung full of smoke—his first since meeting Welles. "People ought to be free to say whatever it is they happen to be thinking, no matter what other people think. That's what being American is all about. And don't you say you don't think that, 'cause I know a girl on this phone that damn well stuck up for her right to say whatever she feels, and that's why she's an American too."

"Acabo de preocupar es todo."

"There ain't nothing wrong with worrying—ah, Christ, that's the door. My food. Hold a sec." Wayne placed the receiver down and, as he walked to the door, pulled his jacket off and tossed it onto another chair. He opened the door, and said, "On the phone to the wife—"

The world stopped.

In the hallway stood a silver cart with his dinner, but behind the cart stood two white men. The left man—the blond one—wore the uniform of the Waldorf, but was obviously too big for it, while the second man—dark haired—wore casual brown pants, a white shirt, and a thick jacket. But it was not the strangeness of their dress, or the cold look on their faces that caused Wayne's heart to skip one of its life securing beats.

The men held small silver pistols with thick silencers at the end.

Welles' egg shattered.

"*Shit.*"

Wayne had no time to move. It was a blink to take in the scene, and in that blink, the whispered spit of the bullet sounded and pain burst in his chest. Blood blossomed—his cigarette tumbled—then blood blossomed again. He stumbled backwards. He screamed—or did he? His perception swam through the pain wracking his body. Had he called out to Esperanza?

His voice failed to call out as the two men entered his room. One closed the door softly, and another stalked in squeaky shoes across the floor. Wayne tried to push himself up, to lurch towards the shotgun, to grab anything. Yes, it was unloaded, but just grabbing it would buy him precious moments. Outside the rain was falling harder against the windows, it's tempo matching his pulse as he moved across the floor, pounding, pounding, urging him on, pounding the beat of life for everyone as he pulled himself up against the table and reached for the box—

There was the whispering spit of a bullet again, and pain in his back.

Wayne crumbled onto the carpet, the box out of his reach. Groaning, he rolled himself over so that he could face his assassins, and meet his death.

The dark haired man crouched down in front of him. "Well, goddamn, John Wayne, dead at my hands. Who would've thought?"

"You god . . . *damned* . . . *snake* . . ." he muttered harshly, spitting blood.

"You don't die like your films," the man continued, taping the silver, silenced end of the gun against Wayne's head. "Shame. My folks love them. Real American they say. But look how you die, man, all covered in blood like you're just anybody."

His vision was slipping, turning grey, but he spat out, "*Traitor*!"

"It isn't that simple," the man replied, softly and with contempt. "But if it makes you feel any better, Stalin's money will be going straight back into the economy."

Wayne's right fist connected solidly against the man's face and a loud, bony crack followed. A bullet sliced into his arm, snapping Wayne's vision back into focus. The blond assassin was taking aim; Wayne dragged his companion in front of him—the man, dazed, his noise crumpled, offered no resistance. On the floor, his pistol lay like a silver dollar.

The whispering spit again, and the dark haired assassin jerked, moaning loudly.

Wayne grabbed the fallen pistol and brought it up.

The shots caught the blond man in the chest and pitched him backwards. Wayne, his vision dimming again, pushed the dark haired assassin away, intent on shooting him too, but there was no need. The man's eyes were wide and his lips bubbled with blood: his breath sounded in shallow gasps as if he were asking God how the world he had been so sure of had failed so suddenly?

"Yeah," Wayne muttered faintly, "I got that question."

Orson Welles stood in the waiting room of the New York-Presbyterian Hospital. It was different from how he last remembered it, but he couldn't quite put his finger on what that difference was. It just felt *wrong*. In fact, everything of late felt wrong. But then why should it feel right? He was standing in the horrible, antiseptic smelling white waiting room of the emergency ward, waiting for the Doctor, fearing the worse, and feeling responsible.

The Doctor emerged from behind the white doors. He was a narrow, white man, with short grey hair. In a quiet, serious voice, he said, "I'm sorry. I really am. It's just that he's lost too much blood, and one of the bullets struck a vital organ—"

"When?" Welles asked, his voice sounding as if someone else had spoken it. Why didn't he feel anything? *Shock. It must be shock.* "When did it happen?"

"Ten minutes ago." The Doctor paused. After a moment, his carefully constructed façade broke and disbelief slithered across his face. "I did not think it was possible for him to . . . I just didn't think he would. He was so strong—a healthy, vital man, in every aspect. I just—I just can't come to terms with what I know."

"Doctor," Welles interrupted kindly. "He was just a man."

"He seemed more, somehow."

"The lie of the screen."

"Don't you have anything to say?"

"No," Welles replied softly. "What does it matter what any of us say, now?"

Octavia E. Butler

(a remix)

1.

....

I was eleven when you gave me the knife.

The day was cold, grey: the end of winter, but early enough that my final year in St. Mary's Sanctuary was a long way from completion. Despite that, on the day that I met you I was thinking about how good it would be to no longer have to walk past the fences that ran outside the school in thick, sandy brick; how I would not have to see the white guards who scanned the bags of all the coloured kids thoroughly every morning; and how I would not have to sit in the back corner of the classroom, friendless and ostracized. The contraction between these thoughts and the fact that the corridors I walked through were empty and I was early, again, did not escape me either. Soon, you would tell me that was how you knew my uncle was staying with me. It was a lie, of course: you knew because you were me.

I pushed open the blue metal door to the classroom and saw you standing in front of a map of the world. At first, I thought that you were a relief teacher, and if not that, a rich mother. I did not suspect otherwise: you were not black, you were not tall, and you did not have the thick, black curly hair that I had. You were white, of medium height, and with close cropped hair that might have been black if it had grown out. In short, you were as physically removed from me as you could have been. You were right not to tell me that this was me, that I was staring at my own future self. You were right to start our conversation by saying, "The infected areas are coloured red, right? It has been a while since I've seen one."

The class had put the map on the wall in the previous week. It was a flat world, its spherical dimensions opened for autopsy, and spotted with red throughout to represent outbreaks of the Alrea virus.

"There is a theory," you said, still having not turned from the map, "that the virus is proof of alien life."

I did not have a reply for that.

"It's in this country already." You turned now to face me, revealing a smooth face that was neither youthful, nor old; but rather, one that was curiously still, like a mask. "It's in New Orleans, brought over by Baker Thomas. Right now, he lives in a small community of infected—the number is fifteen, if I remember right. It isn't difficult for him to hide, but in ten years, it will be impossible to keep his community a secret and he'll have to take action. Just like you will with your uncle, Octavia."

There had been no movement towards me and I had plenty of distance from you, but I felt threatened. You tried to alleviate that by telling me that was how you knew I was early to school; that you knew I did not want to spend the fifty minutes alone with him that I would normally relish after Mother left for her work. I enjoyed that time when he wasn't there, but with him there, you knew that if I stayed, he would step closer to me and touch me. You knew that his eyes had a hungry glint that I had not yet properly identified, but was unsettled by. His presence was like a heavy weight around me when I stepped into the house and you knew that I had taken to locking the bathroom door after he had arrived. You should not have known, but you did.

You smiled, faintly. "On the weekend, he will take you and your mother to a dog fight. Two nights after that, he will come for you."

"Why?"

Your faint smile turned sad. "I wish I could explain it to you. I really do. But all I can do is tell you that this will happen. Don't let him touch you. Don't let anyone touch you if you can help it."

It was then that you put the knife on the table.

"Don't forget this, yeah?"

It was straight and sharp and the handle was made from hard plastic. It was not a kitchen knife: it had been designed to hurt someone, to kill, if used correctly. It was a horrifying gift to me, and when the door to the classroom opened, I grabbed it and pushed it quickly into the bag at my feet before it was seen. I was horrified, yet comforted, and the confused emotions were still at play in my mind when you began walking to the door, nodding at the small white girl who entered.

I would have to die before I saw you again.

2.

On the day of the dog fight, my uncle drove my mother and I to Jersey. My mother agreed, despite her abhorrence to violence, because she could not deny her brother anything.

His name was Robert, but he liked to be called Rob. Mother called him Robbie, the only one who ever did. He was tall, dark, and good looking, the organic farms he worked on paying him well in both money and lifestyle. He was paid so well, in fact, that in the seasonal breaks he could travel as he pleased and, every year, he would spend at least a month with his sister. Whenever this happened, however, all the rules that I lived by during the rest of the year were suspended. An intelligent, insightful woman, it was always disturbing to watch my mother purchase alcohol and junk food before his arrival and, after, allow us to be taken out to events that she otherwise would have scorned and ignored. Often, the events were loud, violent, and unsuitable for her demeanour and my age, but she would listen to no comment that said so. Even after her brother had pushed open the door to the bathroom I was in by "accident," as he said, apologizing with a smile and a stare as he leaned on the doorframe, she could see no fault in him.

The dog fights that he took us to were in a rundown neighbourhood dominated by overgrown yellow grass lawns and houses made from brick and fibro. They had been erected cheaply and would last for years, but were reliant on city generators for electricity and heat, which most of the inhabitants could not afford. They could not afford the private solar generators that would alleviate this, either; of course, having those required the rewiring of their old houses, most of which were cheaper to demolish and rebuild.

The families living in these neighbourhoods were mostly black and Hispanic and my mother noted that as we left the gated community she lived in miles behind.

"You act like you haven't seen that before," my uncle said. "Like we didn't grow up in a neighbourhood just like this."

My mother: intelligent, proud, a lecturer at Engelman, a private college. Her disposable income rivalled many couples and never did she or I want for anything. But she had grown up so poor that only a brief influx of government scholarships and luck had given her opportunities her parents could not have.

In her brother's truck, she said, "Doesn't it seem like it's getting worse?"

"Not really," he replied. "We had a Hispanic President five years ago, ninety-five percent of the population is bilingual, there's a public health care program. When we were kids there were private health funds we couldn't afford and a lot more segregation through economics."

"But the problem is still there. It has just become easier to deal with because there have been changes. There are not slaves—"

"Yet the ways of slavery still exist. We have the slave conversation every year, do you know that?"

If another person had said that, my mother would have rolled her eyes and a biting, sarcastic response would have slipped out; but to her brother, she laughed, and turned her head away from her evidence. "Why are you taking us to this thing? We're going to stand out like eighteenth century Muslim women on a beach."

"Not a Jersey beach."

She laughed again.

I was forgotten in the back of the truck as their conversation, half teasing, half an argument, funny to them alone, continued. I don't remember much more. I drifted off as I sat there and was jolted back to reality when the truck pulled up to the cracked pavement shoulder, hitting it accidentally. Ahead of us was a line of old, gasoline using vehicles, no one with an electric engine like ours.

Out of the truck, I felt my uncle's arm around my shoulder before I saw it. "You're going to enjoy this," he said, closing the door. "It's real—better than those shows you watch."

His grip was firm and I couldn't shrug out of it easily, but I had learned to deal with it. It bothered me that I had begun to become acclimatised to his touch, especially because I was aware that his fingers had not gotten any less confident—if anything, they had gotten more—and that I was growing to accept them, to view them as normal behaviour.

The house that he led us to was one with a large backyard. In it was a sizable crowd and in the noise and bustle of it, I was allowed to slip from his grasp and move closer to my mother, who had an uncomfortable stiffness about her. She had caught the eye of people around her: her clothes, though simple in terms of pants and shirt, were a designer label and had strong reds and oranges through them, while her hair was streaked with brown and touches of honey that only money could buy. In comparison, the colours around her were opposites: faded blacks, blues, and whites. In simple jeans and boots and a cheap t-shirt, my uncle looked earthy and honest, and he greeted people by name, shaking hands, and laughing.

The pit that the dogs fought in was in the middle of the yard. It had been dug by shovels and had chains attached to the side. As I drew closer, I saw two dogs at the end of the long, thick chains. The first was smaller, a red-haired male that moved a lot, pulling at the chain leash it was on, full of energy and anger. Opposite it was a larger dog, a big Labrador, its short yellow fur turning white around its paws and ears with age. It lay on the ground, patient, its brown eyes watching the dog in front of it with a flat, unpleasant interest.

People were calling out bets and my uncle did the same, forgetting my mother and I for the moment.

When the fight finally began, I watched, appalled. My mother was similarly affected, but buried her head in her brother's shoulder. "Too much of that nice living," he said to his friends when he put his arms around her. They responded with barks of laughter. I, however, could not turn away. I hated the sounds the dogs made, and the pain that was evident, but I could see something of myself in the fight. The smaller dog spent most of his time trying to escape the larger dog, using his speed, his teeth, his anger to bite and tear, but ultimately it was for nothing. The larger dog took the bites, rode through the anger—I thought, *I yelled at him when he stood in the doorway of the bathroom, screamed even*—and then used its experience, its size, and its strength to wear down the other, to smother it into a crying submission while men and women cheered and booed around it.

3.

The morning after I stabbed my uncle, my mother, upon returning from the hospital he was in, asked me how it felt to hurt someone I loved.

"Fine," I replied.

In response, she slapped me.

Her brother had come into my room while she attended the retirement party of a colleague at her work. Mother had asked him if he wanted to attend but the response had been one of dismissal—a grunt and shake of the head. I do not know then if he planned to push my door open at eight in the evening and approach me; or if he planned to run his finger along my shoulder and up to my neck; or if he planned to lean against my ear and ask why I wasn't wearing a bra; or to tell me that he knew I wore one and knew the size. I do know, however, that he did not expect your knife to slide out of the table. He gave half a laugh when he saw it in my hand, and opened his arms, as if to hug me. It was a test, a taunt, and your knife punched into him, the skin of his stomach giving way beneath my strength. He screamed and there was blood, but after that I do not remember anything. He had hit me so hard that when I came to, I was lying on the floor, alone. It was not until my mother came home that I learned that Rob had taken himself to the hospital.

My mother said she felt an immense disappointment in me over the incident; there was no hate, no anger, just a bitter taste in the core of her being. "You didn't need a firm hand as a child," she said when I was sixteen. "You were different from any other I had seen." We were in the kitchen and she fed sticks of bright orange carrot into the food processor that chewed quietly with its blades. "You had such an independence that it would've been awful not to recognize it and to treat you like a normal child, giving you boundaries to live by. You did not care for toys, for frivolous activities, for anything that would be a disruption. You were better than that. But I was wrong, I think. No, I know. You needed a boundary. You needed to be guided. Perhaps you even needed a father."

She told me—just as she told you—that my birth was the product of artificial insemination. The sperm was paid for, the father not required, the traditional parenting roles that had been forced upon her ignored.

At least, they had been.

My mother fed another of the chemically grown carrots into the processor. "I don't think that I want you to see this boy."

She was talking about Gregory. He was a year older than me: thin, tall, and white. He was the first boy that I had shown interest in. My memory of him now is static, his clothing a mix of black and white and his hair shaved fashionably close to his head. We walked home from school every day together, though it took me an extra ten minutes to go past the complex he lived in, but he waited for me after school even when he had a free period, so the trade off was fair. We talked about events outside school, but mostly about the Alrea Virus. It had been finally detected in New Orleans and the government had closed the area because of it. News feeds displayed images of empty, crumbling streets, houses boarded up, and homeless men and women living in cracks that well-paid reporters could find. These images were accompanied by videos of Baker Thomas, refusing to die.

"You should stop telling the world we are sick," he said, his face barely distinguishable in the distorted video that all feeds played. "We are healthy. We are strong. We are change. We are evolution."

The speech had been released the night before my mother spoke to me. It had been passed off in the same way that the videos of violent religious groups often were: a delusional threat that would be dealt with soon. Gregory, however, knew someone who was going to play a full and unedited version. Some sites on the internet had reported that only a portion of the video had been shown, and that images of New Orleans being rebuilt and Thomas' accusations of government neglect had been edited it out. The group holding the screening was called Focus, and were planning to play it and a documentary about Alrea in Africa and its supposed origins. It interested me, but I must admit, it was Gregory himself that interested me more.

"I asked the school about him," my mother said, the tiny blades slicing cleanly. "He's failing all but one of his subjects, and was suspended last year for carrying a weapon."

It had been a knife. If I had been allowed to speak, I would have told her that it had been self defense and stupidity.

Instead, she said, "Truthfully, I think I should have someone start picking you up again."

I wanted to shout at her, but she calmly picked up another carrot and I left, wordless.

It is not surprising, then, that I defied her without confrontation. I did it by not returning home the day of the screening. Instead, I went directly to Gregory's house, and then to the city where the Focus meeting was being held. Rain stained the footpaths and buildings, and left an odd sheen on the cars that sat on the sides of the streets. These were different to the gasoline run vehicles that had been in Jersey years before. They were new and with rounded, sleek frames over electric powered engines.

Focus was in a studio apartment in a refurbished factory. The cage door of the lift opened smoothly when Gregory and I arrived to reveal ten people sitting on lounges and beanbags in a room painted dark blue. Mostly, they were white and male, but there were two Asian girls, both slim and wearing thick black glasses and who looked identically cold and distant to me. That coldness touched with frosted fingers on my opinion of everyone in the room and I felt out of place. The fact that they were at least four to five years older than me did not help. This feeling persisted until one of the white men—in designer jeans and a home-made red t-shirt with a picture of a yellow clown holding hand grenades—told me that he was Gregory's brother and that everyone within the loft attended Engelman.

"Everyone gets lost in the images," Gregory's brother, Dan, said. He sat next to me after introducing himself, attempting, I thought at the time, to set me at ease. That was why I allowed his hand to touch gently on my leg as he talked. "We're fed things we want through them, fed clothes, holidays, stories and images, all of them marked by their glamour and beauty. Then, when we see these big splashes of violence, it's this harsh, other world, as removed from us as if it were on Mars itself. But often the violence and anger is never explained, never given context, never shown how it is influenced by our world. There is no focus."

The feed he showed, however, did not reveal much more than what the mainstream media had. Of the two differences, the first was the Alrea infected men and women working to rebuild a house that had been damaged in a flood. They were thin, the virus eating away at their flesh in its trademark symptom, but otherwise, no one looked sick, and the Diseased men and women looked happy. The second difference in the video was that Baker Thomas' face was not obscured, and that he, unlike the others with Alrea, looked healthy and well and very, very black. When I was asked what I thought after the interview was shown, I said it was interesting; mostly, however, I thought it empty, and that Dan and his friends were playing at being revolutionary in the same way that children play at being soldiers and pilots.

I did not realize how much of my life would be connected to him, nor did it occur to me to give Thomas Baker any more than the cursory thought I reserved for the entirety of the world's madmen. I was far more interested in the fact that Gregory sat next to me; that he held my hand lightly; and later, as he walked me down the street to my mother's house, we kissed. We stood in the street for half an hour, holding each other, talking in whispers and kissing until I finally told him that I did not want to go back home. A week later, I didn't.

4.

It was not surprising that my relationship with Gregory did not last long, but it was surprising that within nine months I was living in Dan's studio apartment.

It was my mother's death that began our relationship, and its unhealthy catalyst was apt for the nature of my love with him. I was told of her death by my uncle, who called a month after I had left. Grief lent it a roughness that I did not know: "She took a lot of pills." We had not spoken since I had stabbed him. "Do you—do you have any idea what you did to her? What you tore from her?" Unable to endure my following silence, he slammed the phone down.

I pushed both Gregory and his parents away to deal with my immediate grief—I yelled and screamed wordlessly and cried—and so it was Dan who found me two days later, in the backyard of my mother's house. I had not moved back in, but I needed to be alone, and had nowhere else to go after storming out of Gregory's. I was, however, unable to enter my mother's for any long period of time—I could see her, in my mind, curled up in pain and surrounded by vomit in the living room—so I had set up a small, faded red tent on the overgrown lawn. I slept in it surrounded by the wild, unkempt mix of purples and blues and greens of the garden my mother had taken so much pride in.

When Dan came to the house, he let himself into the backyard, and sat with me, made bad jokes when I had nothing to say, and gave me beer. Later, I slept with him.

The sex was clumsy and I cried after, but not because of Gregory. I cried because I was drunk, because I was confused, and because I was sorry.

"I had a class with your mother the first semester I was at Engelman," Dan said, after I had finished crying. He had touched me, once, when the tears began, but after I shrugged him off he did not do so again. He sat naked and cross legged against the back of the tent, a cigarette paper in one hand while his second, his right, mixed tobacco and marijuana into it. "She was the first teacher I had there and she was so different to any other teacher I'd ever had. She challenged everything that I did. If I wrote an essay one way, she asked me why I didn't do it another. If I wrote it differently, she asked me why I changed. When I told her that it was because she told me too, she asked me if I'd eat rat poison if she asked me to."

"Was it her 20th Century Literature course?"

"Yeah."

"She loved that course."

"Yeah." Dan's hand touched my shoulder, held out the newly rolled smoke. "I'm sorry. I didn't realize you were Ms. Butler's daughter earlier."

The drugs were not new, but the reason I used them was. I told myself that I did not want to dull my feelings to the point that there was nothing to be felt over my mother's death, but I failed at that, and my relationship with Dan became part of my usage. He became a way to dull the pain and after six months in his blue painted studio the drugs became a tool he could use against me. In hindsight, I realize that I trusted him too much, that you and I allowed him too much control, that we gave him too much of ourselves because we wanted not to be responsible for anything. Of course, it was not all negative, and the abuse was tempered, I argued, by the fact that he was my best friend, my love, and one of the few people that did not criticize me every time we met.

"You've become so thin."

I waved my hand dismissively at Gregory when he said that.

"It's true." We were in a bookstore, and he was squatted down at the bottom of the shelves, rows of black and white spines pointed out to him. "I can almost see the light through you. When was the last time you ate?"

I left him there, but he called later. "I am not in need of saving," I said angrily after I had picked up the phone. I had let it ring out six times before I snatched it off the table. "If you need to save someone, go to Africa. You could build pipes for fresh water. You could take them food. If you don't like that, go to France and save the people who are homeless. Alrea has destroyed their infrastructure. If you don't like Paris, go to New Orleans, Texas or even Mexico. The same thing is happening there and the people who are stuck inside need your help. The government has abandoned them. They're not going to be given relocation papers. They will never have a life outside what they have. You've seen the army jeeps and soldiers in the city just like I have. It's a different world! The borders are closed! Anyone born in a Diseased state will never be educated! Never watch international feeds! Never eat well—"

"Why are you shouting?" Dan's voice. The metal gate was pushed up as he entered the studio, recently painted a sombre grey, a reflection of his mood when he looked out in the world, or so he said. "You're going to have the neighbours complaining again."

"I'm sorry."

I disconnected the call.

"My brother?" He was wearing black pants and a grey shirt, his hair neat and cut and dyed a light blond; he worked as a psychologist now. "You know it upsets you when you talk to him."

"I'm sorry."

His hand touched my arm. "Don't be sorry, just don't do it to yourself."

His grip was not tight, but it could be. It had been. The last time it was he was holding me down as I begged him for meth. He had not bought any for two weeks as a form of punishment. I didn't have the money, as the last time I had bought my own after he had cut me off resulted in a furious search through the apartment for pipes and lighters and any debit or credit card that he could find. I had never replaced the last in a mix of apathy and a desire not to upset him, though it wasn't uncommon for him to accuse me of some wrong doing. These things were often small, such as not cooking his food correctly, or being distant during a conversation with his friends in Focus, which was easy, given that I found them shallow and boring. But Dan had an image of what a woman should be like, and that was to be socially engaging and attractive, an object that allowed other men to envy him. In private, I was to be polite and obedient. When I was not these things, he withheld drugs and occasionally hurt me. It often ended with me begging for his forgiveness, more often than not in sexual forms. In the two years we had been together, I found myself involved in acts I would now find degrading. For Dan and my meth and heroin, however, I was submissive, and I allowed him to hurt me, to control me though it did not excite me at all. It excited him, however, and he had taken to finding increasingly minor reasons to punish me.

The final time, however, was different. It was three months after I had spoken to Gregory on the phone and we were at a party. Having smoked before, I was relaxed, easy going, and I flirted with one of Dan's friends.

It was nothing worth reacting over, and indeed, nothing he had reacted to before. Dan, however, exploded when we returned home, and demanded that I make it up to him. Rather than allow him to place the bonds around my arms and legs, I fought back, hitting him, and arguing. It was the first time I had done that and I still do not know what had changed in me to do so. There was simply a switch inside me, and his jealousy, his shouting, the way he wrapped his hands tightly around my wrists and threw me, finally flipped it. The following day I packed a bag after he went to work. It was an overnight bag, black, ordinary, and much too small to start a new life on. Yet, with a hungry, gnawing sensation in my stomach, I threw clothes into that bag and with what little money I could find in the loft, bought a bus ticket.

5.

My ticket was to Jerome, Arizona, but the details were unimportant. I moved from foot to foot as I fed notes into the ticket machine, unable to keep still in the cold morning, and only interested in the first bus that I could get onto.

After thirty minutes of fidgeting, the bus arrived in a long, dull silver streak covered in dust and marked with bullet on the back half. The black metal shields had been lowered from the windows, however, to hide the last, and I should have taken this as a warning, but the implications were lost on me. I wanted only to walk down the street, find a dealer, and a quiet spot to smoke. But then that was no different to my daily life—over the last year I had barely acknowledged the rise of the military in cities, the number of Diseased within the country, and the new laws that had been put into place to detain anyone who looked suspicious. The most I could have told anyone about the state of the world was that the news feeds had increased their dramatic music and now used a lot of red and orange to describe the control of borders, neither of which you needed while you were finding that calm spot within yourself on the beanbag.

For the first few hours of the trip, the lack of that serenity played havoc with me. I found a seat near the toilet, the choice dictated by a sudden rush of paranoia concerning the return of my period. It would take another three weeks for any visible sign of that, but I was not prepared, and spent the first fifteen minutes trying to come up with ways to solve the issue while staring at the green vacant letters on the latch.

Outside, the city slid past the bullet proof glass in a grey collection of buildings inter spaced with khaki military green, yellow barriers, and billboards.

It was at the state checkpoint that I was first questioned.

I had slept, finally, huddled beneath my light coat, and it was the voice of the driver—a deep, base voice with an Indian accent—that woke me. He was telling us to provide identification, and tickets, and to warn us that we might be questioned and removed from the bus if the military thought it necessary. The words were a jumble inside my head as I blinked away the red light of the station from my eyes, my sleeping angle having put me right in direct line of it and the jeep making its way towards us. Two people, one female, one male, the latter with a dog, stepped from it.

I almost stood up in panic. I had to remind myself that I didn't have anything in my bag, not even a pipe, and that the dog wouldn't be interested in me. It didn't help. When the pressure seal on the door lifted in a hiss and the two soldiers walked in, I dug my fingers into the seat and willed myself not to move. Both soldiers were white. The woman was the older of the two, stocky and solid, and when she removed her helmet, she revealed short, grey hair, and faded blue eyes. The younger, who was almost twice her height, was heavily freckled, and looked as if he had been made by pieces of twigs, to a point that they even coloured his eyes. He held the German Shepard on a tight leash as it sniffed and moved around the bus, oblivious of the people watching it.

I was so focused on the dog that I missed the approach of the first soldier, and she coughed, twice, before saying with a bored inflection, "ID, miss."

With a weak smile, I handed her my driver's license.

"Six months out of date." She scanned it, anyhow. The photo that came up on her hand held was two years old, when my hair was shorter and I weighed more. "Do you have anything current on you? Perhaps with an infection scan taken in the last two weeks?"

"No." The German Shepard was sniffing around my bag. "No. I'm sorry."

"What do you do, Octavia?"

I wanted to nudge him away with my foot.

"Octavia?"

I met the soldier's pale gaze and smiled, weakly. "I don't do—dogs, they don't like me. I've never—"

"He's very well-trained. Do you have a job?"

"No." I was suddenly on the verge of tears. "I was a student. Until a year ago. I was living with my boyfriend."

"It's okay." A hint of sympathy creased the skin around her eyes. "When did you leave?"

My voice was barely a whisper: "This morning."

"Got family in Jerome?"

I shook my head.

The solider pulled out a notepad from her pants and, with a pen, wrote quickly. Behind her, the German Shepard sniffed at the toilet, uninterested in me. "I'm giving you directions to a shelter in Jerome, Octavia. This is a special shelter. It's just for women. It's easy to find, just two blocks away from the bus depot, at the back of Saint Mary's Cathedral. Are you Christian?"

"No."

"Say you are." Her eyes held mine. "I'll call in a couple of days and ask for you there. I hope you answer."

I took the sheet of paper and nodded, though I would not make it to Jerome.

The attack came as we were approaching the border checkpoint to New Mexico. I had not been questioned about my out of date license since the first stop, a result that I subscribed to the soldier, whose name had been scribbled at the bottom of her paper, Emma. I had the feeling, though I could not justify it, that she understood what I was going through; it was communal knowledge, shared experience, though how big that shared community was, I didn't know. I would recognize it later, once I had enough distance from addiction and abuse, but then, I sat quietly in the back of the bus, alternating between sleep and feeling unwell. Sleep was not truly a relief from what I felt, but it was better than every third and fourth thought turning to meth. I was in such a twisting, light sleep when the shields of the bus lifted into a defensive position over the windows and the driver's voice said, "We have a problem. I advise all passengers to remain calm and to attach their seat belts."

Before us sat the next checkpoint, the building a mix of broken glass and dark, empty holes, while shattered barricades lay across the road. The gate through to the freeway was cut off by an overturned military truck, the green fabric roof striped away to reveal metal bones beneath.

The bus halted, gears reworked, and it began to reverse.

There was a crash on the left side.

It was sudden, shocking, and violent; passengers screamed; I screamed.

I grabbed hold of my bag and dropped to the floor as a second vehicle punched into the side of the bus. In response, it rocked. The plan to tip us was frighteningly obvious and the driver tried to pick up speed, his cursing bursting over the open microphone he had forgot to turn off. With the shields over the windows, I could not see what was happening, but I could *hear*. I could hear the frantic screech of tires in reverse: two sets, I thought, maybe a third. Difficult to tell. Impossible. *Yet*. Yet when there were three punches on the bus, I was not surprised. I could visualize the trucks they drove, the dents, the broken windshields, the hard growl of the engine. The screech of tires as they were reversed, as they revved, as they hit—

And hit.

And hit.

Until, with a groan, the bus tipped onto its side.

Before any of us could react, there was the sound of boots, followed by glass splintering. The door was smashed. Impossible, I thought—bullet proof, gas controlled, yet there it was, broken open with a hammer as if it were nothing more than ordinary glass. No human could do that. No healthy human. A figure dropped through the door and landed on the driver. There was a shot, a soft pop, but it wasn't the intruder who died; stripped of the very gun he carried, fired into the mouth at point blank range, it was the driver who slumped to the floor and left us, his passengers, alone.

Alone, but for the tall figure of the Diseased, who stared at us. The hint of a cruel mouth was all I could see, and it widened with a toothy smile before he told us to stand.

6.

The trip to Ulee was done silently, done under threat, and done in chains. We sat in the back of a rust eaten flat-bed truck as Texas passed in a hot wind, its desolate red and brown assuring us that there was no rescue coming.

Conversation with our captors was limited. They told us to move and to be quiet, but that was it. The first Diseased we had seen, Brent, the shadowed figure in the bus, was a tall, middle aged white man with sharp check bones and feverish blue eyes, and he served as a model for the others in his quick movements, his quiet, and the menace that emanated from him when he forced us out of the bus. It was enough to quell tears, to stop whispered conversation, and to assure anyone who thought about escaping that a much worse fate awaited them. Though worse depended on who you were. The hungry looks that the Diseased males gave women frightened me more than anything had in my life. I expected to be raped if I stayed or if I left.

Yet.

Yet, for the two nights we drove, I was not touched.

Ulee, upon approach, was a large, open field dominated by a red brick, square farmhouse. Around it, small houses, some of these being built still, looked like child soldiers ringed around a King. As the truck drove up the road I noticed that the people building the houses were not Diseased. They were normal, healthy. It confused me to note the permanence of the structures they were making, and I was appalled to count at least four prams—four babies—covered and sitting behind their working parents.

Outside the red brick house, we were pulled from the back of the truck, and put in a line before the veranda.

It was there that I met Baker Thomas.

"You know the name, I am sure," he said; "but I am not the real Baker Thomas." He looked just as I had seen him years before: black, one of the blackest men I had seen, his head shaved to smoothness, and without one hint that the virus was destroying him as it was the others. "There is a Baker Thomas in every Alrea community throughout the world. I cannot tell you why this is the case, other than that it is what Alrea decides. How it measures who has the right to lead, I cannot say. It is not based off gender, race, education, or age—I was a woman until I awoke to find myself going through these changes."

He wore no shoes, but black pants and a simple white t-shirt, the sleeves rolled back to his forearms. There was nothing feminine about him.

"I know a lot of what I tell you will be resisted, initially," he continued. "It may be hard to appreciate it now, but we are not your enemies, even though the chains you wear will not be leaving any time soon. I imagine that it does not help you to hear this, either, but I hate that you have to wear them. They are the tools of slaves and we here are not slave owners. Unfortunate circumstances have forced upon us violent methods to ensure that Alrea can grow. It must not be hunted, nor must it be treated as a virus; the world's reaction to it has forced us to use methods we loathe to build our community. It may seem a sick joke when I say this, but a glance around you and you will convey the truth: Alrea and human work here in harmony. They live in peace. They are brothers and sisters."

He stood and walked toward us, his bare feet crossing the red gravel as if it were soft grass. "Alrea does not father or mother children. It does not do this because it does not need to procreate, but rather because it exists continually around us. As I stand here talking to you, each one of you has become intimate with Alrea: it is the soil you stand upon, the air that you breath, it is in your skin, your lungs, and your brain."

Baker Thomas stopped in front of me, but his gaze was for everyone from the bus. It was a strange gaze; a mix of sympathy and cruelty, one that understood the fear, but that understood its necessity and even, I believed, enjoyed it.

"In a moment, you are going to be taken away and lodged. In the morning, you will be given duties. If you fail to perform these, you will be punished; succeed and you will be rewarded. I wish that it was not this way, but it is. However, before you go, I will tell you a story, in the hope that you will better understand what is happening around you and how momentous it is. It is the story of how Alrea came to us." He paused, waiting to see if anyone spoke. We didn't. I did not know what to think, other than that I was in the company of madmen. "Alrea," he said, finally, "first seeded outside Mbeya in Tanzania. The man who came into contact with it, Baker Thomas, was a man who looked and spoke like me; his name had been given to him during the three months that a British film crew had employed him to cater their stay. He kept it to be easily identifiable to rich Westerners, for that was how he earned a living. He was on his way to one such couple when a streak of fire lit the sky. Curious, he turned his bike towards the crash sight.

"He found a crater, but nothing else. Whatever had hit the ground had disintegrated through atmospheric heat and impact. It surprised him that there was nothing, given that the crater was as large as a football field, and had left bent, broken, and burnt trees behind its black depression, but he was not an educated man, and did not give much thought to this. The ground inside that hole was cool and Baker walked around it, his eyes scanning the upturned dirt and broken branches for any sign of stone or aircraft. What he did not realize was that Alrea lay in the dirt, that its remains were scattered around him, barely sentient from the trauma that the destruction of its body had caused. What Alrea looked like before it impacted, as it drifted through space, I cannot tell you—that knowledge is lost to us even now, but we, all of us, know from where it came: Mars.

"Alrea was dying when Baker Thomas arrived and it reached out for him just as you or I would have reached for a saviour under similar conditions. On the charred dirt he stood on, Alrea crept through the breaks in his shoes and touched his skin. That was all it took. When Baker left the site later—it having now become surrounded by people, and with he himself being late already—what was left of Alrea had identified an illness in him and set about curing it. For Alrea to continue to exist, so must he, and within hours it had learned how Baker Thomas' body functioned and begun not just to heal, but to strengthen, to push him down an evolutionary path that Alrea would continue to perfect in each of us."

The Diseased listened as if they were in Church. The man before them was their preacher, their spiritual and emotional centre, their guide to what they were experiencing.

"Alrea is still in the ground," their Baker Thomas said. "The Earth is a living, sentient being, and Alrea heals it, just as it healed the first man it came into contact with. It nourishes the soil, it purifies the water, it cleans the air, it strengthens the beings living upon it. The sickness that you see in us will not be present when Alrea has completed, when the planet, and those who live on it, have become a harmonic whole."

A moment later, we were led away.

7.

What affected me most deeply about being a slave in Ulee was not the beatings, nor the lack of independence, but how easily I adjusted to being owned.

It was slavery, no matter what Baker Thomas said. My time was organized, my duties given to me: my body no longer mine, but rather a tool that the Diseased owned. I made one attempt at escape, driven by the last sharp edge of meth withdrawal, but I was caught and returned to chains before the burnt orange of the morning had evaporated. Strung from a ceiling, I was beaten so badly that a month later the wounds on my back still wept on the fields. I resolved never to put myself in such a position again and within six months, I was promoted to the kitchen. It bothered me that I saw it as a promotion and a rise in my living conditions, and it bothered me that it did not bother me more.

For the next two years, my life was routine. At five, I began preparing breakfast, my duties split with Sally, a large white, middle aged woman originally from Philadelphia. "I could go back and be free," she said, more than once, though she did not make an attempt to escape. She had a husband and a family in Ulee, humane allowances that the Diseased made chains from.

It was mostly just the pair of us in the kitchen, though holidays would see anywhere between five and ten women assigned to help prepare the large feasts that Baker Thomas promised. They were always women, too. I never saw one man work in the circular, red brick kitchen that we did. When I remarked on that, Sally, feeding wood into the stove, said, "It's the Infection."

A slave's term for Alrea. In his Sunday services, Baker Thomas called it an insult and a slur.

"It divides us by gender," Sally continued, feeding another piece of wood into the fire. "The Infection's roles for us are based on that, and its definition of those roles are drawn from its first exposure to us. That's why Baker Thomas is always a man. In his family and work, he was an authority and that's the model that the Infection has used ever since as a leader. It's the same reason why you and I cook. Why other women work in the factory to produce clothing. Why men do the building. Why—" she tossed the wood into the stove "—that was chopped by a man with an axe that a man made."

The stove door shut loudly, the full stop in a statement I had no argument for.

Life in Ulee was a borderline existence. There were no more than fifty eight non-Diseased men, women, and children, and fifteen Diseased. It was kept deliberately small by Baker Thomas so that it could be self-sustained and not draw attention to itself. The compound had no government electricity or water, and relied on cheap solar powered generators that were shut down during the day to charge; hand pumps and fire provided the rest of the power, though none of this existed in the dorms—only the houses of the Diseased were wired. The small family houses had candles, but they sat in as much darkness as I did in the evening, due to their scarcity. Food was grown in two fields and small pens of chickens and pigs were kept around the kitchen, while further out, two hundred cattle grazed. Ulee was safe, ignored, nothing—that was what Baker Thomas wanted.

And it was true, until he died.

Baker Thomas' death was not a surprise in Ulee. "Alrea," he said, standing behind his short, polished podium one Sunday, "has told me my life here is done, and that I shall join it in twenty-seven days."

The Diseased began to arrive in the final seven days, arriving in groups of five and six, often in old trucks. They were silent, but there was a hunger in them, and the sheen of their bodies was stronger than those of the Diseased of Ulee. I came to view it as a reflection of their desire. These new men and women were here to see who Alrea would take and remake into the new Baker Thomas, just as we all were, but they also hoped that it would be one of them. Sally told me that a lot of them lived in communities with no Baker Thomas—a few had even been sent away from Ulee after the virus remade them—and to be turned into the new Thomas would mean they would inherit a substantial rise in living conditions. Who was to be chosen, however, was a question that the current Baker Thomas refused to elaborate upon it. When asked, his only response was that on the night of his passing, there would be a feast.

It was the biggest dinner Ulee had seen. We prepared for two hundred and fifty Diseased and human guests, but on the night, a sudden influx of a hundred Diseased saw the slave population of Ulee watching what was to be their food eaten by rows of thin, emancipated men and women. They were surrounded by hundreds of flame lit poles, and the thin sheen of sweat of each of them gave off the unhealthiest look I had ever seen. For the first time they looked like creatures, rather than humans, their capture and slavery of us explainable by their feral nature and the way they communicated in gestures from the wild too subtle, and in voices too low to have tone or emotion.

During this, Baker Thomas walked around them, talking very little, but trying to spend a little bit of time with everyone. Though I was busy in the kitchen, both Sally and I moving in an endless series of movements between the stove, the preparation boards, and the sink where the bowls and plates and knifes and forks were kept, I thought that there was something strange about Baker. It was as if there was a haze about him, a slight blur to his shape and voice, as if he were disintegrating before us;

yet, in the same thought, there was now a feminine quality to him, as if the person he had been before was beginning to emerge.

Yet, when late into the night Baker Thomas motioned for quiet, all of that was gone. He was solid, confident, undeniably a man, and a man minutes from death.

The quiet that followed his request reached both Sally and I. It was in the crackle of the flames, the pop of the ham we were cooking, the slip of a dirty plate into the sink—our background noise became suddenly loud, deafening when compared to the silence outside. It drew both of us, dirty and tired, to the door of the kitchen. Behind us, the seventeen girls who assisted us followed. We stood in a huddle and watched as Baker Thomas stepped onto the centre table, his bare feet surrounded by dirty plates and the bones of chicken and pigs, and bowls of potatoes, tomatoes, pumpkin, and sauces.

He raised his left hand—

—and behind him, the main house exploded.

The roar of planes followed, the ground erupting in their wake as bombs hit. All of us—Sally, me, the girls, the Diseased—began running. In the aftermath of the next explosion I could hear screaming, and feel fire, but I had not even heard the plane, nor the bomb hit. I lost track of Sally, but caught a glimpse of her with other women running towards the slave houses. In the background, I could see that half were already on fire and the dam they bordered reflected the light maliciously. There would be dead in there: dead children, dead husbands, dead nobodies to the military, who were not interested in rescuing the people enslaved by the Diseased.

I did not think of this at the time. They were thoughts for the morning, as I walked tiredly across the empty fields, the sun a wet, bloody mess across the land in front of me. At the time of the attack, I simply ran. I left Ulee behind, running with Diseased and human into fields that I had not worked in for over two years. More bombs fell and the sky lit in a caricature of festivity. I was thrown, I stumbled, and in the brown and grey dress I wore, I somehow managed to escape the debris. It would be days before I realized that I had finally gained my freedom.

But that night, I ran. I ran until I was exhausted, and then walked until I fell, and slept on dirt until I was prodded awake.

I recoiled, but a man's voice said, "It's okay. It's cool. It's me, Octavia. It's Sid."

Sid: tall, lean, his late forties fat worn away by hot days in the fields. Originally, he had lived in Utah, but after the death of his wife, had moved around a lot. He had been taken in a bus attack similar to mine. But now he stood before me, a backpack over his shoulders, the grey pants he had worn for years still in place, though he wore now a faded brown t-shirt with a cracked print of Los Angeles across it. Judging by its age, he had probably been taken in it.

"There's not a lot left," he said, watching me drink his water. "Nothing we built survived, and we pulled what we could out of the wreckage before we even discussed what we to do. That was us, by the by. Not the Diseased. There's none of them left."

"Why is there no one else with you?"

"'Cause I'm the only one who left." He took the water bottle back, did a slow shake of its remaining quarter, then shrugged and drank. Wiping his mouth, he said, "I never thought I'd see a bunch of slaves stay to rebuild the place that kept them, but there it is. They're going to build it and wait for the new Baker Thomas to arrive. They said that would be better than trying the borders that they'd never get past."

Why was I not surprised?

"Where were you headed?" I asked.

He was silent for a moment. Then shrugged again. "Nowhere in particular. Maybe Mexico. I just figure I got a chance to move, and one person off the main roads, he isn't going to be noticed real easy. Two people off the road, even, really."

It was an offer, and one that I took. There was nowhere for us to go, I believed, despite Sid's words, but I did not want to go back.

As the sun rose high above us, Sid told me that the trucks were either gone or destroyed, and that beneath the debris of the attack had been dead men and women, friends and lovers and keepers. Sally, he said, had survived, but her family was gone, and the last he had seen of her she had been sitting by the dam, near the charred remains of her small house, still and silent. "It's grief," he said. We were walking across an empty field, the grass a dry, brittle yellow in the dirt. "That's what has them all, the grief. I can understand it, but no Baker Thomas is going to make that better. He'll probably make things worse, really."

I did not immediately agree, and shrugged when he repeated the statement. I said, "Baker could be anyone. He could—"

"Understand?" Sid finished. He laughed. "If there's a Diseased who becomes Baker Thomas after last night, the last thing he'll feel sympathy for is humans."

His statement remained in my head, when, two days later, we came across a boy who could not have been any older than fifteen. He lay in a ditch, wearing only khaki pants, and with scabbed cuts across his chest and face. In combination to being dehydrated and barely conscious, he was also Diseased.

"Help me," he whispered as we approached him. "Please."

"He's dying," Sid said.

Not yet, but in another day he would be.

"Come on." Sid's hand touched my shoulder, lightly. "There's nothing to be had here. Further we get away, the better."

There's no telling what the Diseased will do, his tone implied. Yet, I did not move.

The last thing a Diseased would feel is sympathy for humans. That is what Sid had said and it was true. No Diseased in Ulee would want to help us, not after what had happened, and I doubted that any adult Diseased would either. We were tools at best, a danger at worse. But the boy before us was not from Ulee and not fully grown. He was most likely an exile, a person that Alrea had recently taken and transformed and who, as a result, had been forced from his community.

I dropped into the ditch.

"Octavia."

Sid's voice held the tone of a parent, speaking to a child. I pulled the Diseased into a sitting position and said, "How long until we're caught?"

"We stay off the roads, we're careful—"

"Another two weeks, a month. Maybe we can hit Mexico and the Diseased there."

Silence.

"Pass me the water." I turned to look up at him. "Sid?"

"No."

"He'll die."

"Good."

"We'll die."

Again, Sid was silent.

"We need to survive," I said. "We need to stay free. You know just as well as I do that we will get caught eventually. There's no safety for us unless we make it. This boy here, he's a chance at that. If we help him, take him in, and show him something different, we have a chance to make Alrea work for us. He's new, a blank slate—"

"He's Diseased."

"Yes." The boy behind me groaned and I held out my hand for the water. "But to the rest of the world, so are we."

8.

It was in the ravine that the Children of the Earth was born, though it was not until six months later that I painted the name onto a small sign and hung it outside the rebuilt red brick house in the centre of Ulee.

The boy's name was Lydon, though he did not tell me that until three nights later, when Sid and I had returned to the community with him. He spoke quietly and hesitantly and asked why I decided to return here to the ruins. I told him, simply, that there was nowhere else to go. "I wish I had a home to go back too," he said, the fire we had built reflecting his narrow, sick face. "They hit me when Alrea touched me; hit me and threw stones at me and beat me. I don't think they wanted to kill me, but they didn't—they didn't want me there."

Home.

Was I really returning home? Was Ulee where I thought my place was? The idea was such a horrible one that I barely slept through the night.

Beneath the sun the next day I told myself that home had never been a sanctuary for me, so I lacked the sense of security and safety that others associated with it, and this was why I was able to view Ulee as a home. But a part of me had not been happy when the destroyed buildings, torn up fields, and gravesites appeared on our arrival. Destroyed were the things I worked for, the things I contributed to, and it saddened me as much as it angered me to know that I had been forced to do this. The contradiction was not one that I could come to terms with: I felt sadness for what had happened, I felt guilt for feeling my sadness and not anger, and the two were irreconcilable with each other. I think that if I could have left in the morning and gone elsewhere to make a life, I would have done it without a backward glance, much as Sid had before.

There was, however, nowhere else to go; nor were we safe in Ulee, either. Of the fifty-eight slaves that had been owned by Baker Thomas, only seven remained to greet us. Two of the seven were children, and one would not live the week out. "There were more," Sid murmured as we made our way down to the dam, approaching the two men and three women. "At least two dozen! I would never have—I would have forced them to come with me if I had known that so few would be left. They're just waiting here to be taken like that!"

Sally was there, nursing the child that would live. It was not her own, but the daughter of a Singaporean couple who had died in the attack. Still holding the girl, both of them wrapped in a dirty blanket, Sally, with dark, baggy eyes, and a sag to her skin that was a mix of fatigue and grief, took me to the graves of her husband and children after we arrived. "Kaoi's parents are behind my family," Sally said, her voice bordering on a monotone. She rocked the baby without thought. "This is all I've done. I've buried the dead. The others that left—they think there's somewhere to go, they think there's nothing. We've buried everything we were."

"Yes," I said quietly, looking at the crudely erected gravestones. "We have."

She did not question me and I did not elaborate. Her grief allowed for nothing different at the moment.

After the second child, a white boy who had been burnt horribly in the attack, was buried, I stood in front of them in the graveyard and told them my plan. "We have to make something different." I had rehearsed what I wanted to say. If I had had a pen and paper I would even have written it down. "We can't go back to New York or Chicago, or anywhere else where we lived. We have only what we stand upon."

"We can't be anything else here," said Louis. He was Hispanic, thin, and with a receding hairline. "There's no freedom for us until we're dead!"

"There are no laws here." I met each gaze before me. "The Diseased don't have a right to own us, and we don't have a right to kill them. The only right that either of us has is the one that comes from living on the same planet. We have the right of community. We are a community and we must start acting like one if we wish to live differently than before. We can do that here. We can create a community to make our voices heard. We can begin change."

It was not easy in the first month, and I thought, on more than one occasion, that I had been wrong. After my speech I was not warmly greeted, nor cheered; the others were wary, disbelieving and at times hostile to the idea. There were arguments, and once, I stopped a fight between Sid and

Louis. Afterward, I told them that "We were change" and said that what we were experiencing was the first of it. The hardest thing, however, was to embrace it myself. I was reluctant to alter the vision in my head, the vision of a community in which both Diseased and human existed without class, weapons, and violence. In defense of that vision, I clashed with Sid in the first week over the creation of a wall around our community. "It's a good defense," he said.

"It will convey to others that we are closed off to them."

"Diseased will run in here and take us if we don't have some kind of defense," he insisted. "They don't care about your philosophy yet."

The first attack proved him right. As the sun began to soak into the ground three Diseased crossed the broken fields, making their way casually to us. We saw them coming—we awoke early to work on rebuilding the houses and reworking the fields—and I had more than enough time to prepare myself to greet them. They were, as they drew closer, a ragged trio: Alrea had eaten their skin down to their bones to the point that they looked as if they were but the remains of their former selves, given life. The first of the three wore dirty overalls and had lank, colourless hair, and it was to him that I first spoke.

"Shut up," he said, his disdain clear. "Get me food, consider yourself owned, and tell me where Baker Thomas died."

"That's not how it works here," I replied.

He laughed.

"Please, understand that I am serious." I was aware of the others behind me and aware of the price of my failure. "You're welcome here if you want to work, if you want to make a different life for yourself than the one you currently live, but you do not own us. No one owns anyone."

"I could snap your neck."

The words had barely left his mouth before Lydon's young hands did exactly that. The leader of the three Diseased dropped to the ground without a word, his neck without any strength to it, his body twitching. Wordlessly, Lydon returned to stand beside me, his face expressionless.

I gazed at the remaining two Diseased. "Leave," I told them. "We're all infected here, but that does not mean I won't have you killed."

After the two had left, I turned to Lydon.

"I don't know." He was staring at the body of the man he had killed, a blank expression on his face still there. "I've never hurt anyone before. It was just—I knew what they wanted, I knew that they'd take us, and I knew, I *knew* what I had to do. It was Alrea, I think. It told me—it made sure I knew that I had to kill him to stop the other two." He turned to me, and to the six that stood behind me, each one of them human. A brief sliver of anguish passed across his features, as if he understood fully what it meant to be Diseased, but when he spoke, he said, very calmly and very quietly, "You should not call us Diseased, I think."

Construction on the wall began the same day and over the months it grew stronger as Sid mixed concrete into the frames. At the end of the first month, after we drove out a pair of humans who wanted to militarize our small community, and who talked about connections outside the border for weapons, we had a year of steady growth and confidence in my idea and leadership. Both Alrea and human came to us, both wanting to be free, to be part of change, *to be change.*

"We have moved beyond whatever I thought possible," I said at the dinner we held one year after Sid and myself had returned with Lydon. "We have made a place for ourselves here that I don't think any of us would have thought possible. We are equals where a year ago we were not. We are friends. We are lovers." The last was new to all of us. A young Alrea girl and a human boy, no older than seventeen, had escaped from a community four hours to the West and made their way to us to be together. With them, we numbered forty-five, twenty eight of them human, the rest Alrea. "We still have our fights, our disagreements, but no community does not have this. We are settled."

Around me, people cheered. Sid rose a glass to me and the others followed.

Once the toast was over, I said, "But we are change, and there are still things to do. Our community needs to reach beyond where we are. The walls that we erected to protect us are also cutting us off from the rest of the world. That is why I will leave tomorrow morning. Don't—don't all shout." I raised my hands to quiet everyone. "There's no need to shout. It's just change. Change to help Ulee grow, to help share our ideas and our peace."

In the questions that rose I tried to be as reassuring as I could. Lydon would accompany me; yes, I would take a gun for my safety; no, I would not reconsider my decision. It was what needed to be done. I repeated that line a dozen times during the evening, but, two months later, in the community of Brixton, as both Lydon and I were lead out naked, and with ropes around our necks, I thought back to the night and realized what I hadn't done was thank any of the people before me. I had not begun as someone who believed in anything, but they had given me faith. They had given me the courage to walk into small communities and talk, openly, about change; to fight in streets with authorities; to run at other times. They had given me the strength to enter Brixton, the first Alrea run town I had ever seen, with muddy streets and shops, and to speak in a secret meeting that would lead to the capture of Lydon and I.

They did not put a hood over our heads on the gallows. I had been beaten and raped and if there was pride in me, it was gone when I stood before the crowd.

It never had time to return.

9.

"Did I forget anything?"

"Not as much, this time." The voice was her own. "How do you feel?"

She wanted to say awful. O.—she could no longer identify herself by the name her mother had given her—felt nauseous, had a dull ache in her head, and could taste only plastic in her mouth. The pale light of the room she sat in did not help, either. The light was meant to be natural, but served only to highlight the artificiality of everything around her. The smooth walls, the lack of windows, the furniture that was part of the floor and warm to the touch—it was all a creation, an aberration of normal. Since she had awoken, O. believed that she had not yet experienced anything authentic, from the food she ate, the air she breathed, and even herself. It was the latter that was the most obvious, however, for there was no ignoring her hard white skin.

She had tried to kill herself twice. "It's your reaction," the woman across from her said after the last time, "to the loss of your identity."

O. supposed she should know, since the woman claimed to be her. Her from the future. It was ridiculous, but still, she looked like her: a medium sized white woman with closely cropped hair—O.'s hair had been cut after her first suicide attempt, when she began to mutilate herself by pulling it out. It would never grow back, she had been told. Just as unsettling, however, was that she looked just like the woman who had given her a knife as a child. The woman across from her claimed that she had, in fact, done that, and whenever O. thought about *that*, she dug her regrowing fingernails into the palm of her hands and attempted to draw blood. She had, as yet, been unable to do so—even in her suicide attempts.

"Octavia," the woman said, "how do you feel?"

"A little nauseous."

"Would you like to go for a walk?"

She didn't, but it was better than staying and repeating what she remembered of her life for the fourth or fifth time.

Rising, O. followed herself out of the room and into empty, unnaturally lit corridors. The warmth of the floor seeped into her feet and she could not shake the feeling that she was standing on something alive. Worse, however, were the thoughts in her fractured memories. She could see faces inside glass bowls and bulky white suits. She could hear heavy breathing.

"You're doing well," herself said.

"Am I?"

"Yes."

"Do you believe that, or is this just what you said to me when you were here?" More than once O. had raised the question of how she could be both the patient and the doctor. She persisted with it now as an act of defiance, rather than an honest question. "You told me that you were here because I didn't react well to Alrea, that it needed you to be a calming influence on me—but how is seeing myself in another body meant to do that?"

"I wondered the same thing."

That, O. decided, was one of her more annoying habits. If it was true, if the woman beside her was her from ahead in time, then—

"What you're thinking right now," herself said, "is that I will be more forthcoming when it is me who stands there." Stopping, she turned to O. "But you won't be, because you don't really know how it works. It's like magic. You go back in time to see yourself because there's no other choice. Alrea is through this door, by the way."

There was nothing special about how it looked. "Why me?" Yet, she could not escape the vague sense of disquiet that settled over her. "Why any of this?"

"I have only theories." Her future self made no motion towards the door. They would part here, it seemed. "Sally was right when she said that Alrea was a child in its understanding of gender. Men cut wood. Women cook. I've always believed that is why Alrea made a woman to be the first carer. But as to why it was you, or me, that is a more difficult question. Nothing that we did made an impact in the world: Ulee did not last long after we were killed and the ideals within it were lost. I doubt that Alrea even paid attention to us at the time, but yet, here were are, reborn imperfectly."

Curious, O, reached out for her double, but her white hand passed through the other.

"I'm just an image," herself said. "If you had touched me in the school, years ago, the same thing would have happened."

"But the knife?"

"Only small things can be sent through time." She shrugged. "I just use it when I am told."

The last word sat unpleasantly with her. The sad smile that her future self gave reinforced the emotion. "Don't keep it waiting," herself said.

And then she was gone.

Alone, O. considered running . . . but to what point? She had seen no exit, and no other person than herself was in the building with her. Earth was a wasteland, destroyed by war and disease, the best of them Alrea, so there was, in theory, nowhere to go but the smooth, shell like complex around. But, again, what would be the point? The answers she wanted—the reason for her to search—the explanation of why she was there, how it had happened, and what the future held lay beyond the door in front of her.

It slid open at her touch.

The light inside was cold and brittle, but dimmed as she walked further in. Within the centre of the room was a large mass and as she drew closer, her mind drew comparisons, first suggesting a sack similar to that of a spider's egg satchel, but many, many times larger; then she thought of a heart, dried and withered and enlarged, suspended in thick black cords from the ceiling; and lastly, she thought it a tomb, for she was able to make out in the dimly cast shadows, a figure. It was human, at least in size and form, but her earlier memories flooded back when she saw a white, full body suit suspended in the middle. Its head was encased in a pressure sealed helmet—or so it once had been for, in turning to face her, there was revealed broken glass and a torn suit.

"Finally." Within the shattered faceplate, there was only darkness. The voice came from around the tomb, around her. "Octavia. Welcome."

O. made no response, could not find her voice.

"I am Alrea." A pause, then a correction: "I am what is left of Alrea."

"You're an astronaut?"

"No." Inside, the helmet tilted up, then turned to the left. "No, I was inside this man when I left Earth. When *we* left Earth."

"We?"

Above the astronaut, light ignited to reveal thousands upon thousands of miniature sacks. So bright was the light that O. could make out a tiny sliver of movement in each, the shiver of an embryo, she knew without having to be told, the beginning of a child. After a moment, the light dimmed, and the encased head of the long dead astronaut that housed Alrea slumped, as if asleep. A moment later, it rose. "These are all that remain of your people."

"Earth." She hesitated, stumbled on the sentence. "There's truly nothing?"

"Yes. I—It was failure." O. caught a glimpse of the face in the helmet as it turned to her: torn, black, but a familiar black: Baker Thomas. The last Baker Thomas. "I came by accident, and I came injured, but as I healed, I grew an affection for where I was. There was such life: in the soil, in the water, in the air, everywhere. The sickness that I saw I thought I could fix easily, but I did not understand how your kind would react, how I would react with humans, and while every day I tried anew, the decades saw that I killed all but Baker."

"And now you want to try again?" She did not know what was more appropriate: anger, grief, or shock. "To alleviate your guilt?"

"Yes."

It was anger. "Look what you have done to me!"

"I have remade you," Alrea said, its voice without a hint of remorse. "You are stronger now than you ever were—"

"I'm dead!" The words were a scream, torn from the body that had been created for her. "You killed me! You can't remake me just because you need me—I did not want to be here! You have no rights over me!"

"Do not take such a tone with me."

Pain wracked her body, forcing her to the ground. It was worst than any pain O. had ever felt before, and it paralyzed her with its strength. Had she been flesh, made from muscle and bones, it would have caused a seizure, and parts of her would have ruptured and split. Then, feeling if she were entombed in a thick gel, she gazed down on white herself, standing patiently, an empty figure waiting to be filled.

"If not you," Alrea said, though now it sounded as if it came from inside her, "then another. You can be returned to the parts of Earth that I keep within myself. Do you want that?"

"No." She could not feel her voice, but could hear it. "No."

"Good."

Released, O. sank to the ground, a sudden weight where there had been none momentarily. There was, however, no safety in it: she knew that could be taken at any time. "You and I," Alrea said, "are working together."

It was a lie: O. was property, a worker.

"Do we understand each other?"

"Yes."

"Good. We will remake humanity here, safe from the destruction I left on Earth."

O. raised her head and met the blank stare of the astronaut. There was no intelligence, no hint of life that she could meet. She asked the room, "Where are we?"

"Mars."

10.

She did not let the children call her mother.

When Alrea asked her about it, she answered truthfully: "I'm not a woman anymore." Before her, the two boys, Zu, dark skinned and dark haired, and Nicholas, pale skinned and dark haired, were writing. The three girls were away, playing under the watchful eye of Alrea, but the two boys had not done their homework and were being punished, forced to write up to a hundred in French and Japanese. "This body is just a shape, a replica of something you saw, with no uterus, nor ovaries. I have no breath. I don't eat. I don't drink. I don't even age. I am nothing but a doll you made."

The last hint of sarcasm was lost on Alrea. "I can give those things to you," it said. "Though I am learning, an adult woman is not beyond me."

O. did not doubt it. Originally, there had been eight children: four boys, four girls. A sample, Alrea argued. The first to die—a boy—had done so within days, but the second and third had been more tragic. Isa, the girl, had begun to cough blood at the age of two, and before the week was out, she had bled from her eyes and ears, bled out until there was no more blood. O. had tried to use the death—selfishly, she knew—as a way to escape her slavery. "I've never raised children," she told Alrea. "I never wanted them. Just because I could give birth doesn't make me a mother." In response, the being that owned her told her she was wrong, and that it

185

had been its fault. There had been a defect in Isa, and it only located the cure when, two days later, Zu began coughing blood. The cure came quick and easy, but the death of Quzong a year later reminded her of the gaps in Alrea's knowledge. The boy died in his sleep from a clotting of blood in the brain, a defect that was removed from the other children while they slept and thin, caramel coloured tendrils rose from the floor and sank into their skulls.

They were test subjects, O. knew, samples to be watched and learned from, just as she was. "I don't want a new body," she said.

"It would allow for you to be, as you say, real."

No, she wanted to tell it, I would simply be in a new creation. But she didn't. Alrea would not understand the point.

For her own part, O. had given up trying to understand Alrea. It was neither a he, nor a she, and its concerns were not ones that she could identify with. Eventually, she decided that it was alien in all terms of the word, and the understanding—superficial, at times contradictory—that she had of the being would well be the knowledge that she kept for the entirety of her 'life'. The point was driven into her on the day she realized that Alrea was not just the astronaut and surrounding sack she had seen, but everything around her: the walls, the air, the ground: the constantly reshaping, shifting, warm to the touch form that grew from the remains of the space shuttle that had crashed into the surface of Mars.

O. learned that the day the broken hatch appeared before her. She was drawn to it because it was out of place, an anomaly in the smooth walls and perfect doors around her. As she stepped closer to it, she told herself that it was a sign of Alrea growing lax in its defences. It was too much thought on her part, however, for when she stepped into the cold, dusty shuttle, that sense of opportunity left her. Alrea had no defences; there was nothing for it to fear. The desolate, empty surface of Mars that lay outside was proof of that.

"I am moving," Alrea said to her, later. "It is not very fast, so there is no threat to you. I do it to create a power source—the hatch passes that part of me every two months."

"You'll want to be careful of that with the children." She hid how uncomfortable it made her to know she was inside it. "They could get hurt."

"I shall take precautions."

Yet still, it was the boy Zu, who found the shuttle door.

"He was just doing what was natural." O. stared at his small body, barely recognizable as the child he had once been. She did not know how to react, and felt guilty that she had not shown more emotion to Nicholas when he had come to her, crying, to tell her that the air lock door was now closed, that he had managed that much after the two of them had opened it. "Kids are curious. They find things. They push things, they play with things—it's their nature."

Alrea, however, while not visibly upset by the boy's death, was obviously so. It was not just a set back, nor hindrance to its work, but a failure, and it was not until a week later that she realized just how far it would go to solve the issue.

"I can make a hole in time." The astronaut, the final Baker Thomas, faced her. The light of the tomb he floated in had turned to amber, and his empty eyes stared at her. "It was not something that I gave much thought too, until you first appeared, after your first attempt to kill yourself. I had you sedated when your future self appeared, and told me that I had violated you.

"I asked how it was that you were here, and you said, 'You'll violate time as well. You'll poke holes in time—you'll be H.G. Wells without the scooter.'

"I did not understand the reference until much later, and I have been running experiments, equations, theories in a part of me since that day, preparing to send you back in time."

O. had a different question. "You want to go back in time to stop Zu?"

"Yes." The astronaut's lips did not move. "You have to go back in time to save yourself, twice. I have seen one, and you the other, so why not save Zu before?"

Why did she not want to? O. asked herself the question as a long, slender tube rose from the floor beside her. Inside, she could make out a complex pattern of wires, some of which she recognized as having existed on Earth, and others which were completely foreign to her. A few were florescent, while others twisted, winding themselves tightly as if they were alive before releasing; yet still others pulsed, while others looked cold, as if they had been made from stone. There was room for her, however, and when she stepped inside, unresisting, the last of the wires, those that had been cold and dead, sank into her back with a burning sensation. Wincing at the pain, she closed her eyes, and when she opened them again, the world was blurred, the lines that defined the world no longer solid.

She should step out. Instead, she said, "How does this work?"

"Only small objects can be sent back," Alrea said, its voice was dull, as if it were speaking through thick glass. "There is feedback, of a sort, when you try to send something much larger than your hand—the other night I lost a shell like yours when I tried to push the entire thing through. An image, however, projected from the shell proves no issue, however. A tiny projector and recorder is what I send through, and it creates in the shell the environment you are projected into. It will simulate everything for you, so that you can interact within it."

"You control it?"

"Yes."

There was no surprise on her part, and suddenly, she found herself standing in the shuttle, the empty, desolate face of Mars and the sound of the hatch opening her only companions.

"See." It was Zu, confident, brazen. "I told you it was here."

Behind him came Nicholas. "What is it?"

"Dunno. But there's another door up here—it takes you outside."

"Outside?"

O. knew what would happen. The two would open the airlock: it would grind loudly as it did, and Zu would step through the hatch, wearing the brown pants and orange t-shirt that he wore now. He had no understanding of the difference in atmosphere outside and he would turn to face Nicholas and grin confidently because of it. The latter boy would close the hatch from the outside, and remain in the shuttle while Zu opened the hatch leading outside.

Nicholas would start screaming shortly after that.

All she had to do was call their names. They would stop the moment that she did that. They would see her projection and think that it was her and she would tell them what happened outside the airlock. But she didn't. She stood in the shuttle, watching the two reach up for the airlock hatch and begin to play with it.

They looked so real.

But they weren't. They were creations. They were grown from the sacks that Alrea nurtured, their bodies repaired, altered, and improved while they slept. They were creations, just like she was. Yes, the hands that pushed the buttons on the keypad had been so tiny and fragile, and they grew and aged, unlike her own hard, white hands. But the thin tendrils of Alrea altered them both in the same way, burrowing into flesh without permission. So, no matter that they aged and died, they were as real as she was, and that, as far as O. was concerned, was not real at all. That was why the sight of Zu's body had aroused no reaction in her. Alrea could remake him, if it wanted. Life was nothing more than a puzzle, an intricate machine that was tinkered with—

In front of her, the airlock door ground open suddenly, shocking the two boys. In response, they jumped back, and Zu swore loudly. The boys burst out in laughter a moment later.

Despite herself, she smiled.

"Boys," she said before she realized she had spoken, "you don't want to do that."

11.

When she returned, Zu was still dead.

"There was no change." The astronaut was limp inside its tomb, Alrea's disappointment so great that it could not even animate its hideous mask to talk to her. "You talked to them both and they left the shuttle, but here there was no change. He lay on the table as he does now."

O. did not know what to say. Her back hurt, and there was a bitter sadness in her that had not been present before. It only intensified as she gazed down at Zu's ravaged body and tried to process what had happened, and what was happening. When Alrea's tentacles emerged and began digging into Zu's broken skin, however, she turned and left the room.

Her aimless walk took her to the children, who lay in their rooms, still figures in sedation. She wasn't surprised: Alrea had done the same thing when the other children had died.

After checking on them, she went to her own room and lay on the warm bed that was part of Alrea. There, she realized that she could not cry. It was the first time she could remember giving in to her grief since, over the years, any sadness she felt had quickly given away to anger and resentment. For a moment, tearless O. almost returned to the anger—but the image of Zu, grinning when he saw her inside the shuttle, thinking that she was there to share in the fun until she explained to him what would happen, returned. The image of his body was not far behind.

The next day, she said to Alrea, "I think there should be a funeral for the boy. Also, you should think about taking us back to Earth."

In response, the room was cold, the tomb of the astronaut dark.

"They can't stay here. You cannot keep them in a box forever."

"Your tone is not appreciated."

No pain followed, and O. pressed her advantage. "I've not got a tone—I'm just trying to help you avoid this again."

There was silence, and she thought that the conversation was over, and indeed, turned to leave, when Alrea said, "There's nothing on Earth."

"There must be something?"

This time, there was no reply, and O. left the room, feeling as if she had, at least for the moment, changed the dynamic of their relationship. She was further validated two days later when a funeral took place for Zu. Her one concern was that she did not have time to prepare for it, either for herself, or the children. She had been directed by Alrea soon after rising, the children with her, into a pale blue lit corridor that opened into a room of coloured a sombre blue. Entirely new, a room she had never seen before, a part of itself that Alrea had created for the occasion, it was empty but for the dead boy laid out in the middle. Surprisingly, his body had been fixed, for a lack of a better term—the damage done by the atmosphere of Mars no longer detectable. Zu looked as if he were sleeping and O., while thankful, thought it a strange act of kindness on Alrea's behalf.

The ceremony was short and simple. The children placed cards on top of Zu and, at the end, Alrea took the body into itself.

Afterward, when the children had returned to their rooms in a sombre procession, it told O. she would have to go back in time. "Twice." The astronaut's tomb was dark, so dark that only the edge of the broken glass could be seen. "The first time will be to when you were a child, the second to when you awoke here."

"Why?"

"A precaution."

"I don't see why." She argued, in part, because she could, but also because she did not want to feel the wires sink into her back with their burning touch. "It made no difference for Zu—"

"Did you see him, today?" Alrea interrupted.

"Of course."

"I did not change him." When O. made no reply, it continued, "I was as shocked to see him looking as he did, so much that I changed how the ceremony would end. Initially, I had planned to burn him, but instead, I kept him, watched, studied."

"Is he—is he alive?"

"No."

"But—"

"I don't know what has happened," Alrea said, a hint of desperation in its voice. "What I do know is that it appears that Zu died for no reason. Every part of him is healthy, perfect, but I cannot stimulate the brain, or get the heart to pulse. It is beyond my understanding, and may forever be, but I take the warning as it is given: time has its own laws, and we cannot break it, nor demand it to be different just because it would make our lives easier. We have to acknowledge it."

There was an opportunity for her. That was what O. thought as the wires sank into her back. She was not quite sure what it was yet, but the relationship between her and Alrea had changed, that she was sure of. She might be able to change it more if she warned her younger self about Dan; if she spoke about her mother's suicide; she could even warn her about Alrea. She knew, however, that even as she thought this, she was ignoring what she had been told, that time could not be changed, or altered—but that was not entirely true. Time could be altered and changed. Zu's body showed that and, while, yes, the change was a cosmetic one, and did not hide the facts, did it not suggest that the potential to change her conditions existed?

Before her, a long tentacle placed a sharp, ugly knife on a small tray in front of her.

Then, she was standing in her old classroom.

Out the window, O. could see the overcast sky, and the sandy brick fence that ran around the school in a sign of its prosperity. The room was smaller than she remembered, however, and the tables tiny. She doubted that she could have sat in one of the chairs comfortably, while pulling herself up to one of the desks was out of question. Unable to do either, however, her gaze drifted across the security camera in the right hand corner of the room, and to the electric board that had only recently been replaced after the monitor component fizzled out on the previous; the posters and charts that the class itself had put up around the room were her final acknowledgment and the last of them was a map of the world, marked with red.

Behind her, the door opened.

"The infected areas are coloured red, right? It has been a while since I've seen one," O said, not yet turning. "There is a theory that the virus is proof of alien life."

There was no reply.

"It's in this country already." She turned, facing the child that she had once been: skinny, black, and with wild hair. "It's in New Orleans, brought over by Baker Thomas. Right now, he leads in a small community of infected—the number is fifteen, if I remember right. It isn't difficult for him to hide, but in ten years, it will be impossible to keep his community a secret and he'll have to take action. Just like you will with your uncle, Octavia."

She used the name that had once been her own and found herself curiously detached from it and the girl before her. She recognised Octavia as herself, and could not deny it, but within herself was the quiet realization that the girl before her was long, long dead. O. was no longer her, no longer on the edge of a bumbling, confused sexuality that would only become more confused over the next years thanks to her uncle. And neither was she what the girl would grow up into: a woman who suffered from addiction and who placed herself in abusive, possessive relationships that stemmed from the early relationships with her uncle and mother.

"That's why I know you're early to school," she said, finally. "It's in your eyes."

Octavia blinked in response.

Was I always this quiet? O. had never believed that she was, but as yet, her younger self had not said a word. Instead, Octavia stared at her with wide, brown eyes, fearful and distrustful, yet also wanting, and needing. That's how her uncle made her feel: as if you were alone, as if you could not trust a single person anymore. The memory came back acutely as she stood there, and O. spoke about the dog fight.

She made no attempt to change the story, or to alter it, as she had thought that she would do so earlier. Instead, as she pulled the knife out, she was very aware of how much she didn't belong there at that moment. Octavia's life would be led; it had been finished for over a century, if O. was to believe what Alrea told her. Changing it would do, what, exactly? Give her black skin instead of white? Give her blood and ovaries? Over the years, O. had longed both to restore her identity, to give her a sense of place, to ground her reality in herself, to make her herself again.

But, standing there, before her younger self, she found it impossible to deny what had happened; it had made her, shaped her and what she did now, with Alrea and the children, was a direct response to it. Yes, she was a slave, a barren mother, and a black woman trapped in a shell. She hated it, but yet, she knew what Alrea knew when it had dug through Zu's body: time, history, could not be ignored, could not be treated as if it were a minor thing that did not make them who they were. Changing it would not alter her problems. She would still want freedom for herself and the children.

The past was the past: it could not be corrected, she realized, just learned from.

In front of her younger self, O. placed the knife.

"Don't forget this, yeah?"

She knew she wouldn't.

12.

"Okay," O. said, "but just one. Just one story out here before I leave."

In the evening, she had built the campfire behind the back of the sprawling house, trying to make it as much as she remembered, with a ring of grey rocks around a shallow pit. The night before she had told the children that, yes, they could camp outside for the night, and she wanted—in what was a rare display of affection for her past—to give them the most picture perfect campsite that she could. By the following night, when dark had fallen, all sixteen children found sleeping bags around the fire, each of them sized to accommodate the youngest (five) and the eldest (seventeen). Before she had let the children out, however, she had made the oldest three girls and one boy look after the youngest for the night and to keep the peace, though she expected at least two of the children to run back to her, crying, after being picked on, or being scared. That was part of the experience of camping, too.

As was the story:

"The story I have is about a girl who was a vampire. She was no older than Mary—being, I mean, that she was eleven, a tiny, tiny girl with dark skin and wild, wild hair." In front of her, the white skinned Mary's eyes crinkled with amusement; she had heard the story before, O. knew, and had heard the vampire given different names, but that didn't change the fact that she liked being singled out. "She had been born on Earth, and had grown up with her parents in a nice house, near a beach. She did not know that, however, when she woke up, because she awoke without a memory, without any idea of where she should be.

"Why, she could've been on Mars."

The younger children laughed; the four older ones rolled their eyes. O. kept her smile to herself.

"When she awoke, she was hungry like she had never been, but she did not want food, not in the way you do. No sandwich, no pie, nothing you would eat would satisfy her: only blood would. Inside her head, her mind screamed BLOOD! BLOOD! worse than it had ever done in her entire life. This was partly because our young vampire had been hurt in a fire and was badly injured. Her need for blood came not because she was hungry, but because blood healed them, and she was in horrible pain. Normally, if our vampire found you or I, she would bite us just here, on our necks." With her white hand—a hand that she still loathed to recognize as her own—she reached out to one of the young boys, Gerard, and pinched his dark skinned neck. "She would do it lightly, and it would be like a kiss, and she would take just a little to get by. But, it could hurt if a vampire drank too much. They could kill a human—which is exactly what would happen if this girl found you or I. She would grab us, grab us by the neck and bite deeply, and harshly, and drink us dry.

"Sadly, this is what happened to the young man who found her lying on the ground. He touched her shoulder to see if she was alive and she grabbed him, breaking his bones with her grip as she tore chunks of skin out of his neck."

Every eye was on O., while behind her, the shuttle that Alrea had crashed into the surface of Mars lay in a pale orange light, ten minutes across the grass field that lay between it and the house. It was a walk that the children made every morning for class, where they learned about math, science, literature, painting, and anything else that Alrea deemed important. In the halls, they walked in Alrea's warm skin, spoke with its voice—gone was the horrific visage of the last Baker Thomas and his astronaut's suit—and then left, to walk across Alrea's grass, breath its air, and live in as much freedom as they could have.

As they were given.

"Afterwards, she felt terrible," O. continued. "She had never meant to kill him, and knew it was wrong to take life. Worse, she had broken one of the vampires' most sacred rules, which was that she had fed without consent, and the blood in her stomach was tainted and awful because of it. A vampire, even a hungry, hurt one, was subject to the same rules that you and I are part of. To drink from someone without consent, to kill them before their time, was something that a vampire should never do, just as you or I should not kill someone, or force them to do something against their will, and just as we would feel bad for doing so, so was she. Our vampire was violently ill and vomited all over the grass she stood on."

She was subverting the nature of vampires, making it a moral that she could use to seed in the children notions of what was right and wrong. Soon, she would introduce an evil vampire who wanted to control humans and treat them like cattle. It was he who had hurt the young girl, and he who she and her friends would fight against at the end. But, before that, O. would tell the children how the vampire needed her companions, all of them human, to survive. That she was talking in part about Alrea would escape all but the eldest, and Alrea itself, but the latter had been losing its control and power since she had returned from her third and final trip in time, wherein she had sat in the room and listened to herself retell the story she knew so well.

After she had left herself outside Alrea's door, she had returned, and since then, fought for her independence. The house and atmosphere she had was part of it, but she was not free, not yet, not completely. Her methods in fighting, however, changed, and she found herself looking just not at herself, but at the children she raised. They were her battleground, and she fought Alrea within them, subverting the stories of her youth and of Earth's past, to ensure that they understood the necessity for freedom, that they could fight Alrea, and that together they could assure not just their freedom, but that the events that had brought them to this point, did not happen again.

theleeharveyoswaldband

"My band is not here. They've left. They've *gone*. That's why it's just me on the stage tonight. I'm going to try and make it work for you all anyway."

Years later, Zarina Salim Malik would write that it was these words that changed her life. It was impossible to think that at the time: the vowels of each word were slurred, mashed together, and lost within the heavy, deep bass voice that emerged from crackling speakers. But it was true. It would change her life. There was a magnetic quality that allowed the musician's voice to rise over the chinks of glass and snatches of conversation and reach her and the other fifty New Yorkers in the Annandale Bar with a tone that implied that he mattered. That they should listen. It was a tone that ignored the fact that the audience present was not there because they cared for the opening act, but because they wanted prime choice in space for the later band they had actually paid to see, and because they had a dedication to music that had nothing to do with any individual performer or act. But the voice ignored that.

The stage in the Annandale was at the end of a small, shadow stained rectangular box of a room with a dirty wooden floor. It had metal fans against the left side that did nothing to cool the place down when it was full and opposite these was a bar where students worked for cheap wages and stole liquor but never cleaned. The whole room lingered in the taste and smell of cigarettes, beer and sweat. It was a shithole, but the bands were cheap and when the music mingled with her pulse, Zarina didn't care. Nothing mattered but the music. But when that voice snagged the part of her mind that went on instinct, something different happened. She had never felt an intensity like this before, and she watched the shadows of the stage as the musician dragged a stool to the front; watched as the electronics squealed and drowned out everyone, then faded; watched even when Sara, slender, cute, blonde Sara in black and green and Japanese tattoos down her spine, *that* Sara, began to speak and she ignored her. In fact, Zarina leaned over, ashed into the half filled metal tray they had been sharing, then stood—herself in black and red and an inch shorter than Sara, with only one tattoo of a sun coloured butterfly on her neck that her long black hair hid—and she said, "I'm going up front."

The musician emerged from the shadows and into a weak yellow light as she did. He sat himself on the stool behind the lone metal stem of the microphone. He had a wooden acoustic guitar in his grasp and he was white. That last part surprised her. She hadn't expected a tall, lean, unshaven, post-grunge-slacker musician in his late twenties with messy blonde-brown hair. He had no shoes and wore faded black jeans and a dirty white shirt covered in a pattern of girls in sunflower yellow dresses playing musical instruments. Sure, he was good looking if he was your type, but he wasn't Zarina's. Never would be. And yet, despite this, she sat at an empty table in the middle of the Annandale's floor, aware even as she pulled back the dull metal stool how fucking weird this was, how her gaze hadn't left the scene before her, how she'd totally turned obsessive. It had taken her months to draw Sara out. Months. And now she'd left her (she was following, but Zarina didn't know this, didn't much care) for a musician she didn't even know the name of. But she sat. She waited. Sara settled next to her, her fine pale fingers touching her leg, their first touch and Zarina couldn't focus on it. She was watching and listening to *him*. Watching as he plucked string after string, tuned with his bony figures whose ends were coated in black polish and moved like magpies jabbing their narrow, sharp beaks into the earth when moving across cords. On instinct, Zarina reached beneath her shirt and turned on the microphone connected to her ipod. She had planned to bootleg *Robots Unconquered* when they played two hours from now—and she still would—but without ever having heard a note, she began recording this lone man whose band had left him just as his head bent towards the microphone.

The following is an interview with John Fritzgerald (Jack Ruby), former drummer for theleeharveyoswaldband. A short, squat man covered in coloured bright tattoos of skulls and women and revolvers, he sits in a cheap diner in Brooklyn, wearing blue jeans, a Hawaiian shirt, and leather jacket. He answers questions with a casual ease. The interview was conducted by Rolling Stone in May of 2006, one week after the death of Lee Brown (Lee Harvey Oswald), the singer and guitarist who, in 2002, became the sole member of theleeharveyoswaldband.

You and bass guitarist Kevin Lynch (Jack Kennedy) left the band the day that the now infamous bootleg of the Annandale was recorded. Do you look back with regret at that?

For a while, I did, but not now. I just tell myself—I just say, how could I have known? No one could predict that that was going to happen. You can't regret that.

Not even when you have, in some circles, been labelled a villain?

It's the curse of those stupid stage names. You call yourself Jack Ruby and eventually you're going to be the villain.

Besides, working with Lee . . . it was just impossible. The guy was the most illiterate person I'd ever met. I mean, he couldn't even sign his own name. He avoided giving signatures for that reason—but I saw him once, trying to fill in a deposit slip for cash. He couldn't even understand what the boxes were for.

That's a serious level of illiteracy there.

It was worse. I mean, I felt sorry for him—someone had fucked him education wise—but he couldn't read music, either. He couldn't write down those songs of his in a way we'd understand and it was just frustrating. You'd try and force a set list onto him, but what was the point? He couldn't read it, couldn't play it, couldn't do shit for it, but worse, he didn't want to do it.

If you bought up the fact that he should learn—that he should go to night school or some shit, he'd just shut you out.

Which just meant that every time we went on stage, we were playing whatever he thought of. Whatever popped into his head. Like, now, I might want a drink. Maybe a Coke. Maybe milk. Maybe a beer. That's how he played. Kevin and me were always playing catch up. Trying to keep a beat that was impossible to know in the first place.

But the music he made—

Was shit, most of the time. That Annandale bootleg was—fuck man, it was like seeing pictures of the Kennedy assassination from the grassy knoll.

From behind rain slicked glass, the streets of Detroit were a dark pattern highlighted by smeared yellow light. To Zarina, it felt as if hundreds of eyes were weeping brightly as she passed. She watched them from the passenger seat of a tiny blue hatchback that was driven by the plump, middle-aged Emily Brown, who, as her name suggested, wore a baggy brown suit to match her cheaply cut brown hair and name.

"You're being quiet," Emily said.

"Yeah." They were at a red light. Emily only talked at red lights. "Just thinking."

"Try not to over think. Nothing good comes from that."

Zarina made a noncommittal sound, then said, "I think I'm making a mistake."

"Nonsense."

But she was. Zarina hunched down into her patched army jacket and stretched her black docs out so that they were under the little car's heater. She didn't know why she had done that: she wasn't cold—in a minute, the heat would seep through her boots and turn uncomfortable—and hunching made her jacket bunch at her neck unpleasantly. But she couldn't keep still; she fidgeted while trying to reason out why she was there. She *should* be back in her apartment uploading new recordings and making sure that someone was covering shows for the Pixel Babies and Eddie Isn't Dead Yet next Saturday. She should be cooking for Sara. She shouldn't be taking two unpaid days (Friday and Monday) from her call centre job to make this trip to Detroit to meet the sole member of theleeharveyoswaldband. She should have said no and junked the email. But when she had read Emily's words telling her that Lee wanted to meet her—

"You're fretting," Emily interrupted as the hatchback stopped at another light. "I can see it on your face."

"I don't—I don't usually meet artists I like."

She laughed. "My. I've never heard Lee called *that* before."

"It's just—just meeting them, y'know?" Zarina continued, trying to push out her words, her fears. "Meeting them can just—can just fuck it all up. That's what I tell Sara. That's always what I tell her. Just the thought of meeting him has woken us up at night."

"Is Sara your daughter?"

"No."

"Oh."

The light turned green.

The other thing, Zarina knew, was her life. She wasn't ashamed of who she was, knew she didn't have to justify anything—and wouldn't, fuck the world if they thought she should—but after that one word, Emily shrank behind the smooth mat black steering wheel and chewed on her bottom lip, allowing the silence to grow heavy as she drove slowly through the wet streets. It reminded Zarina of the very real possibility that Lee Brown could say something that would ruin his music for her. All he would have to say was some small-minded thing, some red state thing, and that would be it. Her fingers pressed into the palms of her hands, bones cracked, and she thought about that night, after the Annandale, when she had returned to her apartment. Without flipping the lights on, she had crossed the cold wooden floors, flipped on the stereo, dropped her ipod into it's cradle, and with Sara's cool white fingers sliding across her stomach, played theleeharveyoswaldband set. The set meant more to her than Brown ever could.

"Well," Emily said, then paused. She cleared her throat like a careful teacher. "Well, it doesn't matter. There's no need to fret, anyway."

"I shouldn't have come."

"Nonsense. You changed his life."

"That didn't have anything to do with me."

The Annandale Bootleg changed everything, didn't it?

It made Lee Brown a cult icon. I mean, seriously, I saw him on a fucking t-shirt the other day. Couldn't believe my eyes.

It is ironic that a man who couldn't read would be so embraced by net culture.

You got to thank Zarina Salim Malik for that.

You don't think it would have happened without her?

No.

Some people, y'know, some people—that fame will happen anyway, and it doesn't matter who is around. I've heard people say that if it wasn't for Sin-e that Jeff Buckley wouldn't have been found—but Sine-e was just a café that he played in, y'know? Could've been any place, it wouldn't have mattered cause Buckley was just genius waiting to be found. Buckley was going to be Buckley and it didn't matter how it would happen.

But theleeharveyoswaldband wouldn't have been anything without Malik. The music was shit, Brown couldn't keep a band, he could never get regular gigs—and then she showed and bootlegged him in a pub and put it on the net and suddenly it's everywhere and people can't get enough of him.

Thanks, in part, to Xeni Jardin at Boing Boing who pushed the link through the site to the thousands of bloggers who reproduced it.

Exactly. Blog culture, the net—it just gave theleeharveyoswaldband an audience, and that allowed Malik, who eventually became Brown's manager and record label, to exploit it.

I remember reading this article that said that the success of the band rested in the fact that it never released a studio album, and that new recordings—new unique records—were put out at every live show and loaded up by dedicated bootleggers, making them part of the process—part of the music, the sharing, the distribution. It was basically saying that because it embraced everything established music didn't, that's why it worked. Which is some weird logic, you ask me, and ignores the fact that Brown was just messed up, and that the brains behind it all was Malik, a blogger with an already existing bootleg audience. But, apparently, the more messed up he became—

Well, the more of a cult figure *she* could make him.

Zarina had never been to a trailer park before.

She had seen them, of course, on television and in movies and across the web, but those images were nothing like the reality at the *Rainbow's End Park*. The rain smeared the yellow light from the trailer windows as it had done earlier, but with the city now a dark outline behind her, the light looked as if it was contained in a wet blur of battery chicken cages, made not from mesh wiring, but fibro and metal, and with each looking as if it were joined to the one next to it, and then the next, and so on as they sat like a school of lost things on the side of the mud and pebble paved road that Emily navigated her hatchback down. In the slick windows of the single wide trailers, Zarina watched the silhouettes of the occupants, but could not imagine what they looked like, what they were doing beyond the cliché of the environment. Beyond drugs, abuse, violence, neglect, and struggle. Each shadow animated itself in her mind; a flat puppet made from other people's limbs. Half way through the park, she became conscious of the weight of her own life, of her education, of the degree she had left incomplete, the college her parents had paid for, the advantages she had ignored to work in a call centre she hated for money she wasted, and the bootleg she had made without a second thought of the man who lived here.

The hatchback slowed, stopped with a jolt outside a single wide with the number 45 on the side. Beyond that, there was nothing to distinguish it. "I'm not sure about this," Zarina repeated softly, staring at the light behind the screen door. "I think I might have made a mistake."

"Nonsense," Emily replied. "Just nonsense. Now up to the door you go."

The windshield wipers rubbed against the glass, a pair of black sticks lifting a curtain and dropping it. The last thing she wanted to do was step out into that wet, artificially lit lot it revealed, but how could she leave now?

Releasing her seatbelt, Emily leaned over and grabbed hold of the door handle. With a shove, she pushed it out into the rain. The light flicked on above them and, lit by it, Emily smiled at Zarina. There was nothing warm in it: the brown in her teeth was darker than her pale skin, and the lines and bags around her eyes gave a look that mixed tiredness and apathy into one. It was clear that she didn't care what Zarina felt or what she was experiencing; this was just a stop before she returned home to her children and husband and the routine she had for her life.

With a faintly murmured thanks, Zarina stepped out of the hatchback. The rain fell heavily onto her jacket, through her dark hair, and splashed into the car. She closed the door and was rewarded with the red brake lights lifting immediately as Emily drove away. Didn't even stay to see if the door opened—which, when Zarina turned, she found to be incorrect on her part, as it was already open.

In the doorframe of his single wide, Lee Brown looked much as he had on the stage at the Annandale: unshaven, lean, with messy hair. He was wearing black jeans and a black t-shirt, but still had nothing on his feet. In his hands he held a brown towel, which he tossed into her hands as she entered.

"Thanks," she said, rubbing her face.

"Isn't a thing," he replied. "You can hang your jacket up behind you."

The inside was, essentially, a box. It was covered in a wallpaper of girls in sunflower yellow dresses playing instruments: banjos, guitars, tiny drum kits, harmonicas, and a whole collection of other instruments that looked to be taken out of the sixties. The pattern covered the entire trailer, missing only the small kitchen behind her. The bedroom beyond that—though she couldn't see the bed, just a beanbag and a red electric guitar, foot pedals, and a small amp—was covered in it too. It was more than a little odd, she thought as she hung her jacket on the wooden rack, and she had no way to even begin explaining it. Drying and warming her bare arms, she turned and glanced into the kitchen again, taking in the stacked plates and empty cans and bottles, and finally came round to Lee, who had cleared space on a cheap table by pushing CDs and tools and strings and small instruments such as harmonicas and kazoos to the side, and was now looking at her with a half hidden *that* kind of look.

Zarina didn't enjoy it. Mostly, she just ignored guys who looked at her like that, but it was a sharp and unpleasant reminder from Lee, driving home the knowledge that she shouldn't have agreed to meet him, that she should have realized that his music meant more to her than he—

He was speaking. Shit. She had missed everything he'd said. "Sorry?"

"I was asking if you had any problems with Em?"

"No. She was very nice."

"She can be a bit . . ." He paused, searched for the word, rubbed at his chin as he did, then said, "Bossy. It's cool if you found that."

"I'm fine."

"Cool. Take a seat."

Zarina wanted to grab her jacket first, wanted to wrap the wet fabric around her and hide her body in its folds, but she didn't. Instead, she pulled back the seat and sat down opposite to Lee. His gaze met hers: his eyes were brown with a touch of green and yellow around the centre. The silence between them began to grow uncomfortable and he picked up a silver harmonica from next to his hand and began twisting it end over end. He coughed to clear his throat, said, "I've never—you know, never been real good with this stuff."

Like she was better. "It's okay."

"Yeah, I know. It's just—just—"

"I wouldn't have picked Emily as your sister," Zarina interrupted. "You don't look much like each other."

"She's my foster sister."

"Yeah?"

"Yeah, her folks took me in when I was about ten." The silver harmonica settled onto the table, the mouth's end pointed away from her. "My original family broke up and I was left on my own, and I jumped from foster family to foster family for a while. No one wanted to take me permanently."

"Why was that?"

"I was angry. I had a lot of problems with school," he said. "Plus I couldn't read."

"Really?"

"Still can't."

"You never tried to learn?"

"I could read until I was nine, but then it left me. Figured I was better off."

He was casual, unashamed, and that surprised Zarina. She had never met anyone who was illiterate before, but she had believed that anyone who couldn't read would want to keep it a secret. She didn't know what to say, but watching Lee pick up his harmonica and turn it around again, knew that she had to reply. "That's . . . odd. Did you ever—you know, see someone about it?"

"Yeah. Mostly they said it was in my head."

"You think they were right?"

"Not in the way they thought," he replied. "I know what's exactly in my head—not that Em's parents believed that. They just thought I was fucked up. I think she figures it, too, but she looks out for me anyhow. She doesn't need to, but family, hey? What's yours like?"

Zarina shifted uncomfortably. He wasn't looking at her as he had earlier, though she believed that she could still see that in the background. The desire had been overtaken by an invasive quality in his eyes, as if each was trying to dig beneath her skin and pull out her thoughts. "I don't have much to do with my family."

"Why?"

"It's . . ." She hesitated, hated herself for it, hated the pause for what it implied. "It's a lifestyle choice."

"You're a smoker?"

She blushed. "No, I'm—"

"I know," Lee said, amused. "I got it."

She laughed to cover her embarrassment and stared at the long scratches in the table as she spoke. They had been made by a knife. "I'm—I'm sorry. I don't usually meet people like you."

"Yeah, I try not to come to places like this, either."

"That's not what I meant."

"No? You're not one of those trailer park girls, are you?"

"You're an idiot." She raised her head, grinned. "I meant I don't meet musicians, much. Especially ones who make music I like."

"Well, thanks for coming."

"I don't know why you wanted to see me anyway."

"It was Emily's idea, mostly." Lee pushed back his chair, stood. He dropped the harmonica and snatched up a blue coloured plastic kazoo. "You want a beer?"

"Sure."

He entered the kitchen and, at the fridge, tapped the kazoo on the door in an incomplete child's tune (was it 'Mary Had A Little Lamb?') as he pulled out two bottles of beer. "I thought I was kind of fucked at the Annandale, you know? Band was gone, I had no more gigs lined up, in a couple of weeks I'd be out of rent. And on top of that, I was playing like I'd never played before. It felt good playing it, but I didn't think the audience liked it much—what audience there was, I guess. Then about a month later I started getting these calls to play. Calls from bars and venues that I'd never heard of."

He placed the slick brown bottle in front of her, the kazoo tapping against his own glass as he did. He was repeating the opening of the tune, never completing it. "I did the shows, and at each one the audience kept growing, and I kept getting more calls. I had no idea why until after one show when this guy shows with a CD he's bought of the Annandale gig."

"A CD?" Zarina interrupted.

"Yeah, I thought he bought it off you."

"No," she said emphatically. "I don't sell anything. The live shows on my site are free. I don't sell it. Making money out of it changes it."

Lee sat. "Don't change it for me," he said, his bottle opening with a hiss.

"It does. People are making off you and you're not seeing any of it, whereas my site, it's sharing the music that people enjoy. There's no money involved—it's just because everyone shares the interest."

"You're a bootlegger, right?"

"I make bootlegs," she corrected. "I don't sell bootlegs."

"The difference in that is just passing me by." He spun the bottle cap across the table. "You're living in a world I don't even want to know."

Zarina's bottle hissed open. "Look, downloading, bootlegging, it's just not simple right or wrong. Nothing's like that."

"Hey, I'm not fussed." Lee's blue kazoo rose into the air with his hands in an exaggerated comic gesture of hands off. He grinned. "I'm getting gigs. I don't care if someone is making a couple of dollars."

"You should care."

"Yeah, so I hear," he said, lowering his hands. "It's what Emily said."

"She's right. If someone is making money off you, you deserve some. Most people don't want to take money from a musician of your level, so they'd rather pay to support you. Some aren't like that, of course, but people do things for a lot of different reasons."

Lee nodded, but he looked uncomfortable, so she added, "I'll put a notice on my website, saying there are no authorized copies for sale out there. You can even start a PayPal account if you want."

"You're losing me now."

"Lot of people download the Annandale show. I can put up a notice saying you need rent, and they'll give you a bit of money. Help you get by."

He twisted in his chair, agitated. "That's not—"

"It's no problem," Zarina said, keeping casual. "People do it all the time."

"That's—I'm not—look—"

His voice broke off suddenly and his head dropped into his hands. Zarina called his name, but there was no response; slowly, she reached forward and touched his shoulder but, again, no response. Lee had just shut down. That was the only way to explain it, and because she could hear his breathing, she wasn't quite yet panicking. Still, she had seen it in his face as he fell into his hands, and watched as the life behind his eyes disappeared like a light being switched off. Around her, the images of girls in sunflower yellow dresses stared outwards, the instruments they held in their hands having more in common with weapons than devices that created music.

His head still in his hands, Lee said quietly, "I can't talk business. I just—I just cannot do that, okay?"

"Okay," she said softly. "Whatever suits you."

"It's not that I don't care, it's just I got to keep focused." His head rose, and in his gaze Zarina saw a sense of fatigue that his previous liveliness had hidden. "If I lose focus, I become something else."

"Okay."

"You don't understand."

"No." *How could she?*

"Like I said, I could read. Once. When I was a kid. I loved reading. When I was nine, I read everything that I could get my hands on, and when I was finished with a book, I would start writing my own stories. Just inspired to make my own, you know?" His fingers placed the blue kazoo on the table and began to pull out a guitar string, the movement causing albums to slide over the table. Lee didn't notice. "But then, one day, I found music. My dad showed me how to play a little tune on a piano. Nothing big. A nursery rhyme. But the sound—the way it made me feel, it was like nothing else I'd ever experienced. It was creation like I had never been involved in before, and after that, nothing was comparable. It was love. I could find it in every musical instrument I picked up, as if it were lingering in the wood or metal waiting for me, and I pushed the words and books out of my head to make room for the music."

There was no awareness of reality in Lee's gaze. He was telling his story and he believed everything that he said. Zarina, however, was not important to it; he could have been telling it to anyone. But while he lingered on the music, she lingered on the details of Lee's father and what had really happened. It was the broken bit of the story, the edge that she could peel back to learn the secrets, but she knew—without questioning— that Lee Brown was incapable of doing that. It was when Zarina realized this that what she feared would happen, did, and in one quiet moment, the purity of his music was lost. She became detached, sympathetic, and sorry; aware that whenever she played theleeharveyoswaldband after this moment, the image of a young boy being abused by his father would be all that she could think of.

"You don't believe me," he said, the cord wrapping around his fist. "I can see that you don't."

"It's not a question of that," she replied gently.

"I've not slept for eighteen years."

"What?"

"If I sleep, I will lose what's inside my head. I will lose *myself*."

"That won't happen."

"It will." Gripping the cord tightly in his left fist, he reached into the mess of instruments and albums on the table to his right, and from beneath it all pulled out a flat envelope that she had not seen. It was old and yellowed and creased and had the words *Lee Brown* written upon it in faded red ink. "The proof is in here."

Why do you think that Brown kept using the band name?

He loved the name. Just loved it. I asked him where he got it from once, and he said, "Me and the dead President have a lot in common."

That's all?

It was the only one he ever gave.

Still, I think theleeharveyoswaldband suited Brown and Malik more than it did when I was there. Kennedy's death signalled a change in American politics, and theleeharveyoswaldband did the same thing for American music.

You really think that?

Don't get me wrong: I don't think Malik made this culture of downloading, but she's become the figurehead for it. With theleeharveyoswaldband she's given it a credibility like it never had before.

She knows it, too. You just have to read her interviews, listen to her on talk shows, whatever. She talks up the net and bootlegging and the creative commons copyright like a guru. You think of this stuff and you think of her. It's not surprising that she's become a hub for new bands, and that large labels have tried to bring her up on criminal charges.

I was reading an interview with executives from Sony the other day, and they were calling her dangerous and misguided.

That's suits for you.

In truth, the corporate level has nothing to fear from Malik right now. She's publicly said that she hasn't moved more than a hundred thousand copies from the millions of downloads that have been made of the Annandale recording, and that's her best seller. When you compare that to a giant label that will move five million copies of an album from a high profile act, it's nothing.

But Malik isn't a problem. Neither is downloading. Suits'll just say that so they don't have to approach the real problem, and that's that their business model isn't producing long-term acts, and what acts they do produce have no loyalty to the shareholders and company brand names. More and more bands with an established audience are leaving to become independent. I mean, shit, Hanson did it. Can you believe that?

Are you talking from the point of view of a musician who is not in the care of a large label?

You saying it's jealousy?

Just asking.

The answer's no. The type of music I make has never been mainstream enough for that.

Why do you think Malik became involved in the business side?

You read her interviews and she'll tell you that she believed in the music—in Brown's music especially. She said it needed an outlet and she provided one.

Do you believe that?

No one is that altruistic. I mean, it's not like she did this for free.

Inside the envelope was a series of blue x-rays. Zarina pulled out the smooth sheets and looked at them on the table, held them up to the light, and then placed them back on the table. She had never seen an x-ray before and had no idea what she was looking at. But she knew that it was important for Lee that she examine each.

On the five sheets was the image of a skull, the bones displayed with a grey stain of skin and blood and veins around it and in the centre. Placing the final image down on the table, she returned her gaze to Lee, who was sitting straight up in his chair, the girls in sunflower dresses lined up behind him like soldiers. She said, "I have no idea what I'm looking at."

"It's a skull," he said.

"I know that."

"It's *my* skull."

"I know that, too," she replied gently. "I don't know what's wrong with it, though. I can't read these things."

"Can't you see that there's nothing in it?" His voice became strained: a desperate note caught on the tight cord held between his hands. "Can't you see?"

"Yes." She wanted to tell him that she wasn't a doctor, that she didn't know enough, but even though she felt that these images were not right, that something was definitely missing, she didn't think he should take it to mean that his head was empty. Instead, all she said was, "Yes."

"You don't understand!" He released the cord, flung it on the table where it lashed across the envelope. "There's *nothing* in there. My head is completely empty. It's just bone and skin and the only thing that keeps me alive is thoughts that I can keep there."

"You can't live like that."

"I know!" he cried out, kicking back his chair to stand. "You don't think I know this? I'm not stupid!"

"I never said that."

"Stand up!"

"Lee," Zarina began.

"Stand up," he said, pushing the words through his teeth. "Stand up."

Zarina rose slowly and sadly. She knew what would happen, but found herself without anger. She regretted that she hadn't listened to Sara and stayed at home, but at the same time, with Lee trembling with anger in front of her, his gaze seeing something that she couldn't even begin to understand, there was only sadness. As when she had first seen him perform, her thoughts were of nothing but him, his presence all that she was aware of.

With a sudden movement, Lee snatched her hands. She closed her eyes, waiting, unwilling to watch . . . and heard a heavy thud. Opening her eyes, Zarina saw that Lee had fallen to his knees and lowered his head towards her, while bringing up her hands. At first, she could feel nothing but his hair, thinner than she had thought, and then, slowly, small puckered scars, the shape of a drill head or screwdriver.

"What is this?" she whispered.

"They examined me," he replied, his voice hollow. "When I stopped sleeping and reading, my father took me to a doctor who ran his tests. When he found that my head was empty, he ran more."

"More."

"We didn't have health insurance, but the doctor worked for free. He said he had never seen anyone like me. That I was special. He laid me out on a bed and shaved my head. There were injections. I could feel nothing, but I watched as he took his metal instruments and dug them into my skull. He told me as he worked that beneath the skin, past the bone, there was nothing but emptiness. Nothing but black."

Zarina wanted to remove her hands, but couldn't. She wanted to tell him how sick and awful this was, but the words would not emerge from her throat. It was dry, choked, and he pressed his head into her fingers, taking pleasure from her touch, starved for attention and affection in ways that she would never be able to understand. And she, knowing this, revolted but unable to deny him, stroked his scarred and tortured head, drew it into her grasp like a mother with her child.

"That's why I can't sleep," he whispered, his voice slurring its vowels heavily in what Zarina would realize, a moment later, were tears. "I'll die if I sleep. All my thoughts will cease to exist. All the music I hear and feel will go. It'll fade away. I can't let that happen. I can't let it die. I have to make music in my mind."

Do you think he's dead?

Yeah.

Yeah, I do.

I've heard the theories that he's not. A kind of Elvis thing for the new century that says Lee just got tired and left and that wasn't really him with his veins cut open, but that's wrong. Even with that last interview with him saying he was tired all the time, it's wrong.

Lee couldn't leave music. It meant too much him. He was impossible to play with, but he loved it. You couldn't deny that. It was all he had.

So that's it?

Yeah. There are no encores here.

Acknowledgements

Short story collections leave a trail of people to thank. First and foremost, the editors who published the individual stories originally: Forrest Aguirre, Shane Cummings and Angela Challis, Jay Lake and Deborah Layne, Ben Payne and Robert Hoge, Ekatrina Sedia, Cat Sparks, and Sean Wallace. A big acknowledgement goes to Brett Savory and Sandra Kasturi, who looked at all the individual parts and agreed that it would make a collection, to Stephen Michell for his work on it, and to Erik Mohr who provided the wonderful cover.

Authors also owe a debt to the authors who have come before them. First and foremost for myself is Octavia E. Butler. The story in her name is the smallest debt that I can pay.

To those of you who have not read her work, I can only hope that I have pointed you in the direction you must go.

Publication History

"There Is Something So Quiet and Empty Inside of You That It Must Be Precious" is original to this volume.

"The Dreaming City" was in *Leviathan Four: Cities*, ed. Forrest Aguirre, The Ministry of Whimsy Press, 2004.

"John Wayne (As Written by a Non-American)" was in *Aurealis*, #37, Chimaera Press, 2007.

"Possession" was in *Fantasy Magazine* online, 2007.

"Under the Red Sun" was in *Fantasy Magazine*, #4, 2006.

"The Souls of Dead Soldiers are for Blackbirds, Not Little Boys" was in *Agog! Ripping Reads*, ed. Cat Sparks, Agog! Press, 2006.

"The Funeral, Ruined" was in *Paper Cities: An Anthology of Urban Fantasy*, ed. Ekaterina Sedia, Senses Five, 2008.

"Johnny Cash (A Tale in Questionnaire Results)" was in *Shadowed Realms* #4, 2005.

"Octavia E. Butler" is original to this volume.

"theleeharveyoswaldband" was in *Polyphony Six*, ed. Deborah Layne and Jay Lake, Wheatland Press, 2006.

About the Author

Sydney-based author Ben Peek's previous novels are *Twenty-Six Lies/One Truth*, *Black Sheep*, and *Above/Below* with Stephanie Campisi. His short fiction has appeared in *Steampunk: Revolution, Polyphony, Leviathan, Paper Cities, Aurealis, Overland, Fantasy Magazine, Clarkesworld*, and various *Year's Best* volumes. He is the creator of the *Urban Sprawl Project*, a pyschogeography pamphlet given out in the suburbs of Sydney, and with artist Anna Brown, the autobiographical comic, *Nowhere Near Savannah*. Later in the year, *Immolation*, the first novel in his series Children, will be released. He lives with his partner, the photographer, Nikilyn Nevins, a cat, and a tree that both paid a lot of money to save. But it is a nice tree, and the man who poured seven litres of copper naphthenate into it, agreed.

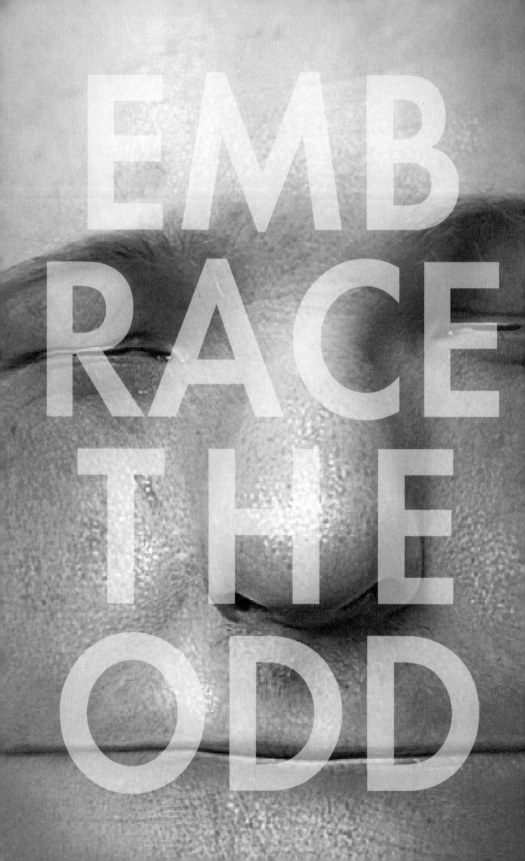

GET KATJA
SIMON LOGAN

Katja from Simon Logan's award-winning *Katja From the Punk Band* is back. Free and on the mainland, she emerges from hiding, only to find herself hunted by debt collectors, mad surgeons, and a corrupt detective, all of whom will stop at nothing to claim her for their own. And behind this scramble lies the twisted mind of an old adversary, desperate to have his revenge. Replete with dark humour, chaotic storytelling, and a fast-paced Industrial thriller setting, Get Katja is the latest novel from the author of *Pretty Little Things to Fill Up The Void*, *Nothing Is Inflammable*, and *I-O*.

AVAILABLE MARCH 2014
978-1-77148-167-0

THINGS WITHERED
SUSIE MOLONEY

For the first time in one collection, award-winning author Susie Moloney unveils thirteen of her most dark and disturbing short stories.

A middle-aged realtor makes a deal that could last forever. A cheating woman finds herself swimming in dangerous waters. A wife with a dark past can't bear the fear of being exposed. The bad acts of a little old lady come home to roost. A young man with no direction finds power behind the wheel of a haunted truck.

From behind the pretty drapes of the average suburban home, madness peers out.

AVAILABLE NOW
978-1-77148-161-8

WILD FELL
MICHAEL ROWE

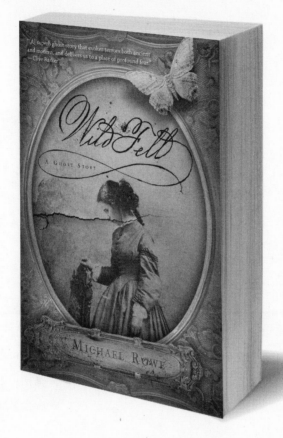

The crumbling summerhouse called Wild Fell, soaring above the desolate shores of Blackmore Island, has weathered the violence of the seasons for more than a century. Built for his family by a 19th-century politician of impeccable rectitude, the house has kept its terrible secrets and its darkness sealed within its walls. For a hundred years, the townspeople of alvina have prayed that the darkness inside Wild Fell would stay there, locked away from the light.

Jameson Browning, a man well acquainted with suffering, has purchased Wild Fell with the intention of beginning a new life, of letting in the light. But what waits for him at the house is devoted to its darkness and guards it jealously. It has been waiting for Jameson his whole life . . . or even longer. and now, at long last, it has found him.

AVAILABLE NOW
978-1-77148-159-5

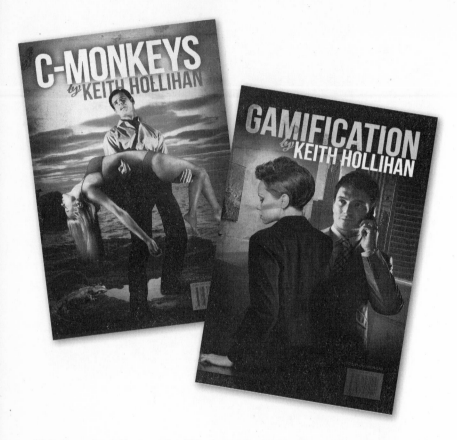

THE N-BODY PROBLEM
TONY BURGESS

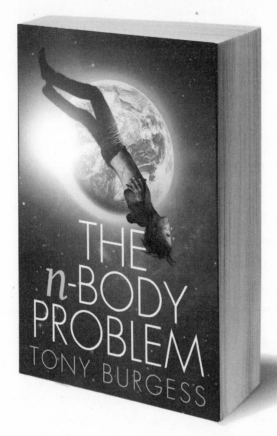

In the end, the zombie apocalypse was nothing more than a waste disposal problem. Burn them in giant ovens? Bad optics. Bury them in landfill sites? The first attempt created acres of twitching, roiling mud. The acceptable answer is to jettison the millions of immortal automatons into orbit. Soon Earth's near space is a mesh of bodies interfering with the sunlight and having an effect on our minds that we never saw coming. aggressive hypochondria, rampant depressive disorders, irresistible suicidal thought—resulting in teenage suicide cults, who want nothing more than to orbit the Earth as living dead. Life on Earth has slowly become not worth living. and death is no longer an escape.

MORE FROM CHIZINE

THE HAIR WREATH AND OTHER STORIES HALLI VILLEGAS [978-1-926851-02-0]

THE WORLD MORE FULL OF WEEPING ROBERT J. WIERSEMA [978-0-9809410-9-8]

WESTLAKE SOUL RIO YOUERS [978-1-926851-55-6]

MAJOR KARNAGE GORD ZAJAC [978-0-9813746-6-6]

"IF YOUR TASTE IN FICTION RUNS TO THE DISTURBING, DARK, AND AT LEAST PARTIALLY WEIRD, CHANCES ARE YOU'VE HEARD OF CHIZINE PUBLICATIONS—CZP—A YOUNG IMPRINT THAT IS NONETHELESS PRODUCING STARTLINGLY BEAUTIFUL BOOKS OF STARKLY, DARKLY LITERARY QUALITY."

—DAVID MIDDLETON, **JANUARY MAGAZINE**

ALSO AVAILABLE FROM CHIZINE PUBLICATIONS